CHRISTOP

Christopher Burns was born in Cumbria in 1944. He is the author of three previous novels, SNAKEWRIST, THE FLINT BED, shortlisted for the Whitbread Novel of the Year Award in 1989, and THE CONDITION OF ICE, as well as a volume of stories, ABOUT THE BODY. His work has been included in BEST SHORT STORIES, 1986 and 1988, edited by Giles Gordon and David Hughes. Christopher Burns is married with two sons and lives in Cumbria.

Christopher Burns

IN THE HOUSES
OF THE WEST

British Library Cataloguing in Publication Data.

Burns, Christopher
In the houses of the west.
I. Title
823.914 [F]

ISBN 0-340-59912-X

10 9 8 7 6 5 4 3 2 1

Printed and bound in Great Britain for Hodder and Stoughton Paperbacks, a division of Hodder Headline PLC, 338 Euston Road London NW1 3BH by Cox & Wyman Ltd, Reading, Berks.

For June and Iain, who went with me.

AUTHOR'S NOTE

This is a novel, not a history. With certain exceptions which I hope are evident, the main characters are fictitious, and occasionally make statements about the tomb and its clearance which should be treated with caution. There is still disagreement, for instance, on what happened during Carter's entry of the burial chamber on the night before the tomb's official opening.

For factual background I have drawn on *The Tomb of Tut.Ankh.Amen* by Howard Carter (three volumes, the first written with A. C. Mace). This has now appeared in a number of editions, sometimes with variant titles. For additional information, and for detail which Carter was unable to provide, I have consulted *Akhenaten, King Of Egypt* by Cyril Aldred; *Tutankhamun* by Christiane Desroches-Noblecourt; *Tutankhamun: the Untold Story* by Thomas Hoving; *The Complete Tutankhamun* by Nicholas Reeves; *Valley Of The Kings* by John Romer; and *Howard Carter and the Discovery of the Tomb of Tutankhamun* by H. V. F. Winstone.

1

He was waiting for me beside the twin statues. Fifty feet above him the shattered face of each throned colossus gazed across the flood plain towards the point of dawn. They had done this for more than three thousand years.

Oxtaby was dressed in sandals, a dusty black djellaba, and a white turban. In one hand he held a short, knuckle-headed staff. As if he were a mere idler beside the relics of a vanished civilisation, he was tracing a series of lines on the ground at his feet. He looked up and then walked forward as I rode my grey donkey down the incline. The air was filled with the repetitive creaking of the hub in a nearby waterwheel as it fed newly planted fields of clover.

'Murchison,' he said as I dismounted, and shook my hand. 'Do you never regret that you do not spend the summer here?'

'Not at all,' I answered. 'My summer was far cooler than yours.'

A fair stubble showed that he had not shaved for several days, and his skin had been tanned to such a deep brown that his blue eyes looked startling within such a face. I would perhaps have taken him for a Circassian and not an Englishman, but beneath the djellaba his skin would be as white as alabaster.

He swung the staff in an arc to encompass the western horizon. 'I enjoy staying here. It's easier to work when every other European or American has retreated. And it does the soul good to see the river rise.'

The floodwater had retreated from the colossi only a few days before, but already the mud around their thrones had cracked into plates. What Oxtaby had drawn there was crude but recognisable. It was an eye of Horus.

He stood beside the base of the furthest statue and placed a hand on the sandstone. The plinth, the throne and the gigantic sculpted feet were all covered with graffiti. 'Akhenaten's father had this quarried a hundred miles south of here,' he said, as if this had just occurred to him; 'did you know?'

I nodded. 'At Edfu.'

'I've been spending time reading the carvings. My Greek is none too good, I'm afraid; I should have paid more attention at college. Nowadays any fool able to pay for a Cook's tour can desecrate a temple with his scribbles, but these visitors were important people – high officials, governors, emperors. Hadrian camped here for days, waiting to hear this statue call to him as the sun rose.'

'Yes, I know.'

He grinned at me like a conspirator. 'Do you think he heard it?'

'I've always doubted that story. Strabo thought it was merely a simple trick arranged by priests. No doubt they delighted in fakery of that kind.'

'A noise like a copper gong being struck; that's what it sounded like. It was after the great earthquake, when this colossus was tumbled and the other one cracked. When they were rebuilt, there were no further cries. Or so the histories say. That's sad, don't you agree?'

'I have to get going, Oxtaby. The train won't wait for me.'

'Of course. But it would be better to go by river, don't you think – just as we sent the first season's finds? That made us all feel as if we were part of a ritual, of a great tradition.'

It was the last time I had felt truly close to Oxtaby. We had brought almost ninety crates down from the valley on a temporary railway, but when at last we reached the river the bank had been too steep for the finds to be loaded directly onto the barges. We slid the crates nervously down the slopes, and the shallows had filled with dozens of fellahin attempting to manhandle the heavy cargo on board. Oxtaby and I had joined them; at the end of the day we were exhausted, drenched, exultant. I stood on a fully laden barge and reached down to shake his hand as he stood chest-deep in the water, and then we began to move away downstream.

'The river was low that May,' I agreed.

He nodded. 'And you went all the way to Cairo with those finds. Did anyone line the banks?'

'People are always curious. There was no trouble.'

'Because you carried no bodies. When the mummies from the royal caches of '81 and '98 were taken downriver, the Egyptians stood on the banks to salute their passing. Men fired guns, and women tore their hair and gave that high, ululating cry they give at funerals.'

'I've heard those stories. But this consignment is nothing like as dramatic as those.'

He gave an exaggerated nod as if to demonstrate the extent of his agreement. 'Tell me, you are only travelling officially, aren't you? There is nothing you are taking in secret?'

'Last year's objects,' I said firmly; 'wooden paddles, ceremonial staffs, with perhaps a few arrows and javelins. For the past few months they have been locked inside the laboratory tomb, soaking in baths of preservative, and it is only now that they have become safe to move. I am carrying Lucas's docket to that effect. I also have consignment notes and insurance certificates issued by the Service. Two men with rifles will guard the crates. I don't envy them; they'll have to breathe preservative fumes for the entire journey. So if you hear any rumours of contraband, Oxtaby, you should scotch them immediately. You'll do that for me?'

'I promise.'

'I have to leave,' I said, and handed him a copy of the *Egyptian Gazette*. 'Take this; I thought you may like to catch up with the outside world.'

He opened it at the page with news from England and read from it. 'Lady Cynthia Mosley is expected to be

3

adopted as Labour candidate for Stoke-on-Trent; there have been complaints about the allegedly immoral nature of the play *Fallen Angels*, written by Mr Noël Coward and starring Miss Tallulah Bankhead; Lord Asquith has been stung by a wasp – but not, fortunately for him, bitten by a mosquito. Do you still think I have any interest in such a world, Murchison?'

'Tear it up if you wish,' I said offhandedly, although I was angered by his sarcasm.

He folded the newspaper and held it in his hand. 'I'll keep it, thank you. And I apologise for my remarks; you should not take them too seriously.'

I nodded reluctantly.

'Are you content with our arrangements?' he asked. 'You have no wish to change them?'

'Everything is as it should be. And you are content that Mrs Plummer and I will make the return journey as planned?'

'Of course. And I'm sure there will be no problem either with Ibrahim or his boat.'

Several white ibis flew in front of us and settled near the waterwheel. The buffalo continued on its blindfolded trudge, and the creak and splash of the wheel kept its hypnotic broken rhythm.

'I have two things to thank you for,' Oxtaby said quickly, as if he wished to keep his gratitude as brief as he could.

'Yes?'

'Lucinda and the Service.'

'You needn't thank me. We may not see eye-to-eye fully now, but we shared a lot in the past. I sometimes think that we shared too much.'

'The Service has offered me a contract for the next season's work. They say that, although I am not required for the lifting of the coffins, I should attend the examination of the body. I know you were instrumental in having me re-employed. I thank you for that.'

'You're too clever to be ignored.'

He gave a small laugh of embarrassment. I did not know

if I believed it; Oxtaby had become a man who appeared to adopt emotions rather than genuinely feel them.

'Besides,' I said, 'Thuillier told me that you worked with Sheik Moussa, clearing the hotel gardens of snakes for the new season. I found that humiliating news.'

'He taught me a lot.'

'But nothing worth knowing. And I must stress one thing – I have had to give assurances about your conduct. Don't let me down.' I pointed at his clothes. 'That means a dark European suit, a collar and a tie. I'm sure you needn't wear a tarboosh, although it may help. And a shave is a necessity.'

'My clothes are stored at our hotel. Hamid is looking after them.'

'Then for God's sake get used to wearing them again. Your sister may find it entertaining to see you dressed like this, but Lacau certainly won't.'

'Did you arrange my contract with Lacau?'

'Lacau is in Europe. If he had still been in Cairo, I might not have been able to speak for you. He dislikes you, Oxtaby. He believes you to be untrustworthy and half-mad. I assured his deputy that you were brilliant but eccentric.'

He laughed, and for a few seconds I saw the man I had once called friend.

'You must forgive me; all the Service should be tolerant of my failings. I love living among the people of Qurna, but I began to miss the company of my own kind. It made me act unwisely.'

I could not help but feel sorry for him.

'I understand,' I said; 'this place is like nowhere else on earth. I have to escape from it in summer. Unlike you, I couldn't stand living in tombs and hovels.'

'My constitution was made for it,' he answered with a half-laugh, so that I did not know if he was joking or not. 'And I'm safe,' he added.

'Safe?' I asked. He had chosen to live among people with centuries of stick fights, thievery and blood feuds behind them; not only that, but it was said that bandits still used

5

the tracks across the escarpment and found shelter in its caves and unguarded tombs.

'Of course,' he answered. 'It will be a wrench to come back to the East Bank and live in a hotel.'

'You're fortunate your sister has money. The Service would advance you none.'

'Perhaps in a few months' time Lucinda will also want to live in the West. I am becoming a popular man among these people, Murchison. Many will think of me as representing them at the unwrapping.'

I thought of protesting, but did not. As far as Oxtaby was concerned, I would have sounded like a character from an Edwardian romance. And it was none of my concern where he and his sister would live.

'So,' he said, 'you have all the details you need.'

'I have her name, the hotel, the dates; I'll leave a message for Mrs Plummer as soon as I arrive, and meet her a day or so before we sail again. I understand a group of ladies is looking after her in the meantime?'

'The lady painters of the Anglo–Egyptian Artists' Society,' he said, his voice reflecting the self-importance of such a name. 'I doubt if there will be an Egyptian among them.'

'Probably not, but it will be good for her to join them for a few days. I'll pass your sister into your care very soon, Oxtaby. And I must be back here for the tomb opening. You need have no worries.'

'Of course. I'm most grateful to you. You have been my saviour on two counts.'

'You're fortunate that Mrs Plummer's arrival coincides with one of Ibrahim's journeys, that's all. Although perhaps, by the end of it, she will have regretted not taking the train to Luxor.'

'And, while she dozes in a railway-carriage, miss the country she has always dreamed about? I don't think so. She will be looking forward to the guided tour. Your approach and mine are very different, but I'm sure she'll enjoy your – ' He stopped, unable to finish the sentence.

'Orthodoxy,' I said drily.

He grinned.

6

I got back on the donkey and tapped it. As it walked up the incline towards the track Oxtaby called to me.

'It's true what I say; the noise was long and sonorous, exactly like a reverberating gong.'

'That's what the histories tell us,' I shouted over my shoulder.

'Yes, but I've heard it myself.'

I looked back at him.

'In a dream,' he said, and I did not know if he was laughing at me or telling the truth.

2

Like all men, I am prey to vanity. Before I met Lucinda
Plummer I stared into a mirror as if somehow my reflection
would correspond with what she would see. While I studied my image I even practised a few phrases that I believed
would show my worldliness, my tolerant cynicism, my
rough–edged charm.

I delayed meeting her until the evening before our
journey south. I had spent my days in the museum, at
a dealer's opposite Shepheard's Hotel, and in the offices
of my employers, the Antiquities Service of the Ministry
of Works. When it was time for us to meet I did not go
up to her room, but telephoned from the hotel lobby.

'Mrs Plummer,' I said, 'my name is Raymond Murchison.
Your brother Clive has asked me to meet you; I believe
you are expecting me. We're travelling south together
tomorrow.'

Her voice was made gritty and sharp by the telephone.
'Mr Murchison,' she said, 'I've been waiting to hear from
you. I'll join you as quickly as I can.'

I sat beside an ornate screen of dark wood and watched
the metal trellis of the lift beside the stairs as it crashed
open and shut with each descent and ascent. The boys who
stood by the lift in their bright uniforms were as silent as
mutes, and their brown eyes were as wide as those of shock
victims.

Oxtaby had shown me Lucinda's photograph, but it
had been taken years ago, before her marriage; I did not
know how those ten years would have treated her. I did
not immediately recognise her as she stepped out of the

lift; there had been other European women before her, all in long pale dresses with cream shoes and beige hats. When she came closer I saw that she was pallid from long days spent in poor light, cold studios, cluttered basements where the remains of antiquity lay beneath dust-sheets. I thought of how hypnotically exotic her paleness would be among the people of this country, and stood up to extend a formal hand.

'Mrs Plummer,' I said cautiously, aware that we were being idly watched by others in the lobby.

She pressed my hand longer than I thought she would. 'Please,' she said, 'you must call me Lucinda, and I shall call you Raymond. It seems, well, *pre-war* to be so formal; don't you agree?'

'Whatever you wish,' I said.

The electricity dipped for a few seconds, dimming the hotel and exposing a liquid sheen across her eyes before the power came up again. There was a murmur of relief throughout the lobby as the illumination was restored.

'It often happens,' I said; 'sometimes the power is lost for hours.'

It was like that, I thought, on the night that Carnarvon died; all of Cairo had been plunged into darkness. Allenby, the British High Commissioner, had asked for a technical explanation from his staff, but it was rumoured that no one could tell him why the generators had failed.

'And this is civilisation,' she said with a slight laugh, as if she was trying to prove that she knew what lay in the future.

'Something like it,' I answered. 'Are you hungry?'

'I haven't eaten much during the last few days.'

'We are due to eat here. You're fortunate; this hotel is quite Westernised. The one we'll share in Luxor is rather more basic, I'm afraid, and with smaller rooms. It has been built in the French style, and there is a shower in most rooms – but not, I think, in the one Clive will have, next to yours. And the balconies are so close that it is easy to step from one to the other. It's fortunate that we have no cat-burglars staying as guests – at least, none that I know of.'

It was a feeble joke, but she had the courtesy to smile at it. Although there was a resemblance to Oxtaby she did not look too much like him. She had the same vivid blue eyes, but her cheekbones were higher and her shingle-cut hair was fairer. Despite her light build she gave an impression of wiry strength.

'Of course,' I continued, 'I understand if you have no appetite – the journey, the heat. I remember I was exhausted for days when I first came to this kind of climate. But we should take our seats anyway; it's cooler in the restaurant.'

I led her through the open wooden doors. We sat opposite each other at a table set for a European meal, with plates made in France and cutlery from Britain. I ordered for us both, as she asked me to do; a fried flatfish, *samak*, followed by lambs' kidneys, mutton, tomatoes and rice.

I could see that she was excited and uncertain about her new surroundings but eager not to appear so. Her decorum and calm were as transparent as the thin film of sweat that had begun to glisten on her forehead and in the well of her throat, and I felt I could sense the nervous beating of her heart.

'My advice is to take plenty of liquids,' I said. 'Lemon squash is fine. Be wary of sorbets and ice-creams unless you're in trustworthy surroundings – they may not be made with purified water. No alcohol just yet, of course – if you don't mind my mentioning that. I understand drinking has become very fashionable among ladies in England. American influence, perhaps.'

She glanced at me with what could have been mild reproof.

'For the next course – well, this item here is a very rich pudding made from rice and almonds, with cream and cinnamon. And this one here is a kind of jelly, again with almonds. But perhaps I am repeating what your artistic friends have already told you.'

'They've warned me about certain foods, certain dangers – of course they have. And everyone is very careful after the assassination of Colonel Stack last year. Clive said that

10

was one reason he did not wish me to travel alone.'

'I see.' Like many other Englishmen, I believed that violent resentment had been quelled following Stack's murder; Allenby, as British High Commissioner, had accused the nationalist government of being implicated, imposed a half-million pound fine on them, and banned all political demonstrations. The government had fallen, and a prime minister approved by the British was now in power.

'Clive said he would have come here if he could,' she went on, 'but that he had business in Luxor.'

I did not tell her either that Oxtaby had no money, or that he was finding it increasingly difficult to leave what he now thought was his home.

'And the ladies have taken you to all the places you wished to see?' I asked.

'Yes; marvellous places. They even have their favourite patch of desert where they can set up their easels and paint the pyramids. And two men came with us to chase away the scorpions and the souvenir-sellers. I wished I could have done more work, but I seem to tire so easily. I didn't think it would be so exhausting.'

'It takes about two weeks even to begin to acclimatise,' I said. 'We have a local doctor, Thuillier, who is often called to tourists in Luxor merely because they have overestimated the sturdiness of their own constitutions. The further south we will go, the hotter it will get. But I shouldn't worry too much; elderly ladies still winter in Aswan. They're convinced the dry air is curative. Considering how the London air was the last time I was home, they're probably right.'

Her voice cooled. 'I'll be thirty years old at my next birthday, Mr Murchison,' she said, looking directly at me. I wondered if her sudden reversal to formality was intended as a kind of warning. 'I hope you don't class me with women twice my age, or more.'

It was an absurd suspicion, and I laughed. 'Of course I don't; I was only trying to illustrate how, once a European is used to this country – '

She interrupted me. 'I intend to make the most of my time here. I may seem like a tourist but I have a professional's eye; I see detail and shading that few others would. I pride myself on my appreciation of design, purpose, achievement. In short, I am here to paint. And you may not class painting as work, but I can assure you that it is.'

'I'm sure,' I said, not knowing why she should be so eager to demonstrate her worth. 'I have no reason to doubt you, Mrs Plummer. More than once, before he knew you were coming here, your brother has told me how proud he is of you.'

I thought she would respond again, but she did not. The waiter appeared, began to spoon portions of fish from a tray and then retreated with a little bow. Lucinda looked at her plate with some trepidation.

I picked up my knife and fork. 'At least here, and in Luxor, we have cutlery. You'll find this fish quite palatable, I think. But a word of warning – don't assume that the filleting will be perfect.'

For a few moments we ate methodically and glanced at each other across the table. Perhaps we each searched the other's face as if it could contain a message that would make words unnecessary.

'Raymond,' she said after a while, 'we're doing nothing but stare at each other. Surely we'll do enough of that over the next day or so.'

I laughed. 'That's true. Although we'll have to share each other's company for much longer than a few days. And you'll find more interesting things to observe than me. As regards being looked *at* – well, you'll soon have to bear closer scrutiny than mine. This is a far cry from Great Russell Street.'

She nodded. 'I expected the bustle and the smell and the strangeness; Clive has written about it. He writes marvellous letters, full of detail and insight and ruminations on whatever has taken his interest. But I still didn't expect it to wrap itself all around me – '

'Like the bandages on a mummy?' I suggested.

12

'In a way,' she said. 'And yet it wasn't protective; it was threatening. I felt . . .' She searched for the right word.

'Exposed,' I said flatly.

'Yes. You're at home here. Clive said you were. There was a letter from him waiting for me as soon as I got here. He told me I couldn't have a better guide or guardian. Of course, if I'd been able to, I would have replied that I didn't want a guardian.' She looked at me to see if I blushed. 'It's nothing personal,' she added.

'He's being generous. We disagree quite a lot over interpretations. As regards being a kind of temporary guardian, I'm afraid he's right. You need – well, a *chaperon*, at least until you know the local customs a little better.'

She separated the flakes of fish with her knife. 'I'm no fool. I realise that I'll not be able to live in the way I have done in London. I intend to adapt. Just as I had to adapt when Rex was killed.'

'Living here may be more difficult than adapting to widowhood.'

I saw her eyes flash, and I raised one hand slightly to check what she might say. The knife was still in it.

'As I said, Clive has told me a little about you, and that includes telling me about your husband. There were so many killed during that war that the mind simply can't grasp the number. I'm sorry, but there were millions like you; this is different. And dangerous in ways that may not be immediately apparent.'

I paused, waiting for another protest. When she said nothing, I went on.

'We are now in one of the great cities of the world. Upriver it's a different story. You'll find that things become increasingly strange, possibly even distressing. Certainly, they'll appear incomprehensible for a while. But there are high numbers of European and Americans there at the moment. They're in groups who, by and large, are insulated from the country. We even have tourists, Europeans and Americans, who expect it to be like *The Sheik*.'

'And now you're patronising me.'

'Not at all. I didn't mean to imply – '

'Yes, you did. Are you always like this, or has Clive asked you to be devil's advocate?'

'I don't know what to say, Mrs Plummer. Clive is one of those Englishmen who find local people more fascinating than his own. I'm not sure what he has planned for you, but I'm only trying to be cautious as well as helpful. But we don't seem to be getting on too well together.'

'No.'

'Look,' I said, 'let me tell you about – '

She placed her knife and fork on the plate; almost immediately a waiter scurried forward and retrieved them along with mine.

'Mr Murchison; I understand that you have a hoard of stories to prove any point you might care to make; most men have. All I want to say is this; I'm not a young girl who thinks she is embarking on a wild, romantic adventure. I'm quite prepared for the lack of hygiene, the strange customs, and whatever else I have to face. Even though I'd never even set foot on this continent until last week, I still have more idea about Egypt than most of the visitors who come here. No doubt that will also be true of all the reporters in Luxor as well. I've read books on the pharaohs; I've studied maps and sculptures and read articles; I've copied the exhibits in the British Museum. I've even read the first volume of Mr Carter's book on his discovery of the tomb; it was published a few months ago. And Clive has written me several letters about daily life here.'

'In that case I admire you,' I said. 'Shall we call a truce? We can hardly argue for the next week or so; and silence would be even worse.'

She nodded. 'Am I being too sensitive?'

'Not at all.'

Suddenly she looked as unhappy as a child. 'I'm sorry. I am being unreasonable.'

Confident again, I put a finger across my lips. 'The next course,' I said.

Another waiter carved the meat at our table, laying suc-
culent slices on the wide gleaming plates. Others measured
out the kidneys, tomatoes, rice.

'I'm not sure if I should eat this,' she said; 'it seems too
heavy.'

'Try to eat a little; not too much. It will be your last
European food for a short while. There will be a cook on
our boat, but he will be an eager amateur as far as Western
food is concerned.'

'When are we leaving?' she asked.

'We take an early breakfast tomorrow and then sail.
There are no lights on the river, so we can only travel
by day.'

She nodded. 'Until Clive told me I was travelling by
boat, I had assumed I would go by train.'

'The next season is due to start in mid-October. I need
not be back in the Valley of the Kings until then, so we
have plenty of time. Besides, I have business on the river.
And it will allow you to see the temples.'

'Sakkara? Amarna? Denderah? Abydos? Do you need to
visit people there?'

'I've already worked out an itinerary. Our first stop will
be at Bedrashen, fourteen miles south of here. From there
you can visit Sakkara and Memphis. Ibrahim or one of the
crew will accompany you if you wish. Of course, if you
would let me be your guide, I should be delighted.'

'You're very generous, Raymond.'

'Not at all. I should be flattered to accompany you.
And since Clive will have told you what to expect from
a dahabeyah, you'll not think either the boat primitive or
the captain a scoundrel.'

She smiled indulgently. 'I promise. Does the boat have
a name?'

'They all have names; ours is no more inventive than
any others. It's called the *Seti*. If you had wanted, we
could have had a *Rameses I* or *Rameses III* or a *Nefertari*.
There will be anything up to a dozen with the same name.
But I know this one well; I have used it before for some
goods I needed transported down the Nile. As for the

15

captains, most of them are called Mohammed. Ours is not; he's called Ibrahim. *Reis* Ibrahim, if you wish to be proper.'

'I look forward to meeting him.'

'You'll find him pleasant. And he speaks good English: many of his countrymen do. Ibrahim tells me that he learned English and French in six months, but that it takes seven years for a European to gain the same proficiency in Arabic. He exaggerates, of course.'

'I see.'

'Ibrahim spends his time taking tourists up and down the Nile. His wife hardly ever sees him. But he has a dahabeyah, and dahabeyahs are not as popular as they were. These days, people prefer to travel by steam rather than by wind. But I think you will like it, even though it is very small. It could take four travellers, but I have arranged with Ibrahim that there will be only you and me. He tells me the *Seti* has new beds, new divan covers in the saloon, chintz on the windows, and new lounging chairs for the deck.'

'It sounds ideal.'

'It's a wonderful way to see the river.'

'A dying way?'

'For foreigners, yes; but dahabeyahs will still be used as barges. Perhaps Ibrahim will do that to his. Or perhaps he will remain in Luxor with his felucca, and merely shuttle visitors across the river.'

'Are you a friend of his?' she asked.

And I wondered if I could describe myself as being a true friend of anyone. The last ten years of my life had left me with many acquaintances, but no real friends. My relationships with Carter and Lacau were professional, although they sometimes masqueraded as something closer. And my occasional cognacs with Dr Thuillier, in his little surgery behind the souk, were shared like fellow aliens rather than spiritual brothers. Of all the people I knew, I had been closest to Clive Oxtaby, but now he was moving away from me and entering a world I could not understand.

'I'm friend*ly* with Ibrahim,' I said, 'friend*ly*. We hardly know each other.'

The river was a thoroughfare for barges carrying cotton, limestone, earthenware pots; for the first tourist steamers of the season, beginning their long journey south towards Abu Simbel; for elegant feluccas, their white sails tapered like a whip; for rowing-boats with men casting a net and then beating the water with an oar to drive fish into it; for dahabeyahs loaded with grain, sugar, hencoops, the crews smoking on deck while chickens pecked around their feet.

To our left the Arabian cliff ran along the edge of the river, while on our right the Libyan bank was low enough for us to see a strip of cultivation, a few miles broad at most, purplish-black with mud or bright green with new shoots, an irrigation canal running through it.

In the morning the sun rose on a surface that seemed thin and delicate, like green silk, and the banks glowed with reds as they took on detail. As the day heightened they began to lose their depth and turn a delicate mauve, and at night, as we moored, the sun fell behind western cliffs that became sharp-edged and velvet-black against a sky of cardinal red. Night gathered swiftly around us, and the land was plunged into darkness but for dim oil-lamps in distant houses. The wooden hull and hemp ropes creaked as we rode safely on the dark infinite weight of the waters, and the trunks and crowns of palms were black against a starry, endless sky.

A strong north wind now began to carry us past hundreds of villages, each indistinguishable from the last, each looking out across the swollen river from behind a protective dyke. Each had its donkeys and goats and camels, its fields of new-planted clover and maize and sorghum, its rough-built houses and tall minaret among palms. Black-clad women stood at the edge of the shallows to fill earthenware jars, perch them on their heads and return up the banks with elegant strides. Children brought water-buffalo from the fields, lashing them ferociously with sticks as the beasts lumbered into water that made their black flanks shine. Men washed themselves in the river before returning to the high bank where they faced Mecca, prostrated themselves on small mats, and prayed. Always there was an aching groan from the timber hubs of waterwheels, and from the distant fields came the muffled thump of shadufs; men had already begun to work at these, drawing water from the reservoirs in a leather bucket slung on the end of a weighted pole.

Sometimes we also passed larger towns, often with a sugar-cane refinery in their midst and a riverbank so strewn with refuse that only a few tough reeds showed through. Boys splashed naked in water that was stippled by slicks of oil, and rats scurried along the crowded banks. The townspeople stopped to watch us pass; their curiosity was so insatiable that the hundredth steamer or the thousandth dahabeyah was still interesting.

As we moved south the air became drier, the light more brilliant; a new clarity made all our perspectives shift. Black-and-white kingfishers sped alongside us, larks rode high over the crops, and butterflies landed on our skin to draw salt. In the evening, flurries of white moths rose from the darkening fields.

Ibrahim stood in the high, curved poop, his hand on the massive tiller, his white shirt blowing in the wind. He navigated a river whose colours changed with the movement of the water and the shifting of the sun, through green to silver and cobalt blue, and he watched us as carefully as a man guarding delicate, fragile charges.

As we approached Amarna I pointed to a stela cut high into the cliff face.

'That's one of the boundary stelae,' I told Lucinda. 'It says that this is Akhenaten's city, a place named in honour of the disc of the sun – Akhetaten, the Horizon of Aten. There's a notch in the cliffs in the distance; that's the wadi where the royal tombs are. Placing them there was an innovation, because the ancient mythologies were built on a link between death and sunset. It was one of the foundation-stones of their religion – you went to the Other World in a burial chamber built in the West, on the edge of the desert, beyond the fields of reeds alongside the river. Yet here royalty was buried in the east, at the position of dawn. I've been on this river and seen the sun rise there, right within that notch. There are some who think that's why the capital was moved from Thebes.'

'From Luxor?'

'Yes.'

'Do we know when – exactly when?'

I always carried with me a notebook full of dates and names, and had checked my entries the night before. '1358 BC,' I said without hesitation.

She nodded as if I had passed a test.

'The old royal way ran along the bank here,' I went on; 'Akhenaten would have ridden in chariots alongside the Nile with Nefertiti, his wife, and their children. Bliss was it in that dawn to be alive.'

She wrinkled her face. 'A Romantic scholar, as well? Is this your Oxford education, Raymond?'

'Schoolboy memories, nothing more.'

We neared a spot where we could moor. One of the crew, Aiman, readied himself to jump in the water and tie us to a tamarisk that grew near the river's edge. The flood had carried away part of the banking and exposed the tree's roots; they reached into the water like dozens of thin fingers.

'On the maps this place is called Tel el Amarna,' I said, 'but there's no great artificial mound covering the remains, so *tel* is a misnomer. Carter worked here with Petrie in the 1890s, when he was just a young man. A lot of the material they found was sold to the Americans last year. I never saw it, but it's supposed to have been quite a jumble – fragments of statues, shards of tile, that kind of thing.'

'What do you mean – which Americans?'

'The Metropolitan Museum in New York, the Brooklyn Museum, the Oriental in Chicago – institutions which are ravenous for culture, even if it comes in pieces that can never be put back together. The European museums don't seem to be worried unduly, especially not the British. I suppose we ransacked half the known world when we could, so a few more statues, a few more obelisks wouldn't make much difference. Carter's dig is privately financed – first by Carnarvon, and now by Carnarvon's estate.'

'Is that why there are so many Americans working in the Valley of the Kings?'

Aiman tugged the mooring rope around the tamarisk and knotted it. 'Mace was with the Metropolitan,' I said, 'and Burton the photographer is. Hauser and Hall are. Breasted founded the Oriental. Newberry comes from Liverpool, Pecky Callender is officially retired as an architect, Lucas is like me – with the Service. Gardiner has his own family fortune, as Carnarvon had. Adamson – well, Adamson is just a tomb guard. He scares away robbers by playing extracts from *Chu Chin Chow* on his gramophone at night.'

As we stepped ashore a few villagers began to crowd around and push fake amulets at us. Among them were young girls with dolls made from sticks and a few scraps of cotton cloth. They were insistent, and took little notice either of my refusals or Aiman's curses.

A young Frenchman in his early twenties stood at their rear, hands behind his back. As we approached he began to smile broadly. 'Mr Murchison,' he said in heavily accented English, taking one hand from the small of his back and extending it, 'how nice to see you again.'

'Laurent,' I said, 'let me introduce you to Mrs Plummer.'

The Antiquities Service had one of its officials present at every dig, and Laurent had been posted to the excavation at Amarna. When we had last met, two more of our colleagues had also been present, but for this second season there was only Laurent. Lacau must have been expecting little of value to be unearthed.

Laurent explained that he had come to collect us, and indicated a nearby donkey-cart. For Lucinda's benefit he apologised profusely for its simplicity as we climbed into it.

He drove the cart through lanes that were so narrow that

the villagers had to crowd into doorways to let us past. At one place, where the road widened, the air was thick with flies. A butcher had set up his tripod in the open space, and from it hung part of the carcass of a goat.

Apart from that there was little activity; one shop-front was open to show rolls of coloured cotton; a nearby handloom was still, its owner looking at us with some suspicion; an old man was being shaved in the street by a barber who looked even older.

We passed a threshing-mill and found ourselves on a deserted track through palms and strips of cultivation shining with lines of irrigated water. A man stood calf-deep in the purplish mud of one field, his head cocked so that we could see he had a blind eye. A few yards away an old water-buffalo was stationary in the mud, a pile of dung behind it. The buffalo was so thin that there was a hollow between the bones of its hindquarters, and a small child lay asleep in it as if in a cradle. The mud on the track had already dried so that, as a lonely wind blew across it, thin clouds of dust whirled about us.

'Where is everyone?' Lucinda asked, looking round the almost-empty fields.

'Excuse me,' Laurent said, running the two words together as if they formed the start of every English sentence, 'the fellahin are all there – look, you see.'

The division between the arable land and the desert was so clear that it resembled a seam running across our path at right angles to us. Beyond it was an arid plain held within the rocky loop of the eastern escarpment. Straggled along the edge of the plain were a number of villagers standing singly or in small groups, often with hundreds of yards between them. Some had already advanced onto the desert, and were squatting beside gullies and ragged fan-shaped depressions in the sand.

'They think it will rain,' Laurent said.

The cart ran onto a slightly raised section of desert floor that was used as a road; we could hear the wheels scrape against tiny pieces of rock.

21

'Wouldn't the people be better in the village?' Lucinda asked.

'The fellahin look for *antika* in the rain,' Laurent said.

'They'll scavenge the gullies and the flood pans looking for brooches, inscriptions, pots, anything that gets flushed out of the ground,' I said. 'It's a bonus for them.'

'They make money by selling those things? Isn't that robbery?'

'Robbery?' I asked. 'Who's being robbed?'

Lucinda looked uncertain. 'I don't know. The country.'

'This is a country that gives away its past. Where do you think the obelisk beside the Thames came from? A man called Mohammed Ali gave it to the British about a hundred years ago. Its sister is in New York. And when you get to Luxor you'll see another tall obelisk just outside the temple – just one, because our friend Mohammed Ali gave the other one to the French.'

'It's still wrong.'

'Perhaps. But giving and selling are part of life here. The Beni Amran, the people who gave this area its name, are part of the same pattern. Barsanti only found the Akhenaten tomb after it had been robbed of every movable object. Some say that the original desecrators took everything, but I have my doubts. These people have lived off the spoils of time for generations. And they're possessive, too. They even smashed up the reliefs in one of the other tombs during some kind of clan quarrel.'

Laurent nodded sagely. 'This is true,' he said. 'They cannot dig as individuals, you see; it is not legal. They must have concession from the *Service des Antiquités*.' Then, as if he wished to impress us by his experience, he added, 'Excuse me, but I think it will not rain. It will not be another Gabbanet al-Kurud.'

Lucinda looked at me inquisitively. I told her the story.

'About ten years ago some villagers from the West Bank were in a wadi some distance away from the Valley of the Kings. It's called the monkey cemetery, the Gabbanet al-Kurud. There was a violent storm, and they discovered that rainwater was disappearing down a cleft in the escarpment ridge and pouring out further down the slope. Shortly afterwards a dealer called Mohammed Mohassib began offering quite unique pieces. The villagers had discovered an unknown tomb, broken in, and begun to ransack it.'

'Couldn't anything be done?'

'I'm told the thieves were arrested, but the prosecution was ineffective and nothing much came of the case. They were soon released. One of them still has a business distributing antika. His name is Sayeed. Your brother knows him.'

'You're not suggesting that Clive – '

'Of course not,' I replied, but I knew that Clive had traded in antika, just like the rest of us. 'Have you never heard it said that police and criminals live in a strange kind of mutual dependence?' I asked. 'Well, it's the same with dealers, archaeologists and the Service.' I pointed ahead. 'Look,' I said.

What was left of the holy city lay beyond a small encampment of awnings pitched among sand coloured like the hide of a lioness. A small group of men stood in the shade of the canvas. One of them came towards us, grinning broadly as he approached. He wore fawn trousers, a cream shirt, and between his shoulders bounced a broad-brimmed hat fastened on a neck-cord.

'Ray,' he said, 'it's good to see you.'

We dismounted. I introduced Lucinda as Oxtaby's sister, and then explained to her that this was Leonard van Diemen; his team had just begun a second season at Tel el Amarna.

'Sure I know Clive Oxtaby,' he said, holding onto Lucinda's hand longer than I thought was necessary. 'I asked him his opinions when I visited Luxor last spring. He told me the whole Aten cult was a complete disaster. He's quite a character.'

'That's one way of putting it,' I said, then turned to Lucinda and added wryly; 'Since van Diemen is an American working for an American university, that means that he has ten times as much money as anyone else.'

Van Diemen laughed and indicated the camp. 'You see how wealthy we are, Mrs Plummer; you see what facilities we have – next to nothing. We even live under canvas; Howard Carter has his own house near the valley. And some of his armed police would be a help right now. If it rains then these people could carry away material we would give our right arms for. We wouldn't even see it; it would just disappear down the plunder trail overnight.'

'You think that it *will* rain, Mr van Diemen?'

'Our people say no, but it seems like the villagers are doing their best to make it. I'm half-expecting a rain dance any minute. We've suspended excavations and even moved to higher ground just in case. My people are spending a few hours completing their notes and hand-washing a few pieces of pot and tile.'

'How are things going, Van?' I asked. 'Anything you should tell me about?'

'I've got an inventory and my report notes complete up to last night. Laurent is impressed by our efficiency, but I don't think there's much that would seriously interest your department. You can tell that to Lacau if you want to. Even he must know that the chances are that anything of monetary value has already been dug up.'

'That's why the terms of your excavation contract are so generous. On the other hand, experts told Carter there would be no other tombs in the valley.'

'Lucky Carter,' he answered wryly. 'But it's said you've got him tied up in red tape on the new concession. He'll get next to nothing when it all ends, won't he?'

I would not be drawn. 'I can't discuss that, Van: you know I can't. And how about your search for order in this particular chaos? Will we have to rewrite all the histories when you've finished?'

He made a balancing gesture with his hand. 'It's difficult recovering truth from wreckage like this. All we uncover is even more speculation. But we can talk about it more tonight – you'll tie up overnight, and join us for a meal? We have some sealed provisions from back home, Mrs Plummer – almost as good as the Fortnum and

Mason's food that Carter and his people eat. We'll not have to rely only on the local fare.'

As he spoke, a sudden gust of wind raced across the sand.

'That's kind of you, Van,' I said.

He nodded. 'All fixed, then. Mrs Plummer, I'll show you what's left of this place, if you like.'

'But the rain?'

'Well, we've been waiting for it for half an hour or so. Ray knows how fast storms move in this country and how localised they can be. Laurent's guess is that we've missed it, and that it's falling some place else on the far side of the hills. Come on, let me show you what there is to see.'

He walked with us along the gritty sand of the old royal way. Rising from it, sometimes lined by shored trenches, were the fractured outlines of the vanished city. Here had been the temples, storehouses and workshops, the offices and stables, the courtyards and gardens; here were the remains of the grand palace, with its state rooms and hypostyle hall; and here, too, had been the mansions of the nobility. Rudimentary geometries of brick denoted reception rooms, a terrace, bedrooms and a bathroom; at the side were the outlines of a grain store, kennels, a yard for fowl, and beyond them the servants' quarters.

I expected Lucinda to be excited by the city's broken outlines; instead she became silent as she studied the crumbled walls, collapsed balconies and dead wells with their mouths stuffed full of sand.

'And you think Tutankhamun was born here?' she asked after a while.

'It's virtually certain,' van Diemen said. 'Of course, in his early days he was Tutankhaten, the Living Image of the Aten. Those were the days when even Osiris's name was never mentioned, because the Atenist heresy was supreme. Only later did he become the Living Image of Amun. He had a few other names hung on him, as well – the Horus name, his falcon name.'

Lucinda surveyed the ruins. 'I arranged to call at Pompeii

25

on my way here. It reminds me a little of that – a city killed in its prime.'

'I guess I can understand why you should think that,' van Diemen said, 'but there's quite a difference. Whatever happened to Akhetaten, it certainly wasn't destroyed by the forces of nature.'

She shook her head as if he had refused to see a symbolic link. 'How long did it last?' she asked. 'A generation?'

'About seventeen years. But as soon as Amun worship regained control then the city of Aten must have been condemned. In this country the worship of one god was an adventure that was certain to fail.'

'Moses succeeded,' she said.

'Moses, Mrs Plummer, was leader of a desert tribe only a few generations away from being nomads. This was a culture that had existed in one place for thousands of years; to most Egyptians monotheism was a blasphemous lie. The renaming of the king was the most obvious way of re-establishing the old religion and the old order.' He turned to me. 'What was the falcon name, Ray?'

I wondered if he expected me not to know, but I was ready for him with a smugly accurate response. 'I think the part of it you mean is He Who Brings Together the Cosmic Order and Who Propitiates the Gods; Heqa-maat-seheptep-netjeru.'

Van Diemen was momentarily crestfallen, and I could not resist a smirk at my own cleverness.

'Clive said in one of his letters that when he began to travel in countries like this he started to understand religion,' Lucinda said. 'He said he began to understand why people living by the Nile used to believe in hundreds of gods. He said that Yahweh and Allah came out of the desert, and that the Akhenaten rebellion was hopeless and doomed from the start.'

Van Diemen shrugged. 'He said the same to me. Maybe he's right. And like most rebellions this one probably ended in bloodshed and destruction. We don't know whether Akhenaten was his own man or a dupe, just like we don't know if he was a true believer or a kind

26

of atheist. One thing we can be certain of; the sun god saved no one in this city.'

He clapped his hands, signalling that we should move on.

'I'll take you to the royal tombs,' he said. 'Would you like that, Mrs Plummer? And can you ride a donkey? It's all right, these are real saddle-donkeys, big, silver-grey ones, not like the fellah donkey on Laurent's trap. There are about three miles to go.'

We rode up the wadi towards the tombs as the sun, descending across the Nile, turned the eastern desert into a blinding saffron-yellow. The donkeys were unusually nervous, and we had to tap them with sticks to steady them. Lucinda fell silent, apparently trying to absorb every detail of this lonely desolation. I could see her study the sand and rock around us, the ravines cut deep into the inclines, even the high unforgiving sky. I left her alone with her silence and talked to van Diemen. I asked about his expedition; he wanted to know about the Tutankhamun clearance.

When we reached the tomb a gust of wind sent grit dancing across its mouth and we had to shield our faces. Van Diemen pulled his hat tightly onto his head and then made sure the donkeys were tied securely to a rail that had been driven into the ground. They tugged at the ropes as if seeking to break free, and then quietened.

'The entrance faces the dawn,' he said, unlocking the iron gate. Then he lit two lanterns and handed one to me. 'Be careful, Mrs Plummer,' he advised. 'There are steps here, and a ramp for the sarcophagus to slide down. Okay?'

He began to descend into the heart of the tomb.

'Will there be bats?' Lucinda asked.

'Dozens,' I said.

'Hundreds, more like,' van Diemen said, and raised his lantern high so that we could see them hanging on the ceiling. One or two of them moved slightly with a trapped motion, as if they had become glued to the rock.

At the bottom of the steps we found ourselves in a bare

corridor that sloped downwards and, at its end, a second flight of steps. 'Here we are,' van Diemen said, his voice echoing eerily in the half-darkness; 'you'll see there's a shaft near here, so watch your step. It's about ten feet or so deep. The royal burial chamber is down there; there's nothing much left of the wall decorations. And off here are three other rooms for Akhenaten's family. Behind you – you may not have noticed it as we passed, Mrs Plummer – is a corridor leading to a few more rooms. I'll show you them all. So welcome to one of the most exclusive suites in the entire world.'

He led us around the chambers and held the lamp near to the reliefs so that Lucinda could see them clearly. Much of the tomb had been defaced, and some of the images were difficult to understand. Van Diemen pointed out the recurring motifs – the disc of the sun with its rays fanning downwards onto the king and his family, each ray ending in a hand; the depiction of vast quantities of flowers, drink and food loaded onto altars to the Aten; a dead princess stretched out on a bier and mourned by her family.

I remembered my own younger sister. Her name had been Virginia. I had taken too large a handful of soil to drop on the tiny coffin. Some of it drummed on the wooden lid, but most fell on the garland of flowers, newly cut that morning, placed there by my mother.

'Who was she?' Lucinda asked. The lamplight made her eyes shine.

'We don't know,' van Diemen said. 'We think it was the princess Meketaten, the king's daughter, and that she died in childbirth. Look, here you can see a woman – a nursemaid, perhaps – with what we think is a dead child in her arms. But their names have been chiselled away. All we can do is guess.'

'Their names were obliterated?'

'Even the pharaoh's body was not safe. When he was found twenty years ago in the Valley of the Kings, all that was left of the goods that were buried with him were four alabaster jars with his portrait on the lids.'

'They were canopic jars,' I interjected. 'The internal

organs of the dead body were removed and stored in canopic jars. Mummies are just the outer shells of the dead. Tutankhamun's jars will be in a canopic chest in the treasury at the back of his tomb.'

Van Diemen nodded. 'They had to keep them safe so that the dead king could be resurrected. Perhaps even tomb-robbers had some kind of respect for the dead. As for Akhenaten's safe tomb, well, I hear that Harry Burton is using it as a darkroom now.'

'And what about Tutankhamun? Were these his sisters?'

'Opinions differ,' van Diemen said. 'I think that he was the son of Akhenaten and one of his lesser wives, a queen called Kiya. Akhenaten and Nefertiti had six daughters. One of them was eventually named Ankhesenamun.'

'Tutankhamun's wife? He married his sister?'

'Half-sister,' van Diemen corrected her. 'To preserve the blood-royal, I guess, but not very good for the health of the family. And perhaps incest had magical connotations, as well.'

'Perhaps,' she said.

When we were walking back up the passageway van Diemen signalled us to be quiet, and tilted his head as he listened to something a long way away.

'My God,' he said; 'it's started to rain.' Immediately he began to run up the steps towards a daylight which had dimmed and become grey.

When we caught up with him he was standing at the rim of the entrance, looking down towards the plain. The lamp was on the ground at his feet.

'I thought it had begun,' he said, half-apologetically. A layer of cloud was sliding across the sky, moving slowly away from us. The donkeys flicked their ears disconsolately.

'The storm has missed us,' I said. 'It could be miles away before it breaks.'

He nodded. He was biting his lip as if disappointed.

'Raymond,' Lucinda said; 'surely it would make no difference – '

I anticipated her. 'The sand won't soak up rain from

a prolonged cloudburst. The top layer turns into a film, into a grease. Excess water, perhaps a few inches of it in a very short time, sluices from the higher ground, falls into the wadi and then surges along it. On the way here you probably noticed huge gouge-marks in the slopes. In a heavy storm those would be waterfalls.'

'The villagers really thought it would happen, didn't they?'

'Maybe they just hoped it would. They couldn't afford not to take a chance.'

'And the tomb? What if it floods?'

'It would be well out of the way,' van Diemen answered. 'Besides, it's not important enough to merit the kind of watertight door that Carter has put up in front of his find.'

We remounted and began to make our way back down the valley, following the tracks we had made earlier. After about ten minutes I saw a white glint in one of our old hoofprints ahead and pointed it out to van Diemen. He rode forward and cleared the sand around the object. 'Anything?' I asked.

He rubbed the find between his hands and then held it in the air. It was a piece of green- and rust-coloured tile as big as his palm. 'Amarna faience,' he said. 'The houses were covered in it. It's nice, but a good Kansas-style storm might have turned up something better. You have keen eyes, Ray; thanks. But I hope the Service won't want to take such a trifle from us.'

I laughed as we rode past him. 'We're not robber barons, Van.'

I saw that he had thought of a response, but did not make it.

'It's not important,' I said quietly to Lucinda. 'And Van will be happy to take anything. For the last three years everything has been in the shadow of the Carter discoveries. Even a biblical deluge wouldn't turn up anything like what has been found in Wadi Biban al-Maluk.'

'That's the Arabic name for the Valley of the Kings, I suppose. Why don't you stop trying to impress me,

Raymond? It has been a long time since I was a schoolgirl. And I'm certainly not a shy maiden, either.'

Her remarks stung me, and I said nothing until she spoke again.

'Raymond, have you ever seen such a storm?'

'Once. From a distance.'

This time she encouraged me. 'Where was it?'

'Not in this country. It was when I was with Clive. In Arabia.'

'Would we have been in danger?'

'We could have sheltered in the tomb.'

'I would have felt better if there had been a little danger.'

I was bewildered. 'All right,' I said, 'there could have been a risk. If the storm had been heavy, if it had lasted for a long time, if the wadi had been longer – '

'I understand.'

She glanced back. Van Diemen had finished studying his piece of pottery but was still a hundred yards behind us.

'I thought of Rex,' she said.

'Your husband? Why?'

'I thought of how he must have died. In the rain and the mud.'

I spoke as gently as I could. 'Clive told me that you don't know. He said Rex was missing, presumed dead, and that was all you were ever likely to find out.'

'Are you going to offer me alternatives? You must know what the likelihood is.'

'It's been a long time. Nine years.'

'A long time? You're used to thinking in terms of thousands of years, and yet you tell me that nine is a long time?'

'You're being unfair; you know what I mean.'

But she went on. 'Are you going to suggest that I should forget him? Or tell me again that there are millions like me? Why do you think I should get some form of comfort from that thought?'

Once more I was reduced to silence.

She shook her head; I could see the glint of tears in her

31

eyes. 'I'm sorry,' she said after a while, 'it's not your fault. It's not even your concern. You tell me whatever you think will interest me, and you always do your best to help me.' She paused for a moment and then went on. 'You're being impossibly nice and I'm being ridiculously sensitive.'

At that moment I was as pleased as a schoolboy praised by a favourite teacher. I wanted to say more, but van Diemen came riding up behind us and began to speak once again about the fate for Akhetaten. I was infuriated at his interruption, but Lucinda asked him for more details. I was unsure if she was genuinely interested, or if she merely wished to avoid having to talk to me further.

'After Akhenaten died there was a period of about eight years in which we're not really sure what happened. It seems that there were three kings in fairly quick succession – Smenkhare, Tutankhamun, and Ay. After that a strong man finally came back to the throne, a man called Horemheb.'

'And Tutankhamun? What happened to him?'

'That's what Carter and his team hope to find out. You're going to be there when they examine the body, aren't you, Ray?'

'Clive Oxtaby will be as well.'

'That should please Clive. Your brother, Mrs Plummer, roots for the old gods. I guess most of us have some kind of sneaking sympathy for Akhenaten, because he seems a bit nearer our own time than any of the other pharaohs. As for Clive, his favourites are gods and goddesses like Amun, Osiris, Horus, Isis, Hathor, Nepthys, Anubis, Nut – hundreds of them. Gods who guarded specific parts of the body, gods who looked after cattle, water, children, the calendar, you name it.'

'And Amun?' she asked. 'What did he guard?'

I was certain she already knew the answer to her own question. She was merely testing him.

'One of the more difficult ones,' van Diemen confessed, and glanced at me.

I was still smarting at his interruption, and was not eager to help him. 'Yes,' I said, 'difficult.'

'He's a kind of vitality,' he said after a few seconds. 'A god of breathing, of living,' he elaborated.

'A life force,' I suggested.

'That's it,' he said, gratefully seizing the phrase, 'a life force. Amun breathed life into the world and every creature in it. Mind you, it was typical of the Egyptians to have as their animating spirit a god whose name means Secret or Hidden.'

'He's associated with the ram, so is often shown as having a ram's head,' I said. 'Sometimes he's shown as having the head of a serpent, or the head of a frog, as well. And he's the god of creativity.'

'Of painting?'

'I suppose so.'

'*Suppose*, Raymond? If he's the god of creativity, then he must be.'

Suddenly I was angered by her teases. 'And he's the god of sex,' I said. 'Of copulation,' I added, in case she had not quite understood.

'How interesting,' she answered, determined not to be shocked.

'The Egyptians viewed sex as symbolic and ritualistic as well as procreative and pleasurable,' I said airily, as if I discussed such subjects all the time with attractive women. 'In burial chambers the dead king looks upwards, and from the undersides of coffins or shrines the figure of the sky-goddess Nut looks down on him. Her body is spangled with stars and arches across the heavens. The king copulates with her in death to re-engender himself.'

It was van Diemen, not Lucinda, who was made uncomfortable by such images. He began, too obviously, to talk about the shrines rather than their decoration.

'The Tutankhamun shrines were wonderful,' he said; 'placed one inside the other like Russian dolls, but these were gilded boxes. Ray told me that Carter said he could peel them like the skins of an onion. Isn't that right?'

'That's right,' I said.

'I'm due to visit the site myself in a month or so,' he went

33

on. 'I can take the train and get a room in the Winter Palace. I couldn't leave this country without visiting Carter and his people at least one more time.'

'Yes,' I said, 'I'm sure.'

And I thought of how the outer golden shrine had almost entirely filled the burial chamber, and how the narrow gap between its sides and the walls had been littered with emblems of a lost life and a journey of death – figures of Anubis, a bouquet of flowers withered to ash, steering paddles for the vessel of rebirth. Even when these had been numbered, photographed and taken away, there was still only little more than two feet of clearance between the painted walls and the gilded cedar.

There was not one shrine but four, with the sarcophagus at their heart. Each shrine had a door and was floorless; each gilded surface was decorated with animals, gods, quotations from the Pyramid texts, the Book of the Dead, the Book of What Is In the Other World. Here were Isis, Osiris, Anubis, and other guardian divinities. On the lid of the inner shrine the sky-goddess Nut looked down, her wings spread so that she could settle onto the body of the dead king.

When the team had reached the sarcophagus itself they found it to be nine feet long and just under five feet broad and high. The lid was made of granite, but the box itself had been cut from a single block of quartzite, the sacred stone for the royal dead. Both the lid and box had been painted a golden yellow.

Carter arranged the construction of an elaborate pulley system to raise the lid, and early last year the granite slab was finally hoisted from its resting-place. Beneath it were linen shrouds spangled with stars, and beneath them the shining magnificence of the outermost coffin.

On the next day the tomb was shut down.

All through that evening I regretted my attempt to shock Lucinda. Van Diemen and his colleagues did their best to entertain us, but much of their conversation was about either the rigours of Egyptology or American sport and politics. Whenever they spoke to Lucinda they were charming but over-deferential, and I wondered if they had been made uneasy by her presence.

When we returned Lucinda squealed as she stepped onto the gangplank of the *Seti*, for a large rat scampered beneath it along the margin of the river and then slipped into the water. 'I hate rats,' she said; 'they remind me how things must have been in the trenches.' She had seen rats before, but had shown no reaction.

I sat with her in the lounge, wondering what I should do next. The oil-lamp glass was yellow; duskiness gathered in the room, softening her features and turning her skin amber. It was as if we were alone in the draped, heady richness of a seraglio, but I did not know what she expected of me. Uncertainty made me rash, and I reached out and took her hand.

She flinched; I had made an approach she might have to fight off.

'Don't spoil things,' she said, and her voice trembled slightly. 'Please.'

My thin confidence cracked apart. I laid my other hand on top of hers like a friendly clergyman. 'Tell me about Rex,' I said. He camouflaged my hopes, but he was the last person I wanted to talk about.

Her blue eyes were as dark and wide as they had been in the tomb.

'There's nothing much to tell. We were only married for a short while before he went back to the war. He was killed at the Somme.'

'How long had you been married?'

'We were married on the third of April, in 1916.'

They had only had a few weeks. By the end of June Rex Plummer was in another country, waiting with thousands of others while an unrelenting bombardment of a million and a half shells fell on enemy positions. On the first day of the new month the British advance began. It was planned to be the decisive breakthrough in a stalled war. Men climbed from their trenches and walked towards the enemy in a line thirteen miles long and a few yards deep; one of their captains even kicked a football across the shattered landscape. Then German troops emerged unscathed from their dug-outs and began mowing down the advancing soldiers. Very few reached the barbed-wire, and those that did found it still uncut, and dense and coiled enough to halt any further advance. More than half of the troops were wounded or killed, and at the end of the first day about twenty thousand dead and dying lay unrecovered in the raw mud of no-man's-land. Rex Plummer had been among them.

There was nothing I could say to justify such carnage.

'Have you a photograph of him?' I asked.

'Of course. I carry it everywhere with me.'

'May I see it?'

There was a locket around her neck, tucked into her clothes. She pulled it from the top of her dress, snapped it open and held it out to me. I took it between my fingers; the silver, warm from her skin, felt light as an alloy. As I bent to look at the image I could smell her body more clearly than I had ever done before.

'He was handsome,' I said, and she nodded.

I could just see the military collar on Rex's portrait; above it his face had a particularly English kind of bland good looks, sharpened by a moustache clipped short at the corners of the mouth. His expression was slightly reserved, as if he had not wanted to be photographed.

Perhaps, I thought, this was the face of a man who would have been content as he stood on duckboards in a muddy trench among rats and rotting sandbags. But as I continued to look at it the face began to seem disturbingly familiar, and I wondered if somehow I had met Rex Plummer a decade or so ago, before I had known either Clive Oxtaby or his sister.

'When was this taken?' I asked.

'Just before our wedding. He hadn't been to the front by then. He took me to see the exhibition trenches in Kensington Gardens. They were clean, tidy, and well-protected. In a way, they were even comforting. He told me the front would be much worse than what I saw. I didn't know how much worse until long after he had been killed.'

I handed the locket back to her, and then wondered what to do with my hands. I joined them together and placed them awkwardly on my lap. I could still sense her warmth on my skin.

'I can't have met him,' I said, 'but it feels as though I must have done.'

'He looks familiar?'

'Yes.'

'Afterwards, everyone said we married each other because we looked alike. But we didn't, really. He looked like Clive.'

Now that she had told me the resemblance was both obvious and eerie, and I wanted to shiver at this odd parallel.

'Of course,' I said. 'If Clive had a moustache, the likeness would be even more striking. You weren't related?'

'Not directly, but perhaps distantly. My great-grandmother and Rex's had the same maiden name, and they both came from Oxfordshire. We didn't know that until after we were married. But sometimes I wonder if that was what really attracted me to him, without my knowing it.'

She breathed deeply, and when she exhaled there was a tremor within her breath. Then she reached across and touched my wrist with her fingers.

'He wanted to go to war,' she said. 'I was proud of him.'

'I see.'

'We went to the little railway station near our home. It's a fine place – the name is spelled out in white cobblestones on a grass bank and everything seems to be always newly painted. The station-master even keeps geraniums in window-boxes outside the ticket office and the waiting-room. I said goodbye to Rex on the platform.'

I nodded. This time she was looking straight at me as if determined not to look away. I did not dare glance down in case I broke the spell. My hand lay just underneath her wrist, and I could feel her pulse within it.

'I forced myself into thinking about what would happen if he were killed; it was senseless not to try to imagine that. Friends of mine had lost husbands, brothers, even fathers. But try as I might I could never think too seriously about it. It was as if it were just a kind of silly dream – not even a nightmare, because all the time I placed myself at the centre of the tragedy. The beautiful young widow, robbed of happiness while still in the first flush of youth – that's how I saw myself. I even felt a little like that when the telegram came. Do I shock you?'

'Of course not.'

'But you and Clive were fighting too. Some of your friends must have had wives and fiancées back home; they probably took their photographs with them, too. Doesn't it distress you that a wife could think like me?'

'No. I'm pleased you can be so honest. But that's not all you felt.'

And now she did look away, and she withdrew her hand from mine as well.

'No. I cried for weeks. During the day I was composed, calm; when I went to bed I cried until I was exhausted and fell asleep. It was a routine like an addiction, and I couldn't break out of it. We lived together for only a few weeks, and yet I missed him terribly, hopelessly. I wanted him for everything. I even wanted him for the habits that he had and that I found irritating. He used to read his newspaper, tell me things out of it, and then comment on them – as if somehow I was incapable either of reading it myself or making up my own mind. I hated that; and yet, afterwards, I would have given anything to hear him do it again. I missed his presence; I missed our future together. I wanted him back in his favourite chair, I wanted him beside me in our bed.'

'I understand.'

'How could you understand? You've never been married, have you? You've never lost anyone really close to you.'

I did not answer. The cabin had grown dimmer.

'That was unforgivable of me,' she said after a while.

Again I said nothing.

'I don't even know where Rex is. Buried somewhere under a white stone with no name on it, maybe. Possibly not even his regiment's name, because there would have been nothing to identify him. And I'll never visit his grave because I don't know where it is, and I'll never find out. There must be thousands of unknown soldiers. That's one of the worst things about it. If I had seen Rex – if I had seen him dead then I might not have recognised him. It makes me shudder to think what he might have been like. That he might not even be in a grave at all. Perhaps he never had a chance to die as he should have done – with his friends, not alone and lost in a barren landscape. I would have liked him to die in someone's arms. I would have liked someone to hold his poor head as he breathed his last.'

Her intensity was such that I felt nervous about speaking, and cleared my throat before I did.

'If you want a military man's answer to that,' I said, 'then I would tell you that he was probably killed by a single bullet, two at the most, from a machine-gun. His identity just got lost in the confusion. That happened to thousands.'

'You think so?'

'You can be pretty certain about it.'

And I thought of the only time that I had been shot.

For more than two weeks we had trekked across land-scapes of scrub and sand, beds of limestone, broken lava. Our days had grown so monotonous that we scarcely thought about our purpose, and the latest intelligence had put the Turks at a hundred miles away. So my mind was drifting when my camel breasted the ridge and began to descend the other side. A few yards away, on a slope of disturbed sand, a Bedouin woman was being bayoneted by a soldier. For a few moments he did not see me, and I watched in a kind of frozen horror as he eased the blade into her again, probing the resistance of the flesh before he leaned on the rifle butt. Nearby was the corpse of a man who had been killed in the same casually efficient way. Suddenly there was an odd feeling in my shoulder, as if I had been clubbed by an invisible enemy, and almost instantly I heard the noise of a shot. Stupefied, I looked further down the slope. Four other soldiers had gathered there and begun to fire at me. Smoke drifted almost lazily from the rifle-barrels, and I heard the crackle of shots and the whirr of bullets passing through the air alongside me before the camel went down and I was pitched forward into the sand.

'Rex may not even have known about it,' I went on, trying to be convincing; 'bullets travel faster than sound.'

'The whole air must have been full of noise,' she said. 'Machine-guns, shells, screams. It must have been like wading through a river of sound.'

'Lucinda,' I said, 'it happened. You can do nothing about it now.'

She nodded.

'If Rex were still alive you might never have come here. Clive might still have invited you – but you would never have been able to come under the circumstances that you have.'

'You think not?'

'You would have settled down to a suburban life, and arranged that Rex's meals were always ready for him when he came back from the office on one of the trains that stopped at your little station. And he would have read his items from the newspapers to you and carved the roast beef on Sunday. Afterwards, if the day was sunny, he would take you for a walk in the local park to hear the brass band play. He might never have wanted to go abroad again. When you had a letter from Clive with an Egyptian postmark, Rex would say that it was a country full of wogs and flies; but you would remember your father's library, and his books on archaeology, and how you and Clive dreamed of seeing the Nile when you were grown up.'

'Clive told you about that library?'

He had talked more about the library than he had about her.

'He told me the names of some of the books that were in it,' I said. 'The *Histories* by Herodotus; *A Popular Account of the Ancient Egyptians* by Gardner Wilkinson; biographies of Belzoni, of Champollion. He boasts that he even read the first two-volume edition of *The Golden Bough*.'

'We certainly had a copy; I remember him reading the section on Osiris to me. And we had Auguste Mariette, *The Monuments of Upper Egypt*; Samuel Manning, *The Land of the Pharaohs*. And there were novels about explorers among desert tribes, stumbling across priceless treasures. I've been in love with this place for a long time, Raymond. I was fascinated by it as a child. It seemed so different from everything I was ever likely to know.'

'It *is* different from everything else. There's nowhere on earth quite like it. You worked hard to get here; as hard as anyone and harder than most.'

'You're telling me that I'm only here because my husband is dead.'

'I'm saying you're here because you made choices after his death.'

'Those are both facts. I couldn't deny them.'

I waited. The darkness seemed to close itself around us. I dared not take an extra step.

'I'm tired,' she said; 'I must go to bed.'

I felt that I had been suddenly dismissed, and stood up too quickly. 'I'll say good night to you,' I said.

I only hesitated a moment. I had the sense that she was about to say something else, but I would have felt foolish if she had not and I had waited any longer.

I left her and went back on deck. The planking creaked slightly. Aiman lay asleep at the feet of Ibrahim, who was scanning the dark shore as he smoked the last fraction of an American cigarette from a pack given to him as a minor bribe by van Diemen.

'Laurent,' he said to me, inclining his half-closed fist at the shore.

We went down the gangplank. The lantern was turned down low and the air reeked of silt. Ibrahim dropped his cigarette in the water; I heard its momentary hiss. Laurent stood quietly on the riverbank near to the tamarisk. He took a step towards us as we approached. His pale face was

41

coloured bronze by the lantern-light; he looked excited, as if he relished the secrecy and romance of such a meeting.

'I did not think,' he murmured, 'that with the lady . . .' He allowed his voice to tail off, and looked at me for approval.

'Quite right,' I replied. 'This has nothing to do with Mrs Plummer. What can you tell me?'

'Nothing from van Diemen's team. They say theirs is a dig for academics, not for exhibitors, and that this is proved by the terms of their concession. But I know that for this season they have extra funds from their museum. I think it is expected that they return with something of value. Something not only for professors.'

'I understand.'

'So, to please and interest them, the villagers talk of a signet ring being pulled from the ground, with the face of Nefertiti upon it.'

'Like the one sold forty years ago – the one that is in the museum in Edinburgh? Are the Beni Amran still copying such rings, Laurent?'

He gave a Gallic shrug. 'Who knows? It is less ambitious than last year, when they said a gold and lapis pectoral had been found. The ring is just, you know – just speech.'

'Just talk.'

'Quite so. To keep the Americans interested. All the Nile knows they will pay very high prices. It is said that even Howard Carter is surprised at how much money such men have.'

'What is whispered on the Nile is exaggerated. As usual.'

'Is it an exaggeration that Lord Carnarvon's private collection has far more than a thousand items, many of them selected and approved by British archaeologists such as Carter? I have heard that since his death Carnarvon's wife and daughter have decided to sell this collection.'

'They want to sell it; that's true. Go on.'

'Is it true that Carter has itemised and valued the goods, and that everyone expects the Americans to offer more than one hundred and fifty thousand dollars? Because some say that this is a very low price; on the open market a museum would have to pay much, much more.'

'No one knows what the final bid will be, Laurent. I do not expect it to reach one hundred and fifty thousand dollars. The British Museum will be offered the entire collection for twenty thousand pounds. A true value may be higher than this, but Carnarvon's family no doubt wish the goods to remain in Britain.'

But in one of his moments of confidence, Carter had told me that he hoped and expected the British Museum to refuse. He would then do what he wanted to do, and sell the goods to the Metropolitan. He believed he could easily obtain one hundred and fifty thousand dollars; for the Americans it would still be a bargain.

Laurent nodded. 'I understand. And I am told Lord Carnarvon had items found in the Gabbanet al-Kurud.'

'Did he? I don't know, Laurent. All that took place when I was working out of Cairo with the Arab Bureau. I thought that the Metropolitan bought all those objects.'

Laurent became even more sly. 'It would be probable that Carnarvon had *some*. Carter was his agent even then. It is also rumoured that in the collection there are items taken from Tutankhamun's tomb. I tell myself that surely this is not true.'

I laughed. 'Of course it isn't. The tomb cannot have contained such items. Every one is noted down, measured, photographed, catalogued. The Service knows everything that has been found in that tomb.'

'We did not know about the lotus head.'

After the tomb had been closed I had been in the storage tomb when another of the Service's employees had found a gessoed wooden head. Oxtaby had been working next to the man; we had exchanged a momentary glance. The head was of Tutankhamun emerging from a lotus flower, and it had been packed in a Fortnum and Mason's wine-crate as if ready for shipment out of the country. I had not thought that the affair was so widely known.

'We knew about the head,' I said wearily. 'It was catalogued under a general description. Anyone with a detailed knowledge of the documentation procedures would appreciate that. Certainly Lacau did.'

Laurent nodded but did not appear convinced. 'It is said, too, that the Metropolitan is very interested in manuscripts, papyrus, that they have paid large figures for these. Perhaps van Diemen's museum will pay large figures, too.'

For more than ten years there had been rumours from Aswan to Cairo that the Metropolitan had paid a vast amount for a rare Coptic manuscript. Like many others working on the ancient sites, Carter had been unwilling to believe the increasingly extravagant figures that he heard quoted. He told me he had worried that unrealistic payments would distort the trade he had so carefully nurtured. But the spoils from the monkey cemetery had cost the Metropolitan more than fifty thousand pounds over five years, and on the day that Carnarvon died Carter had received almost one thousand pounds from them for the purchase of a papyrus from one of the dealers in antika, Maurice Nahman. He had levied a twenty per cent commission on these exchanges.

'In this country, everything is for sale,' I said.

Laurent dropped his voice still further. 'A few days ago there was a dealer's boat on the river. This man and van Diemen, they talked. He had come down the river, perhaps from Luxor. He belongs to one of the West Bank villages – Qurna, Qurnet Murai, Al Khokha.'

'Who is this dealer?' Ibrahim asked.

'You know of him, Ibrahim. His name is Nasir. His uncle was Mohammed Mohassib, who sold treasure from the Gabbanet al Kurud. It is said that he will be the best dealer on the river in two years, maybe three. Like his uncle, he pays his suppliers with gold coin.'

'I know of him,' Ibrahim said. 'He is a scoundrel. I tell you what he does – he takes his treasures and he divides them many ways, but he pretends there are only two divisions. And he says to one person – "Look at the treasures I can sell you, but someone else wants the other part of them." Then he says to a second person – "Here

are treasures, but another part must go to someone else."
And the price goes up, because each person wants the full
treasure, not just part of it.'

'And when that person has bought,' I said, 'then Nasir
discovers a third part of the treasure, and a fourth, and a
fifth. There is no end to his treasures, and no end to paying
for them. What has he offered van Diemen?'

'I am not certain.'

'What would you guess?'

'From what I overhear, I think two canopic jars, perhaps
a head of Osiris made from onyx.'

As he said this Laurent glanced round as if he feared being
overheard by someone else that none of us could see.

'Good enough to begin to satisfy his museum, perhaps.
Only two canopic jars?'

'Only two. I think they must be Eighteenth Dynasty.'

'What else?'

'I have heard van Diemen talking of a papyrus.'

'A special papyrus?'

'I am not certain, but I think it must be very special.
Perhaps not even Nasir has seen it. I stole a look in van
Diemen's diary. Should I not have done this?'

'Of course you should not. What did it say?'

'It said nothing and everything.'

'Just tell me, Laurent,' I said, exasperated.

'Mostly it was what is written in his official reports.
But on one page there were no words, merely figures.
He had added them up. The figure at the bottom of the
page was one hundred thousand dollars. With a question
mark beside it.'

'That's mad. Nothing is worth that. Nothing.'

'Indeed. You say that an entire collection has been valued
at less. But I must report this figure to you.'

'What kind of papyrus?'

'I do not know. I have only heard van Diemen talk
openly of a Ptolemaic one he brought down from Cairo,
but it cannot be that one. He says it fell to pieces within
days.'

'Those are cheap; they are dug up in their thousands

in the Fayoum. A really expensive papyrus would tell us things we did not know about the ancients, about their history or their beliefs.'

'I have heard tales of an Other World papyrus.'

'Everyone has heard those. They are like the tales of Goha that fathers tell their sons and mothers their daughters: they give amusement, but no one would truly believe them.'

'And no one has seen this special papyrus?' Ibrahim asked.

'Who knows?' Laurent asked.

'The oldest trick among men,' Ibrahim said scornfully. 'What fool would buy a thing he had not seen?'

'I hope van Diemen would not,' I said. 'Laurent, what do you think – another rumour with no substance?'

'It is possible.'

'There will be no papyrus,' Ibrahim said dismissively. 'Van Diemen used to believe only archaeological reports and white men. Now he has added Nasir to his list.'

I nodded sympathetically. 'He's probably right, Laurent.'

Laurent smiled and spread his hands as if in a stoic acceptance that his news was not worthy, but I could read the disappointment in his voice.

'It seems I have nothing exciting to tell you after all,' he said. 'What do you want me to do about all this?'

'Nothing. It is not worth our while to pursue Nasir over a few items that will finish up in a display case in America. If van Diemen needs his little pieces of treasure so badly, let him have them.'

'It is not worth reporting to Lacau?'

I shook my head firmly. 'Lacau hates to be bothered by unsubstantiated anecdotes. I'm sorry. You are working well, Laurent, and this is not the most pleasant of postings, but this rumour is something which we can let rest.'

He shook my hand, I thanked him again, and then he walked quietly but despondently back towards the dark village.

Ibrahim and I went back to the boat and sat opposite each other. Ibrahim kicked off his slippers and put his feet

46

up on the seats. Mosquitoes flickered around the lantern and crawled on its glass sides.

'Well?' I asked.

He spread his hands resignedly. 'Perhaps.'

'Perhaps it is true.'

'Yes.'

'Is Nasir such a scoundrel, Ibrahim?'

Ibrahim laughed. 'Of course he is not. He is a relative of mine, a distant cousin. If you wish, and if God wills it, I can arrange that you are introduced to him. It will take some weeks, for we both sail the Nile, but for different reasons. You did not wish Laurent to think him an honest trader, did you?'

I shook my head. 'I thought I lived a complicated life until I met you. I divide my loyalties, but yours are in splinters.'

He laughed again, and drummed his bare feet on the planking as if delighted by my comment. Aiman woke, turned over, and went back to sleep again.

'Perhaps your cousin is playing what we call the waiting game,' I said.

'Or perhaps there is no papyrus. This is more likely. He is like a fisherman, and you and van Diemen are like the fish. Not only you, but Carter as well. And you will all swim into the nets that he casts.'

'What you mean is that he only has ordinary plunder, looted from a tomb we will never locate, and that he will eke out the finds, a little here, a little there, year by year. And because we hear persistent rumours about an Amduat papyrus, we will buy these things. Why? Because we will be foolish enough to think that if we humour him he will give us first refusal on such a treasure.'

'You think that a papyrus exists of What Is In the Other World?'

'Perhaps.'

'And if it does exist, Nasir will keep it for ten years, more. And watch the price go up. Men always want what they cannot get. If they believe it to be almost within reach, they can no longer think straight.'

I nodded.

'Does Clive Oxtaby know about this papyrus that is so valuable, this ghost which lives only in men's dreams?' he asked.

'It would be very much his kind of interest.'

He shook his head as if we were all fools. 'Do not go down this road, Raymond. There is no end to it. What you think is a treasure will be nothing but sand.'

'We'll see what Nasir has to tell me when we finally meet,' I said.

He spat over the side of the boat. 'You will pay each other compliments which neither of you believe, and circle each other like jackals, but in the end you will each come away with nothing.'

'What's the matter, Ibrahim? Do you think I will mistake a handful of sand if it is offered to me?'

'If you recognised it for what it was,' he said with a wide grin, 'then Nasir could always sell it to the Americans.'

I heard little more of Rex until, early one morning, Ibrahim moored the boat near Baliana and we set off on hired donkeys to visit the temple at Abydos.

At first there were five of us, with two pack donkeys trailing behind on a rope. Ibrahim had decided to buy further goods for the *Seti*, and he brought along Aiman to help with these. Ali, another crewman, was delegated to carry Lucinda's equipment.

We approached the village on *bund* tracks, narrow embankments of earth raised higher than the inundation levels. A thin blue mist dispersed around us, revealing dark thick soil, green with new crops. Hundreds of pigeons rose and flapped around their towers as we rode into the village, and people came to the doors of houses to watch us. Ibrahim pointed out to Lucinda something I had not noticed before – a column inscribed with hieroglyphs, broken at a height of three feet, obscured by a giant hollyhock growing beside a house wall. He and Aiman rode with us as far as the temple perimeter before they left.

As we entered the first courtyard a pair of hoopoes scattered out of our way, running along the ground for several yards before they flew onto a low wall. Like a guard, Ali positioned himself on a large stone between the two outer courtyards. Lucinda wanted to sketch a view of the square-columned portico of the main temple, so Ali called on a passing youth to hold her parasol as she worked. The boy stood blinking at her as if he had unaccountably become involved in an extraordinary and puzzling ritual.

Lucinda's sketch was completed, and the youth was given his money and ran away down the incline of sand and flagstones into the village. I studied her work. At first I had judged it to have no special qualities, but the longer I looked, and the more I thought about its artist, the more pleasing the drawing seemed to be.

'Satisfied?' I asked.

'Not quite,' she said. 'Raymond, be a true friend and stand against the stone over there. I'll put human figures in later, but I need some idea of scale.'

I did as she asked, and stood self-consciously beside an inscribed wall while Lucinda squinted at me and made a few additional marks on the paper. Behind her Ali grinned widely, relishing the strangeness of my situation.

'I have to breathe imaginative life into these dead stones,' she said when she had finished; 'I have to see the exotic where others could only see ruin.'

'I see. And how will this exotic image shape itself?'

She pursed her lips slightly. 'The ancients wove linen so that it was transparent, didn't they? And women sometimes wore dresses which exposed their breasts?'

'I'm sure you already know that to be true.'

'I thought perhaps a bridal scene – pomp, vivid colours, a hint of cruelty; the bride would be young, too young in our eyes; the pharaoh attractive but frightening, all-powerful. I'll call the painting something like *The Sacrifice of Abydos*. Its owners will be able to prove to guests that they are historically aware as well as good judges of art.'

'You came prepared with ideas.'

49

'I've studied the market.'

'And what will you make of this site?' I gestured at the honey-coloured stone and the deep shadows. 'Will you leave it as barren as this?'

'Was it always so desolate?'

'This was fertile land, not desert – black land, not red. There was a canal up to these walls, so the temple was famous for its gardens and pools. Osiris is the god of vegetation, as well. There, I've given you a little more information for your painting.'

'Thank you. I make sure I produce what is wanted, Raymond. I'll romanticise this, soften it, people it with detailed figures. I have to make money. Photography is taking away the living of artists who record only what is to be seen; on the continent new painters are producing work which is not even understandable. Everything is changing. The war marked the end of a lot of things.'

'But your kind of painting – hasn't that kind of style ended as well?'

She nodded. 'It depends. Alma-Tadema and Edward Poynter still have a huge following, you know. I can always sell my work to enthusiastic collectors. And I paint well; I research, I copy exhibits in museums, engravings from books. I've made a special study of David Roberts. Sometimes I think that the best life for me would be in the United States, in Hollywood.'

'Working on Valentino's films?' I asked, unable to contain a sneer.

'Or *Intolerance*. Or *The Ten Commandments*.'

I had seen the first film years ago, in Cairo, and had smirked at the statues of giant elephants supposedly built in Babylon.

'Who will buy a painting like this, Lucinda?' I asked.

'There is always a demand for Orientalism. Mr Carter's excavation has created a lot of additional interest. Someone will buy *The Sacrifice of Abydos* because to them it will be like drinking a cocktail of richness, cruelty, and beauty. And sex, too. The Near East is still harems, virgins, eunuchs and incest, as far as my buyers are concerned.'

50

She did not look up from her work, and I said nothing.

'Of course, you could explain to them all kinds of detail about the Egyptian view of sex, couldn't you?'

'I suppose so,' I said.

'Why not? You seemed as if you wanted to talk about it when we were with van Diemen.'

'I'll tell you whatever you want to know.'

She ignored me, and bent towards her work.

'Of course,' she said after a while, 'whether or not this will actually be *like* ancient Egypt is another matter.'

She finished the sketch and we entered the temple. The interior was roofed and gloomy, but broad shafts of light shone through gaps in the stonework and illuminated part of the columned hall with pools of brilliance.

The wide walls both hollowed and imprisoned my voice. 'Seven gods,' I said, 'some of them amalgamated; Amun-Ra, Osiris, Isis, Horus, Ptah, Ra-Harmakis, and Seti himself. The temple was planned on the number seven – seven doors, seven chapels. Your brother would say that was a magic number to the ancients, but that doesn't explain why Rameses had six of the doors walled up.'

I pointed out the paintings on the white stone – Seti, his flesh the colour of red mud and his hair and crown a delicate yellow, Isis wearing a robe of Marian blue, Osiris portrayed in a series of elaborate and puzzling ceremonies. In a gloomy corridor of stone, light spilling into its far end, I showed her a relief of Seti and his son Rameses making offerings to the seventy-six god-kings who had gone before them, their names fixed for ever in a geometry of cartouches.

'The Abydos king-list,' she said; 'I never thought I would see it.'

At the rear of the temple we ascended a vaulted staircase and went back out into the open air. Here we could look across a deep hollow that contained massive blocks of red Aswan granite, a flight of broken steps, some twentieth-century scaffolding, and spears of vegetation in a pool of dark stagnant water. Some of the blocks were assembled into architraves but others had tumbled as if a giant, grown suddenly bored, had swept away much of a building he had been artfully constructing.

'The Oseirion,' I said; 'the tomb of Osiris. Originally the temple was built so that the inundation flooded it and flowed across stones that represented the original mound of creation. Now there's usually water at the bottom because the water table has risen since ancient times. It makes it virtually impossible to excavate it fully. Apart from that, any archaeologist would be worried that excavations would harm the foundations of the main temple.'

'It's fascinating,' Lucinda said. 'Difficult to sketch, however.'

'It was the ambition of every Egyptian to visit here before he died,' I told her. 'The model boats found in tombs were linked to journeys to Abydos after death. And there was a mound of earth at the centre of the main temple, a heap of alluvial mud like the primeval mound from which life was said to have begun. This temple, this whole area, the burial chambers in the Wadi Biban al-Maluk – they all have to do with generation and resurrection. It's also said that, at night, barren women still come here to bathe. It's supposed to work.'

'That's touching. I rather like the idea of a secret ceremony. It would be lovely to paint that by moonlight.'

'Ibrahim swears the legend is true, and that Aiman had an aunt who was made fertile by coming here.'

'Perhaps I should have visited this place before Rex was killed.'

I looked at her. There was a steely twinkle in her eyes, as if she were forcing herself to joke about her past.

'You would catch something from that water,' I said; 'I doubt if it would be pregnancy. It's an absurd superstition, that's all.'

'Not so absurd if you grow up with it; and not if you live among people who think that womanliness is indistinguishable from motherhood. I know a little about that superstition. Some people assumed that Rex would have made me pregnant before he left. Because he did not, it's thought that I must have something wrong with me.'

'In view of what happened, it was good for you that he didn't.'

'But I wanted him to,' she said quietly; 'I would have even gone into that pool for him.'

'I think you're being as romantic as your paintings now.'

'Do you think so? I would have loved to have had a child. If it had been a boy, I would have felt that I had to call him after his father.'

'And a girl?'

'I would have called her Virginia.'

For the second time in a few days I was vividly reminded of my sister. Disturbed by the presence of death in the house, I had been unable to sleep and had gone into her room with a lighted candle. My father had fallen asleep on his vigil and the room was filled with a rich, sweet smell that had an edge of sickliness. I had already seen the body; it was laid out in the coffin in a nightdress of the purest white. But this time Virginia was there, too; she was standing beside her own corpse and wearing an identical nightdress. One hand rested on the wooden edge of the coffin, and her wide eyes were staring directly at me. This had happened more than twenty years ago, but I still remembered every single detail.

'What's the matter?' Lucinda asked. 'You look unwell.'

'No,' I said, and the word caught in my throat so that it sounded gruff. Fearing that there were tears in my eyes, I turned away. I had not wept since I was a much younger man.

I was angered that I should be so affected by such an absurd coincidence. Angered, too, by the way she talked about Rex. These emotions came upon me with an unaccustomed force, and I did not at first recognise why I was feeling them so keenly.

I turned and walked back into the temple. She did not follow me. After a few yards I turned and called her name.

'You're annoyed,' she said when she joined me again.

'Not at all.'

'Of course you are. Do you think I can't tell?'

I strode across the uneven floor of the hypostyle hall. Angled rods of sunlight pierced the gloom, and the filaments of spider-webs shone like traceries of steel within them. I halted beside one of the massive pillars and turned to her.

'Clive told me what to expect. He said you were modern in outlook, intelligent and independent, that you'd gone for self-improvement after your husband had died. All that is fine by me. He didn't tell me you still have an obsession with a dead husband. Rex is gone, Lucinda; he's dead for ever. It's as if you keep his file open on your desk all the time, shuffling the papers in it to try to prove something. But you may as well put the file away. You have nothing to learn from him now.'

'You're telling me to forget him,' she said. And then, in a tone of outraged dignity, she added, 'How dare you.'

'Don't try being superior. It won't work. I've been away from English manners for too long.'

We stood glaring at each other. I wondered if I was throwing away whatever chance I might have, and calmed slightly.

'Of course I'm not telling you to forget him; you must never forget him. But it's as if you use him as a kind of justification, a kind of proof. You're your own woman now. You could never have been that with Rex. You must realise that. There's no reason to feel guilty just because you have put yourself at the centre of your own ambitions.'

I saw her lips purse.

'You don't have to brandish his name all the time,' I went on, 'and you don't have to pretend that you wanted a child by him. Even if you did, then you must know by now that you're better off without one.'

'Raymond, are you jealous?'

I waited before I answered. 'That's ridiculous.'

'Do you think I'm a fool, and that I cannot grasp the facts of his death after nine years? Of course I can. But if I talk about Rex all the time, it's because I'm nervous – perhaps even scared.'

'Scared? Of living in Luxor?'

'No.' She drew a deep breath. 'Scared because I have not seen Clive for a long, long time. Despite all his letters, despite what I'm told about him, I simply don't know what I shall find.'

'However long it is since you've met, Clive will always be your brother,' I said. 'There's nothing to worry about.'

But I was not sure if I believed what I said.

As we returned to the entrance I began to wonder about Lucinda's fascination with the civilisation that lay in dusty, broken pieces along the length of the Nile. The Egyptians had built their world, not only on the river, not only on a panoply of strange gods, but on convictions about bodily preservation and rebirth. They had taken their dead far from the rotting silt of the river into the dry, desiccating heat of the desert's edge. Rex Plummer's death was beyond doubt, but his remains were beyond recovery, location, even identification. At almost every site, the contrast must be hitting his wife.

Osiris was killed, dismembered, and the fourteen parts of his body distributed about the fertile lands. Isis, the sister he had married, searched for them along the length of the Nile, finding them all except for one. Some versions spoke of Isis then breathing life back into the dead god; others, of the parts being buried where they were found; yet another, of the body being bandaged together to make the first mummy. Whatever the version, it was his wife's act of grief and worship that enabled the god to pass into the next world.

3

Oxtaby was not waiting for us at the hotel, although I had half-expected him to be there. The lobby was empty but for a small group of newspaper reporters seated next to an ornamental palm in a brass pot. They sat glumly, legs outstretched as if their very clothes were uncomfortable, and the hats which they had placed on their table were discoloured by sweat. On the far wall were hung several framed copies of tomb paintings, and in the ceiling a fan with blades as large as an aeroplane's sliced through the dead air.

'Mr Murchison,' one of the reporters said as soon as I entered, 'what can you tell us?'

It was as if I had never been away.

The others began to ask me the same kind of question, repeating variations in a ragged chorus like men used to rejection but still hopeful. I had got to know them when the excavation had first begun; two of them had once struck each other in a struggle to be first on the wire at the Eastern Telegraph office.

I held up my hand to ward off any further questions. 'I haven't been near the tomb for weeks. You people know more than I do.'

'We know it's going to be uncovered soon, probably tomorrow,' one of them said; 'Carter already has his reis hiring labour to move the stones blocking the entrance.'

'Really? It was bound to happen about now, I suppose.'

'Come on, Raymond, you can tell us more than that. You're with the Service.'

'We're promised daily bulletins,' another said, 'but

what we need is something with more individuality, more zest.'

'I don't know any more. Honestly. I'm sorry.'

They nodded as if no one believed me, and began to study Lucinda.

I spoke to her and, like a zealous guardian, made sure my voice carried. 'This way, Mrs Plummer,' I said, as if mention of her married name would dispel any suspicion of impropriety, and walked with her to the reception desk. Ali and Aiman walked behind us, so festooned with travel bags that they resembled figures in a carnival. The hotel porters walked beside them, uncertain whether or not they should snatch the luggage.

I stood with Lucinda as she signed the register and was given her key while the porters finally took control of the bags.

'Clive's room is on one side of yours, and mine is on the other,' I said, showing her the number on the key; 'I always have the same room. Don't I, Hamid?'

The man behind the desk nodded and placed his finger-tips together in a delicate gesture. 'Mr Murchison has stayed with us for years,' he said. 'The man who was last in your room, Mr Murchison, did not wish to leave, but I told him no choice. A gentleman such as yourself, from the Service . . .' He spread his hands as if there could be no competition between my custom and anyone else's.

'Good man. Mrs Plummer, let me know if you have any difficulties. There should be none – Hamid here can sort out most things. And don't go out on your own. Not yet, anyway; not until you're more used to the place. If neither Clive nor I are here, the reporters will help. Most of the other Westerners are at the Winter Palace. The Americans there have parties every night, I'm told.'

'I thought Clive would be here,' she said, and for a moment it seemed that she felt lost.

'He wasn't to know our time of arrival,' I explained; 'we can get a message to him if you want. But it's late afternoon now, and there are boats across the river all the time. He'll probably be here soon.'

57

She nodded.

'From these rooms you can look out across the water to the West Bank,' I said as we ascended in the lift. 'Behind the screen of cliffs are the Valleys of the Kings, the Queens, the Nobles; the whole area is riddled with memorials and mortuary temples. Some people would give their eye-teeth for rooms like ours. Influence, you see; we're important people, at least for the next season or so.'

'It will be all over soon, won't it?'

'This season and next will see an end to clearing the tomb. There will be years of academic work afterwards.'

'But you'll not be involved, or Clive.'

I shook my head. 'Not me. I'm sure Clive won't be, either. Lacau will have posted me to another dig, or put me behind a desk in Cairo. As for Clive – well, Clive's his own man.'

The lift stopped and a small boy in a crumpled uniform opened it for us. I walked with Lucinda to her door. She paused and looked at me. Light flooded the end of the corridor, but it was gloomy where we stood.

'We were in each other's company for such a long time,' she said; 'I'm sad that it's ended.'

I wondered if she was propositioning me, and my heart quickened. 'So am I,' I said.

'But we'll see a lot of each other. You promised to guide me round Karnak.'

'Clive will want to do that.'

'Yes, but I'd like you to do it.'

I nodded. 'Of course. We'll try to go when there is no one else to disturb us. At times there are far too many tourist parties.'

'Yes. The East Bank must be like a little piece of empire.'

I smiled. 'Even the American wives act like memsahibs. Everyone is involved with the clearance in one way or another. Those who aren't directly involved meet up to play bridge or parlour games or to arrange outings. And there are receptions to organise for important visitors when they arrive. It's as if Egyptians had nothing to do with their

58

own history, because they're ignored. The Astors and the Connaughts and the Queen of the Belgians just see the workings of the English class system and the American infatuation with any kind of nobility.'

'I think you're being cynical just to impress me, Raymond. Be like Clive. He may have the same dislikes as you, but he has more belief.'

We said our goodbyes and went into our own rooms. As soon as I had closed my door I leaned against it. I felt that a term of judgement had at last ended, and that I had somehow been found wanting.

The room was comfortingly familiar. I walked up to the small rectangular mirror on the wall, looked at myself, and wondered if Lucinda was doing the very same thing in her own room. Then I turned to the copy of a London newspaper which Hamid had had placed on the dressing-table. It was several days old, and the paper had turned slightly brittle with the heat, but I smoothed it out on the bed and read the headlines before I did anything else.

Afterwards I stood in the shower. The waterpipe clanked; nothing came out of it for several seconds, and then a trickle splashed onto my face. I waited for a few more seconds, and then water came out with full force. I stood beneath it for several minutes until I was refreshed, and then I put on a thin cotton dressing-gown. I could hear the muezzin call from the mosque that had been built above the temple in the middle of town. Soon his voice was lost within the chirping of thousands of sparrows; each night they flocked in from the Nile to roost in the crowns of roadside palms.

I went onto the balcony to watch the sunset. Distances were foreshortening as the colours deepened, and the Theban hills filled the entire horizon. The range was darkening through shades of purple, and above it an unblemished sky moved from scarlet to crimson. The sails of returning feluccas were silhouetted against the glittering river, and a hot desert wind blew into my face from the land of the dead.

Lucinda did not call, and I did not leave my room.

Instead I ordered a light meal and sat on my balcony. The wide stone balustrade was still warm to the touch, so I draped a towel across it and sat with my feet on that. Horses pulling carriages were trotting along the road below me, and a man walked by with a string of camels behind him. Guarding the camels were two small boys who could not have been more than five. A black-clad woman with a child sat beneath the sycamore in the tiny garden in front of the hotel. The child lolled in the crook of one arm, exhausted or dead, and the woman held out a thin hand to every passer-by. Most ignored her.

There was an electric light just inside my room; I sat as close to it as I could, swatting the occasional mosquito as I read the newspaper. Often the reports were like news from another world, and I no longer felt I knew what it was to be English. Today, after so long on the river, the newspaper had a strange fascination.

There was even a long piece about what was planned for this year's work. The writer used the word *excavation*, which we had all stopped using some time ago. *Clearance* was the correct term; the actual digging had long been complete.

These were the latter stages of the team's excavation of the tomb of the Egyptian pharaoh Tutankhamun, the report said. Three years ago steps down into the rock had been uncovered, and since then a series of memorable events had taken place. The finds in the antechamber alone had been unique in their splendour; the squabbling with Egyptian authorities over excavation rights had been unprecedented; and the whole affair had been dogged by rumours of a mysterious curse that had allegedly already jeopardised the lives of several of the team members. Most notably the expedition's patron, Lord Carnarvon, had died shortly after the discovery.

I smiled to myself. There had been excitement and drama enough at the tomb without the ridiculous tale of a curse. I had even heard it reported that an actual written curse had been found inscribed on the entrance to the burial chamber. This was untrue; I knew that it was untrue. All that had ever been found were necropolis seals, including those of the jackal and the nine bound captives. There had been no curse. A posturing novelist, Marie Corelli, had prophesied doom for anyone entering a sealed tomb. She would have been ignored if Carnarvon had not died a few weeks later and if another novelist, Conan Doyle, had not echoed her views. But Carnarvon had been a sick man for years, so sick that he had been unable to fend off the effects of blood poison from a mosquito bite.

Early last year, the report went on, it had seemed to many that the most exciting archaeological find ever made in Egypt would fall victim to both the bureaucracy and greed of the Egyptian authorities and the obstinacy of the Anglo-American team and its leader, Mr Howard Carter. Ever since the discovery the Antiquities Service had sought to restrict and frustrate the archaeologists. A new list of instructions, culminating in a refusal to let the team's wives visit the tomb before anyone else, had so angered Mr Carter that he closed and locked it on 13 February. When he did this, he left the huge sarcophagus lid suspended by ropes over the coffins which still contained the dead pharaoh.

The closure of the tomb was an ill-considered action which he must have had cause to regret. Less than ten days later Pierre Lacau, the director-general of the Antiquities Service, had his men break into the tomb and carefully lower the lid back onto the sarcophagus. Lacau then had the locks on the tomb replaced with the Service's own. Other tombs being used for analytical work and for storage were also entered and their locks replaced.

Carter and his colleagues were therefore denied access to the very place in which they had laboured so diligently and for so long, as well as to the treasures which they were scrupulously preserving and cataloguing before they were handed over to the Cairo museum.

There was a slight cry from the next room; I stopped reading and listened. It had been a woman's voice, so it must have been Lucinda, but I could not tell if the cry was of distress or pleasure. Soon, however, I heard another voice – this time a man's, and one which I recognised. Clive Oxtaby had come to see his sister at last.

I folded the newspaper so that I could read it more easily.

Only in January of this year had the dispute been settled and a new concession granted to Carter's team. It was understood that the new contract enabled the archaeologists to keep duplicate items, that is, should the tomb be found to contain several examples of the same object, then the Antiquities Service would not press its legal claim for sole and full ownership of every item found in the tomb.

I could not help but smile at the wording. I doubted if Carter would officially be given anything, and it was now impossible for him to take it.

The remainder of the season had been spent in preservation work that was being undertaken by a team led by Manchester-born Alfred Lucas, now a chemist with the Antiquities Service. It was understood that certain items, most notably a linen pall portraying a night sky spangled with stars, symbolic of the goddess Nut, may have been permanently damaged because it had effectively been abandoned during the term of the dispute.

I could hear Lucinda and Oxtaby talking, but could not distinguish what they were saying. Then I heard Oxtaby's voice say, very clearly, 'But of *course* I did.'

Within the next few weeks the team would begin to empty the sarcophagus. The late Lord Carnarvon had already said what his team expected to find – two or three coffins made of gilded wood, and within them the mummified body of a young man. The body would have gold bracelets, rings, pectorals, and his fingernails and toenails would also be inlaid with gold. This young man, believed by his subjects to be a god, had died more than three thousand years ago. After the sarcophagus was emptied, there remained the last room to clear. This was the so-called treasury; this, too, was a trove of riches.

One could only speculate about what would be found within the sarcophagus. It seemed certain, however, that the latter stages of the emptying of Tutankhamun's tomb would be even more exciting than the earlier ones.

'Clive,' Lucinda said, 'I'd hoped things had changed.'

I looked up rapidly. But then she must have moved away from the window, for whatever she said next was distant and indistinct.

Overcome by curiosity, I stood at the very edge of my own balcony so that I could hear their voices more clearly, but there was only the noise of fabric rustling, and perhaps a wardrobe door being closed. Oxtaby, I thought, must have left his sister alone. And for one wild moment I wanted to vault the balcony like a hero, and present myself at her french windows.

I forced a smile at my own imagination, and went back into my room and lay on the bed.

I must have fallen asleep dreaming of treasures and theft, because I woke convinced that it was raining. But there was no cloud in the high and starry sky, and the river sparkled under a cold, high moon.

Before I saw the work-gang I could hear the noise it made; the mouth of the valley rang with the stony crash of rock and gravel being heaved from panniers and carts.

Millions of years ago water had gashed and scoured the valley, marking it with fissures and gullies. Now there was no water at all, merely bedrock, grit, and sand. Dozens of members of the Theban royal family had been placed in coffins at the end of tunnels into the rock, and had lain there awaiting resurrection like larvae at the end of burrows. Now their resting-places had been opened by people whose motives and appearance they could never have imagined. The blocked tombs had been emptied, the sacred necropolis turned to a nexus of dusty pathways. In the well of the valley, as if all the other tombs were somehow focused onto it, the sixteen steps down into the house of Tutankhamun were being cleared yet again.

At the end of each season the tomb was re-sealed and the stairwell packed with rubble and gravel which was watered so that it baked as hard as brick. Now men and boys, more than a hundred of them, were lifting the blocking from the entrance. They worked with picks, shovels and their bare hands. Carter's two foremen, Ahmed and Hussain, were issuing a series of excited orders. They marshalled the workforce as if it were little more than a band of slaves, and handed out tokens for each full basket dumped in the chosen areas. The newly built retaining wall around the entrance was clear, and men were already standing on the upper two steps of the tomb.

Carter leaned on his cane and watched it all, his bow-tie knotted impeccably and a hat placed squarely on his head. It was as if he were surveying an English race-meeting, but the temperature was already well over ninety, and his grey striped suit was beginning to be covered with dust settling out of the air.

I shook his hand. To me Carter had always seemed an avuncular figure, approachable yet stubborn, a man prone to self-doubt despite his extraordinary success. He was short and well-built, with a thick moustache, and he still spoke with a strangely comforting Norfolk accent whose stresses carried over into his Arabic.

'You'll reach the timber-blocking by tomorrow,' I said.

'I hope to,' he answered. 'There are many tons of rubble to shift, Murchison. It takes time, even for these people.'

'And then you can tackle the coffins. And the body inside them.'

'I'll have a whole month to think about the body,' he answered testily. 'Pecky Callender and I have spent the summer redesigning a lifting system for the coffins. We're confident it will do the job very quickly. If your man Lacau had not gone to Europe, or if he had let his deputy stand in for him, then we could have arranged to have the mummy examined earlier.'

'Lacau wants to be everywhere,' I agreed. 'Jesuits have a keen sense of history.'

'It would help if he had a keen sense of timing as well. It seems that it is his intention to keep us all waiting. It was a poor day for Egyptology when it was agreed that the post of director-general should always be occupied by a Frenchman.'

'Gaston Maspero was a good friend to you.'

'Up to a point. But his successor is more than a thorn in the side; he is a lance deepening a wound.'

'You're being unfair,' I answered. 'Lacau may have a bureaucrat's mind, but his heart is with the science of Egyptology. And he's not your enemy. If he'd wanted to, he could have destroyed your reputation when we found the lotus head. That was very lax of you, Howard.'

He prodded the sand vigorously with his cane as if he were exterminating a troublesome insect. 'Lacau is a man who has no financial or academic commitment to the clearance,' he said, 'merely a sense of personal aggrandisement and cultural avarice.'

He looked straight at me, daring me to object, but I refused to be drawn. Carter was a man of much kindness, but he was also capable of sustained bitterness. At such times it was politic not to respond to his provocations, for he might then endanger the very things we all strove for.

'So your professors of anatomy are arriving in early November?' I asked. 'It may take you that long to free the body. The unguents could have glued it within its coffin.'

'I need no lessons in possibilities,' he said.

'Of course not.'

He was silent for a moment, and then cleared his throat. 'The museum has told me that our last shipment reached them in satisfactory condition.'

'Perfect. I pitied the guards. Lucas's preservation work is extraordinary, but they must have breathed formalin for the entire journey.'

'Lucas breathes it every day of every week; paid guards have no cause to complain. But it's true that his work is first-class. He and Newberry would have liked to have done more with the shrine pall, but its salvation was almost totally wrecked by your Service – the duroprene could only preserve a little of what remained.'

'That's sad,' I said neutrally. Carter had once been a

member of the Service himself, but had resigned more than twenty years ago. He had refused to apologise to the French after a scuffle between his Arab employees and some French visitors to Sakkara. After that he had for some years survived as a dealer and artist before Carnarvon employed him as a practising archaeologist once more.

'I am continually astonished by what officials do not know,' he continued. 'In Cairo, they were fixing the wrong wheels onto the chariot axles – imagine that! And these are the people who are judged expert enough to look after our finds.'

'They'll improve. They have to.'

'If they do, it will be long after my day.'

He was silent for a while, and then spoke again.

'You're a good man, Raymond. I appreciate your loyalty and trust. Certainly you have done things for your mother country and not merely for the Service. But I hear that you were not alone in your journey up the Nile.'

'Ibrahim's business has always been with tourists.'

'And the tourist is Clive Oxtaby's sister.'

'Mrs Plummer, yes. I was a kind of guide, and a kind of chaperon as well. Even those tourists in groups were made nervous after Stack was shot dead. It would have been foolish for a lady to travel alone. She paid me handsomely; and I was due holidays from the Service.'

'And where is Mr Plummer?'

'Dead. Killed at the Somme. I understand he left his wife the money which has allowed her to travel here. Like you, she's a watercolourist. And quite successful, I understand. Although her paintings rely more on the imagination than yours.'

'Mine are of tomb paintings or reliefs, and are done from necessity and for the accurate recording of our finds; I think perhaps we would have little in common. Besides, over the last three years we have had difficulties enough within our community and its satellites. Envy and frustration have sometimes walked hand in hand with us; I would not wish to increase their grip.'

'I take your point. But I've seen some of her work, and

to me it seems competent. Assured, even – but perhaps I'm no judge. I'm sure she'd like to study the paintings in the tomb, if it could be arranged. When the coffins have been lifted, of course.'

He was silent again for a while.

'Your friend Oxtaby,' he said eventually, 'I thought he was like us.'

'Like us?'

'I thought that he had no relatives; no connections.' He hesitated slightly before the last word.

'Howard, you have a large family. How many brothers have you? And a sister, as well.'

'I mean that I thought he was – ' And again, there was a slight hesitation. 'His own man.'

Carter was fifty-one years old. Since he was seventeen he had been working in Egypt, so that he had spent an entire life bound by the necessities of his profession. Now, as his greatest work neared its end, perhaps he was growing more sharply aware that many of his colleagues had children to return to. Sometimes I saw myself like him.

'I knew about his sister,' I said. 'He used to talk about her. Not much, but a little.'

'Here?'

'No. When we were in the Bureau.'

'I hope she settles him down,' he said. 'The man has undoubted talents, but he seems incapable of directing them properly. He should have kept quiet about the lotus head. For God's sake, didn't the man *realise* what had happened?'

'There were others in the storage tomb, Howard. I was there myself. He could hardly have ignored it; there were several witnesses.'

'And after that he had what you would call his break-down, didn't he? Heard strange voices talk to him in tombs, began swearing and hitting out at other Englishmen, started to think he was an Arab born within the wrong skin?'

'It wasn't quite so dramatic, Howard. You've had plenty of trouble yourself with others, especially with officials. And you like to live on the West Bank, just as he does.'

'I like to live with a modicum of comfort, and not in a temporary hovel, like some kind of jackal. Lacau did right to sack him. It's one of the few things on which I was in full agreement with that Frenchman.'

'You used to be less critical,' I said. 'Remember the Christmas celebration we held at the Winter Palace after the discovery? We all had a fine time; Carnarvon had even sent us English plum puddings to eat. And Oxtaby entertained everyone with his tricks. He could deal out cards in ways that deceived all of us who watched. And he demonstrated what a gullible man would call mind-reading. There were even those who suspected him of being a professional conjuror.'

'He's stronger in the techniques of conjuring than he is in common sense, Murchison. Even the people of Qurna are beginning to be wary of him.' He looked directly at me. 'A word to the wise,' he said, and then gave a dismissive snort, as if he was slightly embarrassed in even talking about Oxtaby.

'Not according to him. He says that people are waiting for him to be present at the unwrapping of the king.'

He laughed out loud. 'Which king? Ours here?'

I nodded.

'And which people? The villagers of Qurna have even less claim on this tomb than your Service has; they're descendants of Bedouin, not of ancient Egyptians.'

'Oxtaby is back with the Service, at least for this season. He's too knowledgeable to ignore, even if he does hold some foolish views.'

'And who spoke for him, Murchison? You?'

'Yes. To Lacau's deputy.'

He shook his head sadly. 'I hope you don't have cause to regret doing so. I thought you and Oxtaby had argued so violently that you could never be close again.'

'That's not true. There was no argument, merely a difference of opinion. The kind professionals often have.'

'You were once like brothers.'

68

'Not like brothers who confided in each other.'

'Nevertheless your tolerance of him has always intrigued and astonished me. Save your life, did he? In the war?'

'We shared some bad times.'

But I had lain there winded and stunned as a sudden fierce pain began to burn in my shoulder. The soldier with the bayonet came towards me; he seemed to take an age to wade through the soft sand, and yet I was so utterly convinced that I was going to die there, on the slope of that dune, that there seemed no reason to resist what was inevitable. I merely watched him come for me. At that moment, Clive Oxtaby crossed the ridge behind me, and a line of Arabs came with him.

I thought that Carter had finished talking about Oxtaby, but he suddenly flushed with anger. 'The Egyptians will have their officials present. Like you, Oxtaby will attend *only* as an employee of the Antiquities Service. He represents no one else. Certainly the villagers of Qurna would not want him.'

He took a swing at a loose rock with the end of his cane, but missed it.

'His views are not foolish,' he said darkly, 'they are insane. This is a scientific study, not a theatre for the ravings of a madman. His very presence at the autopsy would undermine my authority.'

'He has given me assurances, Howard. You'll not be troubled by him, or by anyone else.'

'Troubled? Has he not done enough already to trouble me? His acts are like treason, from someone I once thought had the manners of an Englishman.'

'It was your own actions that led to the discovery of the lotus head, not Oxtaby's. And preventing the lid from smashing down on the sarcophagus was an act of prudence and not treason. If you were less quick-tempered you would never have left it like that. You have a lot to thank Oxtaby for, as you have a lot to thank me for.'

'We have agreed never to speak of that.'

'I don't intend to.'

He was silent for a few moments. I assumed he was

69

thinking how, along with Carnarvon, Carnarvon's daughter Evelyn, and Pecky Callender, he had illegally entered the burial chamber before the official opening. They had spent the night hours transfixed by the variety, beauty and strangeness of the funeral goods, and been unable to resist bringing a few small items with them — a gold signet-ring, a statuette of a girl, a tiny bronze dog, ivory figures of a gazelle and of a horse, some cosmetic boxes and perfume jars. I had been the man entrusted to take them secretly to Alexandria. If I had been discovered I should have been discharged from the Service, and Carnarvon and Carter would never have been allowed to renew their concession; but I had been paid well.

'Howard,' I said, 'there is a rumour on the river that another important discovery has been made, but that this one is secret.'

He remained impassive. 'Rumour,' he repeated.

'There is little else to act on.'

His eyes searched me out.

'Rumours can be ignored,' I said.

'This land is full of hearsay and fabrication. Some even believe the tales of Goha to be true. It is always wise to disregard most of what one hears.'

'Agreed.'

'What kind of discovery?'

'That's difficult to say. I believe van Diemen has been offered items at his dig at Amarna, but it appears they come from the south.'

'From here?'

'Possibly. A man called Nasir is involved. His uncle was Mohammed Mohassib.'

He nodded slowly. 'A dealer with pedigree,' he said.

'Laurent, the Service's man at Amarna, believes that Nasir is asking an extraordinary price for a papyrus, but no one has seen it. Laurent has merely seen figures in van Diemen's diary.'

'You don't think it could be a version of the Amduat?' Suddenly he gave a wide, nervous grin, as if he had been discovered committing a petty crime. 'That would be too much to hope.'

Carter had heard rumours, too. 'There are a few other items included,' I went on; 'canopic jars, a head of Osiris. But Laurent thinks the total value of Nasir's sale is about one hundred thousand dollars. There must be something highly valuable somewhere in the deal.'

'Will he buy?'

'He's inexperienced enough to accept a ridiculous sum. But we agree that this is a country of rumour, that there may be nothing to this story. On the other hand, if it is true, then Nasir might not approach us because he believes the Service will take everything from him. Which it would do.'

'Undoubtedly.'

'If we try to find out more – '

'You'll do that? Secretly?'

'We cannot keep this just between you and me. Ibrahim knows already, but he can bring Nasir to us. And Clive Oxtaby is our best judge of material relating to the Other World.'

'I don't like Oxtaby's involvement.'

'I believe it to be essential. And Oxtaby can also make an approach through his own friends on the West Bank. We must know as much as we can about the papyrus if we are to assess its value correctly.'

'If this fails, Raymond, I want nothing to do with it.'

'Howard, neither do I.'

We were silent for a while. Two more steps to the tomb had been unearthed, but there was no let-up in the speed of the men digging out the entrance.

Carter cleared his throat. 'Taken a shine to Oxtaby's sister, have you?'

I was taken aback by his insight. 'Is it so obvious?' I asked.

'You are always so keen to help Oxtaby; I wondered if this time you were doing it to impress his sister. But she must not be told about the Other World papyrus.'

'I can guarantee I'll not tell her.'

After a while he spoke again. 'I used to believe that there was something special between Lady Evelyn and myself. Of course, there was nothing. She was merely captivated by the find.'

'And you?'

'And I,' he said, 'I am a man who has spent too long away from his home.'

That evening I met Oxtaby for the first time since our meeting by the colossi of Memnon. He was wearing the double-breasted suit I had last seen on him more than a year ago, although now it looked slightly too large, as if he had lost several pounds in weight. He was clean-shaven, with a collar and tie, and shoes that had been polished; he could have been mistaken for any other member of the Service.

As soon as he saw me he strode across the lobby and shook me warmly by the hand. I wondered if his gratitude was staged for the benefit of the reporters who were now crowding the hotel. The overnight train from Cairo had brought a further six or seven, and some were already seated near the small bar. One began talking loudly about the difficulty he would have in filing his stories. Oxtaby and I looked at each other and smiled. In that moment we shared an unalloyed complicity; we were old hands, each of us.

'Raymond,' he said, calling me by my Christian name for the first time, 'you've been a real friend. Lucinda thoroughly enjoyed her journey. But now I'm afraid she will know almost as much about ancient Egypt as I do.'

He laughed; it was not unconvincing.

'I enjoyed it as well,' I said. Smooth as any lounge-bar hero, I added, 'It's not often one has the company of an intelligent and beautiful woman, let alone under such pleasurable conditions.'

'Lucinda *is* quite beautiful, isn't she? She takes after our mother, I think; unlike me. You find her exciting; I can see that you do.'

I smiled noncommittally, disturbed that he should speak in such an unguarded fashion about his sister.

This time his laugh was almost like a jackal's bark. 'Some men would think it inappropriate to hand over their sister to a man who was a stranger to her. But it is always said on the Nile that you are honourable, Raymond.'

'I'm not sure if you're paying me a compliment or insulting me.'

'A compliment, of course. I hope her presence didn't get in the way of any other purpose.'

'Trade? You know how sensitive that is.'

'Ah, but you can tell me. We understand each other on such matters.'

I shook my head. 'I'll not tell you here.'

'The garden should be pleasant at this time of evening,' he said, 'and the river will be quiet.'

We walked out into the cool dark air. An old man was watering the grass with a hose, and the beggar-woman and her baby had moved to the middle of the path, which was also splashed with water. Oxtaby pressed a coin into her hand as we passed, and she began to thank him.

'For your child,' he said to her, anger in his voice. 'That baby is dying,' he said to me, 'I'm sure of it. We are up to our necks in relics worth thousands, perhaps millions, and children die on the street.'

The night smelled of bougainvillaea and horse-dung. We ignored the carriages that stood outside with their oil-lamps lit, and crossed the road so that we could look out over the Nile. The moonlight made the water shine and darken like the scales of a fish, and on the far bank there were tiny pinpricks of illumination. Deserted feluccas tethered to the bank slowly thumped together and then parted, and further downstream a steamer shone with a hundred lights.

'Oxtaby,' I asked, 'do you know a man called Nasir?'

'Scores of them.'

'This one is the nephew of Mohammed Mohassib. They say he's becoming a very important dealer. Even better than his uncle or Maurice Nahman.'

He turned to me, and in the moonlight his face looked bloodless.

'Yes, I know him. I met him once, when I was crossing the jebel. He had two other men with him. I thought they must be up to no good, but I would have had no proof. They gave me the impression they would split my skull if I tried to interfere. I found out later that Nasir has two lieutenants, Akhmet and Deesa; one of them is a burly bodyguard, the other is smaller and more vicious. I'm sure those were the people I saw with him.'

He paused, and in the silence two feluccas grated so roughly against each other it sounded as if their wood was splitting.

'I was in native dress; that probably helped. We had a short, very civilised conversation, as one often does on such tracks. Why do you ask?'

'Have you heard anything about his deals?'

'I heard he was concentrating on Americans because they are richer than us. And maybe he's wary of dealing with people like Carter. Or you.'

'Have you heard about a papyrus he could be offering? Perhaps concerning the Other World?'

'A copy of the Amduat? Written down on papyrus rather than tomb walls? Those rumours are nothing but fairytales. Aren't they?'

'Probably. Would one of your men know?'

'Sayeed? Maybe. He and his family have hawked grave goods for a century or more. I've heard that Nasir is a generous man, and that he makes sure his uncle's old colleague lives well. Sayeed may even be a channel for some of Nasir's lesser pieces. Why are you so keen on this, Raymond? Greed? Or are you just doing your job and reporting everything to Lacau?'

'A concern for the progress of knowledge, that's all.'

'And if this concern puts money in your back pocket, then so much the better? Because you're working for Carter, aren't you? You're not going to tell Lacau a thing.'

'He doesn't have to know.'

'Tell him nothing. He deserves to know nothing. But, if you're asking me to help you, then you must tell *me* everything. I need to know as much as you do.'

I told him about the visit to Amarna, about Laurent's belief that van Diemen had bought objects from Nasir, including two canopic jars, and his speculation about the papyrus. Then I told him what Carter had said.

'Lucinda doesn't know?' he asked.

'There would be no reason to tell her. And Carter insists that the fewer who know, the better. That's sensible.'

He shook his head in parody shock. 'Keep secrets from my own sister,' he said.

I said nothing.

'You know,' he said after a while, 'in fifty years' time Carter will seem an anachronism. The idea of Europeans and Americans emptying a tomb like Tutankhamun's will seem as bizarre as Nubians digging up Stonehenge.'

He seemed to consider this for a moment.

'But they'll still need people like me,' he added.

'Why you?'

'Because I'm special.'

'We're all special; each one of us. Some of us are leading authorities, and those that aren't soon will be. You know what the Americans call this? Their meal ticket. They know their work here has made them famous, and that these last seasons will make their futures even brighter. University departments will offer them new jobs at high salaries, institutions and societies will want them to lecture on their work, their home-town newspapers will print their photographs on the front page yet again.'

'And what will you get from this? Nothing? Is this why you are so eager to get a percentage of an expensive sale? Perhaps you're keen to get back to England when the clearance ends?'

'I'm a servant of the Egyptian Ministry of Works, just like you. I don't expect anything other than a salary. Carter will get the rewards.'

'He may get royalties from a book which can never tell the full story of what has happened here; as for the Service, he'll be lucky if it allows him a few arrows, a tiny cup, and maybe a box that once held food for the afterlife. Tell me – you're much higher in the Service than I'll ever be – tell me if Carter will be given what he hopes for.'

'I can't say. Even if he doesn't, then he should be knighted.'

'*Should*. I doubt if he will. Carter has ruffled too many feathers. Acting like a hero is one thing, but being sullen about it is another.'

'He's popular with the people. Crowds are turned away from his lectures.'

'Since when have the people had anything to do with who gets honoured and who doesn't? I would want no honours from the British. I prefer the respect that I am given by the people of the West Bank.'

I nodded. 'Perhaps you're wise.'

'And that's where I'll start looking for your new version of the Amduat,' he said.

We went back to the hotel. As I passed the beggar, I gave her a few coins from my pocket. The child in her arms had lost all consciousness, and there was a shadow across its face. The mother's thanks followed me to the hotel door.

Inside the bar we found the only spare table and ordered drinks. When the boy served us Oxtaby told him to charge it to Lucinda's room number.

'I'm sorry,' he murmured; 'until the Service pays me something, I have virtually no money. All that you see is camouflage.'

'I would have paid,' I said. 'We can't expect Mrs Plummer to.'

He waved one hand in front of him as if he were dispelling mist.

'It doesn't matter,' he answered; 'she'll probably become richer than either of us.'

I was about to say something else, but he began to speak again.

'I must tell you something important. I have almost mastered a new trick; one that will astonish even the jaded. I say *new*, but it has its own antiquity. My time with Sheik Moussa was well spent, despite your evident embarrassment that I assisted him. When I have perfected it, then perhaps I shall demonstrate the trick to you.'

'I wish you weren't so keen on displays of music-hall fakery. Lacau is far too solemn for such entertainment. It does you no good.'

'I said my trick had antiquity. Akhenaten and Moses were both charlatans possessed by mad ideas, but at least Moses got his people out of this country. How? By a series of conjuring tricks and prophecies learned from the priests.'

'Maybe. We'll never know the truth about that.'

'Truth?' he said, almost coughing. 'Truth,' he repeated again, more slowly, as if he was testing the word.

I looked across the room. Lucinda had come downstairs and was making her way to our table. She was more formal than she had ever dressed on the *Seti*, and she looked tired, as if she had not slept at all.

That afternoon Oxtaby had guided her around the temple of Amun-Ra in the middle of Luxor. 'Clive has a way of bringing the past alive,' she told me; 'it's as if his imagination is alight with ancient history.'

I nodded. I would have liked to hear her praise my own skills.

'Raymond detests my way of bringing things alive,' Oxtaby said drily.

Lucinda looked surprised. 'Is that true?' she asked.

'Your brother's being mischievous,' I told her. 'I have no doubts at all about his factual knowledge – it's as good as mine. I'm sceptical about his interpretations.'

'He's being diplomatic,' Oxtaby said.

'Not at all. Egyptology has to cope with vast ranges of time. The early dynastic periods started about five thousand years ago, and the last of the native pharaohs reigned up until about 340 BC. With a time span like that, it's not surprising that there are whole areas that we know very little about, whole areas which are still being argued over.'

'You're skirting round the issues. Raymond is only interested in hard fact, Lucinda. That's how you would put it, wouldn't you?'

77

'If I had to, yes,' I agreed.

'And that's what you're good at. You like things you can measure and slot into place, as if all of the dynastic history of Egypt was a jigsaw scattered by the Romans and the Arabs and the Turks, and all we had to do really to understand was dig the pieces out of the sand. But it's not like that at all. This was a people governed by spiritual beliefs quite foreign to present-day excavators, content to believe contradictory myths about, say, Osiris, without thinking that confusion at all odd. When anyone looks closely at what has survived, they must be struck by what remains puzzling and mysterious. Inside temples, on rolls of papyrus, and even on body ornaments there are pictures we can't understand and configurations of symbols which no one has ever been able to explain. Even the necropolis seal is a mystery to us.'

'But we usually *have* been able to explain them,' I said. 'The Ptolemaic temples had the rituals chiselled into their walls.'

'Late versions,' he said dismissively, 'half-destroyed by Christians.'

'And their myths aren't all that strange. Many of us grew up with ideas about judgement after death, about salvation, and an afterlife.'

'All of which had their roots in the ancient beliefs. It doesn't need a philologist to see that Christian ideas of resurrection spring directly from an Isis cult that was still strong in the Middle East of two thousand years ago. But what exists in the West now is watered-down belief. Compare its hesitations and its compromises to the beliefs of Eighteenth Dynasty Egyptians – they were the ones who raised the cult of the dead to its highest level; they were the ones who began to record elaborate magical formulae for the protection of the dead king.'

I wanted to use his last name, but for Lucinda's sake forced myself to use his first.

'Clive, these were practical people. They may have had a complex religion, but it was tied to the practicalities of life on the land and of what they measured of the world around them. This was a race who built Nileometers, for heaven's sake; they could forecast the river's effect on their economy by noting its rise at known points. A superstitious people wouldn't be able to do that.'

'Superstition?' he asked, and spread his hands like a man displaying wounds. 'That's a Western idea. The product of a particular way of classifying societies, with primitive people on the bottom and the English at the top.'

I shook my head. 'I don't feel superior.'

'Of course you do,' he snapped, so curtly that Lucinda reached out her hand and touched his arm as if to restrain him.

'I'm sorry, Raymond,' he said after a short pause, 'that was ill-mannered of me. You have your job to do, of course; I understand that fully. But I want more than you. That's why I was happy to leave the Service for a while.'

I glanced at Lucinda. I had never mentioned that Oxtaby had been discharged; I wondered what half-truth he had told her.

He turned to her. 'If Raymond had taken you around the temple, he would have given you an entire mass of detail.'

'He's promised to take me to Karnak,' she said.

'Then go with him; it will take days to see it all. And Raymond will check all his dates and then he will deal out fact after fact, like a man setting down cards. I used to be the same. But what is much more interesting, much more *vital* is what lies beneath all the facts. There's another world underneath the external one of ruins and inscriptions. What was the motivating force of this civilisation? What kind of mystery drove them on? They must have believed in a kind of real magic, in a union with spiritual forces. Everything they recorded meant something; they weren't interested in mere diversions.'

Lucinda looked back at me. 'Clive always did have a vivid imagination,' I said.

I need not have spoken. 'A long time ago,' Oxtaby went on, 'when Raymond and I worked in the Arab Bureau – '

'Not the war,' I said; 'please.'

But he continued. 'We were crossing a barren stretch of desert on camels. You remember this, Raymond?'

'We spent two years crossing deserts, thousands of miles, backwards and forwards, up and down. Most of it was pointless.'

'On this particular day we were crossing lava beds, mile after mile of them, the two of us and about thirty Arabs. I saw a round, dull object in front of us, the colour of silt, no bigger than a cricket ball and even harder. I knew I had to pick it up, but I didn't know why. It was a ball of rock – a geode. I took it back to our base and had one of the engineers saw it in half. The rock was hollow, and the entire inner surface was encrusted with brilliant crystals. It gave me an insight into what the ancient religions were like.'

'Clive,' I said wearily, 'I've heard this analogy dozens of times.'

'But I haven't,' Lucinda said.

'Religion,' he went on, 'belief, a sense of a guiding force, call it what you will, is central to most civilisations. Today we rationalise it so we can understand it better, but the true ancient religions were a kind of mystery. The rituals took place in secret; they would never have been watched by the people, like a service in a modern church. That idea was literally unthinkable. From the beginnings of its dynastic history Egypt was hidden, infolded. The mortuary temples that are now open to the sun and the wind had mud-brick walls to protect them from unwanted gazes. And the main sections of all the temples were roofed, dark, with inner sanctuaries. Statues of the god-kings had stone rooms built around them so that they would be enclosed in secret chapels for all eternity. The only men who saw them were the priests. They were allowed to peer into two spy-holes, like watching eyes, and to blow incense through them. What we see now, and what we oversee, are ruins.'

'It's all we have,' I said.

He looked up at the ceiling, as if he were drawing

a fiction from the air. 'Imagine what it would be like three thousand years from now, if we knew nothing of the history of Europe, nothing of Christianity – and we found a razed church with a smashed altar, fragments of stained glass littering the ground, a gold cross in one corner, a battered communion cup, some torn vestments. That would be a large amount of evidence to survive. But from it, would we be able to recreate the form of a service? Of course we wouldn't. As for deducing the form of the *religion* from such relics, why, that wouldn't even occur to us. We would see the remains of the body, but the mind would have eluded us for ever.'

'That's a poor argument,' I complained. 'And you left out the Bible because that would have been even more likely to survive. And we have the Pyramid texts, we have the Book of the Dead.'

I did not dare mention the Book of What Is In the Other World.

'That's rather like having the letter to the Corinthians, and nothing else.'

'You're putting your argument too strongly,' I said.

'Really? What does the world think of Carter's clearance of the tomb? The descriptions and discussions are all about the richness of the finds, what they looked like, how they were to accompany the king into the next world. They want their readers to think that the Egyptians believed that the tomb contents would somehow dissolve and be transported to a kind of heaven. Well, the treasure was certainly there for the next world, but there was nothing crass or unsophisticated about the people who put it there. The hoard was both everyday and royal, but it was also secret, mysterious, inseparable from divinity.'

He stopped as if he had exhausted all he had to say. We stared at each other for a few seconds, and then he dropped his eyes.

'An Amduat papyrus would be priceless,' he said.

I held my breath.

'What's that?' Lucinda asked him.

'It's a kind of guidebook to the next world,' Oxtaby

81

answered. 'When a king died he passed through a field of reeds and went on a journey through the twelve hours of the night. Each hour had its own characteristics, its own incantations. At the end of his journey he was reborn with the rising of the new sun.'

'And it's a book?'

My mouth was so dry I could not trust myself to speak.

Oxtaby shook his head. 'Not really. The Amduat is painted on burial chambers, mortuary shrines, grave goods. You'll have seen copies of parts of it in museums. Tutankhamun's tomb has the opening sections on its walls.'

I wondered if I had misjudged Oxtaby; perhaps he was going to talk about the Amduat papyrus even now, only minutes after he had promised secrecy.

'It begins,' he said, 'with the words *The writings of the inner sanctum, the places where all the gods, souls, and spirits meet, what they do.*' He looked across at me. 'Raymond?' he asked quietly.

I continued for him. '*The gates of the West; the knowledge and the power of those that are in the Other World; what is done there; knowledge of the sacred rituals; knowledge of the mysterious forces.*'

This seemed to be sufficient answer for Lucinda, for she moved on. Only when I began to relax did I realise how tense I had been.

'And your geode,' she asked. 'What happened to it?'

'Lost,' he said brightly. 'Someone must have swiped it, I think. It was difficult to hang onto anything but the most basic essentials in those days. Isn't that right, Raymond?'

I saw that he was pleading with me for a truce, and that he no longer wished to talk about our differences.

'That's right,' I said quietly.

In a few minutes he left us to talk to one of the reporters. For three years now Oxtaby had earned furtive money telling such people about the importance of Carter's find and the place of Tutankhamun in the politics of the Eighteenth Dynasty. When he did this he avoided his own wilder

82

flights of fancy, perhaps believing that such idiosyncratic views, if printed, would eventually be traced back to him.

'What did he tell you about the Luxor temple?' I asked Lucinda. 'That it was a symbolic representation of a man's body?'

'Yes. Would you disagree?'

'I see no evidence for it.'

'It wasn't just theory, Raymond. He pointed out – '

'Yes, I'm sure he did. But your brother has ideas that are unsound. He sees the peristyle hall as a kind of ribcage and the inner sanctuary as a kind of skull. Like all half-mad theories, it's difficult to disprove.'

'He has reasons for drawing those conclusions. The phases of the moon are carved into the bases of the columns, and Clive says that in mythology they're linked to the act of breathing. And the sun is linked to the beating of the heart. So that the sun – '

I shook my head, exasperated. 'Should I tell you what Clive's theories are like?' I asked, and then momentarily hesitated.

'Go on,' she said.

'I'm not talking about him behind his back; he already knows what I think.'

'Tell me.'

'I owe Clive a lot.'

'I'm sure you do.'

'And I probably understand him better than anyone else on this stretch of the Nile.'

'Anyone but me. I understand him in the way that only a sister can.'

Something about the way she said it made me pause, but then I continued.

'He once told me you had very unusual childhoods,' I said. 'I believe he was proud of that.'

'We didn't realise how different it was. Our mother asked us not to talk about it to friends; she said that they wouldn't understand.'

I was puzzled by this comment, but did not wish to be taken off my point.

'What I'm trying to say is this – you were brought up in a rational household. You were encouraged to see mankind as something that made itself. Probably you were told that, if you had questions, you would find no answers in the Bible. Whatever there was to know lay buried in history, and in the workings of each human brain. At the end of your time you would die, as millions of others had already died, and there would be nothing but oblivion.'

'So?'

'So Clive studied the first nation-state in the world – the one whose ruins are lying all around us. And at first he did it with the cool eye of a professional.'

'The same eye as you have?'

My discomfiture was momentary and inexplicable, but I pressed on.

'He's forgotten detachment. Even turned his back on the rudimentary procedures that we use in excavation, preservation, analysis. Instead he's surrounding himself with arcane scraps of knowledge, ridiculous theories drawn from unsound premises. It leads to all kinds of mad conclusions.'

'Mad to you.'

'Mad to all of us. Your brother is becoming a zealot for the irrational. It's as if, after all these years, he has finally discovered the seductive power of religious thought. With each year that passes he gets drawn deeper and deeper into a way of life which is – well, beside the point. He mistakes the simple for the complex, and the shallow for the profound.'

She shook her head, and for a few seconds I thought there was pity in her gaze.

'Poor Raymond,' she said; 'you just don't realise how original Clive is.'

It would be worthless to argue further. 'Maybe not,' I said.

She touched my wrist with her fingers, and I drew it away quickly. 'But I know you have done a lot for him. He says you always do your best to help him. I appreciate that. It means so much to me. You'll carry on trying to help him, won't you, Raymond?'

I smiled thinly.

'It would mean a lot to me. I sense that he's under some kind of terrible strain. Please say you'll help.'

'Yes,' I promised, 'I'll always do what I can to help.'

Oxtaby walked back towards us across the lobby, hands thrust nonchalantly into his pockets, his head tilted back as if he had not a care in the world.

Lucinda leaned forward and whispered. 'And poor me,' she said, 'having to live with someone convinced he is a genius.'

Later that night I stood again on the dark balcony. Behind me the screen of white curtain hung motionless. A bat flew back and forth along the front of the hotel. A hundred yards away the river was black, fast-flowing, stippled with moonlight. The woman with the child was slumped beneath the black sycamore.

I stood for a long time before I heard voices, and even then I had to strain to listen. Carriages were still being driven along the gloomy corniche, and someone on a hired bicycle without lights rang its bell incessantly as he rode it proudly around the palms.

' – talents are forensic,' I heard Oxtaby say.

I stood as near to my balustrade as I could. All I had to do was lean across it, reach out, and I could easily touch the one around Lucinda's balcony.

'Perhaps they're right,' she said.

In the pause, her clothes rustled, but there was no sound of a footfall. I thought that she must be walking across the room in bare feet; for some reason I found this thought stimulating.

'They're pathologists,' Oxtaby said, his voice slightly muffled.

I held my breath, leaned against the retaining parapet, and then toppled forward so that my hands spread on Lucinda's balustrade and took my weight.

'They like examining dead things,' Oxtaby said.

'Murchison is only interested in the skeleton, and I'm interested in the soul.'

'And my soul?' Lucinda asked.

He laughed. 'How can you ask?'

'That's not an answer.'

I tilted my head, trying to hear more clearly. Craned like a bridge across the drop into the garden, I felt neither vulnerable nor guilty. For most of my adult life I had been involved in surveillance, assessment, deception.

The voices became indistinct again, as if they had moved to a far corner of the room. I pushed myself back onto my own balcony. After I had retreated it took me several seconds to realise that I was involuntarily clenching and unclenching my fists.

For a while I could hear nothing but a murmur that was as tempting and mysterious as the noise of a distant sea.

I put one foot up on the top of the balustrade, looked down into the garden, hesitated for a second, then stepped out over the drop. Everything inside me was alert, and I felt that the purpose of the world was merely to wait until I should turn my attention to it. I balanced on Lucinda's balustrade for a moment, then stepped down onto her balcony and pressed myself against the dark wall.

I could only see a little of the room – a pale wall with an oval mirror hung on it, the corner of a dressing-table. I memorised every detail instantly, as if my mind had taken a photograph of what I saw – the smudge on the mirror glass, the chip of varnish missing from the dressing-table, the way the electric light was directed onto the wall. When spying, the mind becomes filled with absurd detail. A hairbrush had been placed on the dressing-table, the handle pointing out towards me; if I were asked about it years later, I would still be able to describe it accurately.

Oxtaby's voice became clearer. 'This is where you belong,' he said. 'Eventually you'll understand. The others have no hope of insight. Merely by what you do, you have more right to be here than either Murchison or Lacau.'

'Or Howard Carter?'

'Especially Carter.'

'I can't believe you. Besides, if Rex had been alive – '

'Rex is dead. And we must both be glad that he's dead.'

The bat flew so close to me that for a second I thought I could feel the slight breath of its passage.

I could hear Lucinda's voice tremble. 'Clive, inside you there has always been a coldness. You're like – '

She stopped. I saw her hand, and part of a bare arm, reach out and pick up the brush.

'Like a reptile,' she said.

I was so close to the wall that a speck of grit fell on my lips. I licked them, and felt it on my tongue.

'I don't know how you could make such an accusation,' Oxtaby said. There was hurt in his voice. 'You wouldn't even be here if it weren't for me. There was nothing wrong with Rex. He was the same as thousands of other men – quite kind, sometimes thoughtless, needlessly proud. He overestimated things.'

'Such as?'

'His own intelligence. Your love. His own chances of survival.'

I could hear the soft rasp of the brush through Lucinda's hair.

'He wasn't the man for you,' Oxtaby said.

'I still want him, Clive. I've always made that clear.'

There was a short period of silence. I did not know what was happening, and feared that one of them might come to the window and discover me there. I eased myself fractionally from the wall so that I could step back onto my own balcony.

As I did so Lucinda began to talk again. 'Raymond Murchison is more attractive than you said he would be, but he doesn't have much idea how to treat a woman. He vacillates between being brusque and being far too obviously charming.'

I pressed myself back against the wall.

'He would be happy lecturing you,' Oxtaby said. 'His confidence would be boundless when he did that.'

In that second I saw Lucinda's face in the mirror; her reflected eyes were looking straight at me.

My heart began to race, but her voice neither broke nor wavered; I began to think that she could not see me, only a patch of darkness.

'Yes. I thought that was rather sweet. Do you think he's ever had a white woman?'

'He's never talked about such things,' Oxtaby said. For a few seconds his voice became muffled again, as if something was passing over his mouth. 'I'm told there are European girls in the Cairo brothels,' he went on. 'He may have gone to them, for all I know.'

My breathing was light as a fevered child's, as light as Virginia's had been on the day before she died.

'Why should you be interested?' he asked.

Lucinda's eyes still stared at me; I could see the light swim in them. 'I'm not,' she said.

I stepped onto the balustrade, but could not stop myself from glancing back.

Lucinda had remained motionless, and I could no longer see her face, only the upper quarter of her body. It was naked. I could see the texture of the skin across her shoulder and the swell of her bare breast.

My lungs tightened, and my balance slipped beneath a sudden attack of vertigo. The hotel gardens seemed to tilt as if the surface of the earth was nothing but a skin over a gigantic piece of moving machinery. I half-stepped, half-jumped across the gap, was certain I would fall, and stumbled onto my own balcony. My feet buckled, I sprawled, and then I picked myself up.

I pushed aside the white curtain and fell onto my bed. All strength had gone from my muscles. The ceiling fan rotated above me, its low whirr filling the silence of the room.

Some years ago Oxtaby had insisted on taking me to a brothel. I never talked about earthly delights, he had said; surely this was not because, at my age, I was still innocent about such things? I denied him so hotly that I could do little else but accept the challenge, but all the way through the dark narrow streets I cursed myself for being his fool.

Arab and Nubian girls in bright clothes stood by the lamplit doorway or sat outside on mats. I could hear noises coming from behind the screens of carved wood across the upper rooms. The women had kohl-thickened eyes, like ancient priestesses; gold discs were sewn into their clothes, and their flesh smelled of sandalwood. To me they were both opulent and squalid.

Oxtaby chose a young black girl, perhaps seventeen years old, with a face marked by cicatrices. I lied and said there was no one who took my fancy. He teased me, and told the madam that I was such a devout Englishman that I could only couple with white girls. She promised to bring me one, a Circassian girl, very expensive, very young.

Oxtaby and his partner went upstairs; I sat uncomfortably on the divan until the Circassian appeared. She was about six years old. I refused her disgustedly and went back out into the street. Vertigo struck me and I had to lean against the far wall to steady myself. The girls watched me warily, as if they feared I would collapse.

I could hear Oxtaby talking in the upper room. I wondered if he could see me through the gaps in the trellis, and if all his carefully articulated obscenities were neither for himself nor the girl, but for me.

4

The raising of the coffins was a complicated, agonising process that took day after long, exhausting day. They were as ponderous as small boats, and yet we feared they could be as fragile as dried papyrus. Only those directly involved in their lifting were allowed inside the burial chamber, so I watched from the antechamber with a small group of officials. For several days we stood on the rough planking that had been laid across the floor, shoulder-to-shoulder like refugees awaiting salvation, each of us breathing the others' breath, our clothes heavy with sweat.

Carter and his team bent over the outer coffin like precision jewellers. Above them was a scaffolding of beams and pulleys with blocks for automatic braking, and from behind their heads high-power lamps were angled directly into the sarcophagus from tall metal stands. It was so humid that I could hear moisture droplets sizzle on the incandescent bulbs.

The outer coffin was made of cypress covered with gilt and gold-leaf, and was more than seven feet long. On its lid the dead king was portrayed as Osiris; his hands, folded across his chest, held the crook and flail, symbols of the ruler as both kindly shepherd and unrelenting scourge. From the brow of the head rose the divine cobra and vulture, symbols of Lower and Upper Egypt.

The lid of the coffin had been fastened to its base by silver pinions. These were laboriously removed, and then ropes were tied around the four handles fixed to the lid. We watched in a silence that was almost holy as the lid was gradually lifted free and the ropes creaked slightly with the weight.

The light shone on a black shroud strewn with withered garlands as dry as ash. Although it was obvious that there was a second coffin underneath, the shroud was left in place. Many-coloured facets of glass inlay could be seen glinting beneath the decayed linen, and further down the body a golden hand protruded, clasping the base of a flail.

The second coffin was almost seven feet long, three feet deep, and without handles. It lay so tightly within the base of the first coffin that there was not even space for Carter to slide his little finger between them, and the pins that fixed the lid to its own base could be only partially withdrawn. For a while it seemed impossible to go further without cutting through the wood, but eventually it was decided to lift the entire contents of the sarcophagus so that they could be examined more easily. Steel rods were passed through tenons in the outer base, and all the coffins were raised together.

It took eight men at the limits of their strength to lift the enormous weight. The ropes moaned like hawsers in a storm, but there was no breath of wind in the sultry confines of the tomb. Wooden trestles were placed across the sarcophagus as soon as the coffins were free, and then, gradually and painstakingly, they were lowered onto these. The planking sagged as it took the full weight. Only now was the shroud rolled back on the second coffin.

This was revealed to be even richer and more splendid than the first. Here, too, were the crook and flail, the cobra and the vulture, this time covered with gold foil and inlaid with glass the colour of jasper, turquoise and lapis lazuli. The head of the king was shown with a striped *nemes* headcloth, and on the face was a strange, emotionless expression, both regal and vulnerable.

But Carter knew he had merely postponed the next essential stage, the removal of the second coffin from the base which enclosed and held it as tightly as an outer shell. With the lack of coffin handles, the minimal clearance, and the narrow confines of the tomb walls, the problem seemed insoluble. There were two full days of brooding before a solution was reached.

Copper wire was threaded around the partially withdrawn pins in the lid and the entire assembly of coffins was raised again by these. As it hung within its cradle of ropes the trestles were moved away from the sarcophagus, the shell of the outer coffin was prised free and lowered as if into a stone trough, and the second coffin and its contents were eased back onto the swiftly replaced trestles. With marginally more space now available to them, the team could remove the second lid.

There was a third coffin inside, shrouded in linen but for a burnished golden head with its cobra and vulture. The face was more youthful than the faces on the external coffins, and the workmanship was so smooth that recognisable reflections could be seen flowing across the gold as men bent close to examine it. When the shroud was removed, however, it was found that gallons of unguents had been poured across the surface of the coffin, covering it in a black shiny mass of solidified oils.

It was suspected even then that the third coffin was of solid gold. Still held within a shell formed by the base of the second coffin, it was lifted into the antechamber. Its weight confirmed what Carter had been heard to remark – that this was bullion of inestimable worth.

Many of the official spectators were now asked to leave. I had to relinquish my place to Lacau, who had just returned from his European trip. For a short while we waited together beneath an awning of bleached canvas which had been slung on poles near to the tomb entrance. The valley was thronged with reporters and observers in straw hats and solar topees. Most of them wore dark glasses, like so many blind men. Armed soldiers stalked the paths as if in constant expectation of a raid. The soldiers were unsure of their own powers; some were deferential, others haughtily dismissive. Electric cables snaked between two khaki tents, across the wall surrounding the tomb, and then down the steps. Nearby a petrol-engine rasped and chattered.

Lacau was a tall, handsome man whose presence was enhanced by a full grey beard. 'If your countryman had listened to reason, the coffins could have been opened last year,' he told me as he waited to go back into the tomb.

'Carter has many problems.'

He surveyed me for a while, as if a searching gaze would bring any imperfections to the surface of my character. 'No more than the rest of us,' he answered. 'And you may have given back to the Service a problem it could well do without.'

I feigned innocence.

'You know very well that I am talking about Clive Oxtaby,' he said. Then he indicated a path through the crowds that led to the summit of a spoil-heap of pinkish shale overlooking the tomb. 'Let us walk up there,' he said.

We edged our way past the army tents and a line of reporters who stood beneath umbrellas raised for shade. Several of them asked us questions as we passed, but Lacau held up an imperious hand to silence them. As we set off along the path a man with a camera and tripod came down it. He was sweating so much that his dark suit was covered in wide stains, and his red face gleamed as if it was being boiled.

We slowly climbed the bank and stopped on the littered rock at its summit. No one else was in earshot. Lacau looked impassively across the valley.

'Pierre,' I said, attempting familiarity.

'Oxtaby has been a trouble to our organisation, and when my back was turned you fooled my assistant into having him re-employed. Why?'

'With respect, I know he will be valuable. He is an expert in funerary – '

'So is everyone else who will be at the autopsy. And there are already too many people. Carter has complained about the number of spectators at the lifing of the coffins; in this case, I sympathise with him.'

I took a deep breath. 'The autopsy will be held in the tomb of Seti II, in the outer corridor. We both know

93

the laboratory tomb was chosen because of its nearness and size. It has already been agreed that there will be more than a dozen officials who have to be present. The two doctors will conduct the examination, of course. But apart from them, Carter will have to be there, and Burton the photographer. A representative of the Cairo museum needs to be present. As well as you and me, there will be others from our department – our chief inspector and Lucas, our chemist. Who else? The provincial governor? The undersecretary of state to the Ministry? And everyone has unofficially agreed that Thuillier should be allowed to attend at least part of the examination. Does one person extra make all that much difference?'

'Hundreds want to be present. Why should such a man as Oxtaby take precedence?'

'Because he knows more than anyone else about – '

'About ritual magic,' he interrupted me. 'So I believe.'

We stared down at the tomb, and the high cliffs behind it. A circling kite began its call.

'At least Oxtaby will know more than the provincial governor or our man from the Ministry,' Lacau said with a smile, and for a moment I thought he had relented.

'Perhaps even more than the effendi from the Cairo museum,' I suggested.

'I doubt it.'

I let him be silent for a while; at last he spoke to me again.

'Sometimes, Murchison, I wonder if I trust you. You are too close to Carter.'

'This is a country of rumour; I cannot be responsible for lies that people may tell about me. I am not Carter's friend. Mace was close to him until his health failed; Callender still is. As regards the Service, Alfred Lucas is much closer than I am. But Carter is a strange man, and many find him unlikeable. Despite their apparent civility, he and Gardiner detest each other.'

'I don't think you have given me an answer. If I did not know that Oxtaby was detested by Carter, I should be even more suspicious.'

'Carter and Oxtaby dislike each other; that's true.'

Lacau put his fingers to his beard and stroked it carefully in a preening, self-admiring fashion. 'Murchison, you have conspired to have your friend present at a moment that will live in history. You claim that he is an expert, but he is less of an expert than many others who have been refused admission. For the Service, this arrangement does not seem to be a very good one.'

I said nothing, but looked down on the men clustered around the entrance to the tomb. Like people awaiting a revelation, they had scarcely moved.

'I have half a mind to forbid him to be at the autopsy,' Lacau said. 'More than that, I am considering revoking his contract of employment.'

I immediately thought of the promise I had made to Lucinda, and imagined her disgust and distress at my failure to protect her brother. Perhaps she might never speak to me again. And then I thought once more of what I had seen from the balcony.

'I should be most grateful if you did not do those things, Monsieur Lacau,' I said.

'Why?' he asked. 'Give me a reason.'

I was thinking rapidly, but before I could answer he spoke again.

'It can't be because of Carter. Is it because of Oxtaby's sister? I heard you wasted some of your holidays accompanying her down the Nile.'

'That was a favour to Oxtaby, too.' I drew in a breath and held it within my lungs for several seconds before I expelled it. 'I feel responsible for him,' I confessed. 'He once saved my life.'

'In the war?'

'Yes.'

He nodded. 'I know all about the Arab Bureau, Murchison. It was full of dreamers and misfits like Oxtaby and Lawrence. For me there is wide taint of the charlatan in both men's characters.'

'And why did we fight the Turks?' I asked. 'Why, we did it so that their empire could be divided between my

95

country and yours. In his own way, Oxtaby helped deliver entire countries into French hands. And now you talk of refusing him a small favour.'

A bareheaded Egyptian in shirtsleeves came into the light from the well of the tomb and began looking around the entrance.

'I must go,' Lacau said; 'they are uncovering more of the third coffin.'

I thought he would leave and say no more about Oxtaby, but as I tailed him down the path he turned to me.

'Murchison,' he said, 'for your sake I shall let the arrangement stand. I understand what you feel you owe Oxtaby, but a man cannot be in debt all his life, and nor can a country. It has been a long time since the war; we should consider all debts to be discharged.'

Inside the ruins at Karnak there was a little café that sold fruit, squashes, and pastries cooked in a clay oven set up next to a tumbled block of inscribed granite. At the end of our visit we rested in the shade of its awnings while the smells of cinnamon and guava drifted across us.

Lucinda seemed both tired and happy. I had told her that this had been known as the birthplace of the world, that stars had been painted on the temple ceilings, and that the shapes of the columns mirrored the stems of reeds through which all would pass on their journey to death. I had guided her around the obelisks and the courtyards, the avenues of sphinxes, the columns and architraves; I had taken her to the edge of the reed-covered pond that had once been the sacred lake, shown her the battle scenes chiselled into the high, biscuit-coloured walls, and indicated the remains of the builders' ramp behind the first pylon. I paused before the gigantic statue that was of both Amun and Tutankhamun, and followed with her the supposed route of the boy-king's coronation. All the time I watched her like a man denied what he most desires.

'Lucinda?' I asked.

At first she ignored me, but when I spoke her name

again she finally looked at me. I watched as her eyes came back into focus; they had been staring into a distance that was out of my sight.

'Lucinda; are you all right?'

She nodded, but even this simple motion was uneven, as if her muscles had been bruised, but there was no sign of injury.

'I was watching that lizard over there,' she said.

I glanced to one side. 'It's a chameleon,' I said.

She nodded, but without interest.

'I'm pleased we came here,' I went on. 'I thought Clive would have insisted in telling you his own version of all this.'

'No,' she said, 'not at all.'

Suddenly I noticed that she was holding a small amount of sand in one palm, and that the fingers of her other hand were rubbing it absentmindedly.

'Are you sure you're all right?' I asked.

Immediately she dropped the sand and dashed its remaining few grains from her skin. 'There's no need to worry, Raymond. I'm fine.'

I thought of her image in the mirror, alluring and forbidden.

'How is the work?' I asked, to fill the silence that had grown between us.

She waited a while before she answered. 'I'm still painting, if that's what you're asking. I have to. When Rex's money is exhausted, it will be my only income.'

'Some people find Egypt overwhelming, and take weeks to come to terms with it. Lassitude afflicts them, and they can do nothing. But you've worked a lot.'

'Because I had a good idea what it would be like here. In my childhood I knew it.'

'Your father's library, you mean?'

'Partly. But it was more than what I actually read; it was the experiences I had. Clive and I shared a different kind of childhood.'

'I know.'

'No, you don't. It was much more intense than other

97

children's. We relied on each other. We even had our own language.'

'I don't understand.'

'It was a kind of private language. At first it was just silliness and children's slang, but then we started reversing words or stealing them from foreign-language dictionaries. Often we just invented them. To everyone else it was nonsense, gobbledegook. We loved talking about people when they could listen to us but not understand a word we were saying. There was freedom in that. It was so exhilarating we used to feel drunk with our own cleverness. Did Clive never tell you this?'

'He said you were close. I didn't know how close.'

'In every way, Raymond. No one has ever been closer to me than Clive. Not even Rex. It's an extraordinary feeling when someone knows everything about you. It makes you feel safe and scared at the same time.'

'Everyone has secrets. Even Clive can't know all there is to know about you.'

'I'm sure you have secrets, Raymond. You're that kind of man. Even if you were married, even if you had the most intense love for someone, you would still have to keep something from her. Clive and I were different.'

'You mean that you would tell him everything?'

'Wouldn't you have liked a sister like that? One you could share everything with?'

'I don't know,' I said weakly.

'We were physically close as well,' she went on.

My mind began to fill with images that both disturbed and excited me.

'Lucinda,' I said, and had to clear my throat to complete the sentence. 'There's no need to tell me all this.'

'But I want you to understand. I feel it's necessary that you understand.'

I nodded.

She breathed deeply, as if readying herself for an ordeal, and then spoke.

'Our parents had their own ideas about education; Clive and I had our own private tutors. It was planned that we have a good and natural childhood. So we were encouraged not to be ashamed of our bodies. Even though we had well-off parents and lived in a house with its own grounds, Clive and I were closer than slum children.'

'Lucinda, I – '

'Hear me out, Raymond. When I married Rex Plummer – '

She stopped, as if wondering whether to go on. The use of the surname made it sound as if she was talking about someone quite distant from her.

'When I married Rex I acted as he expected me to act – shy, virginal, unused to men and certainly unused to their intimacy. For him I was shocked, embarrassed, tearful. But I had grown used to nakedness because Clive and I were often naked. In our household it was an approved sign of maturity, of a kind of moral cleanliness. If one knew about the bodies of the opposite sex, if these bodies performed their natural functions in front of one's eyes, then the mind would be clearer and less prejudiced. It would spend less of its capacities in speculation and needless excitement, and be focused on what was true.'

My heart had quickened, and in my imagination I stood once more on her balcony, peering like a thief into her room, the dark fall below me.

'So you could tell no lies to Clive, but you lied to Rex,' I said.

'It made him happier. I have no regrets; he had little time left.'

'And today? Is there still that physical closeness?' I wondered if she could tell that my mouth had dried, or if she had noticed that I was tapping the side of the table rhythmically, like an impatient lover.

'It's a doorway, Raymond. Clive has always insisted on that.'

I was puzzled. 'A doorway?'

'To the soul. He learned about my body a long time ago. It's matters of the spirit that concern him now.'

I wanted to be both sympathetic and impassive, but I was angry and jealous and humiliated, and at the same time puzzled by the depth of my reactions.

'There's a world beyond all this, you know,' she said, and gestured to the columns around us. 'Clive's right. This is merely what has been left behind. They're just remains.'

'Of course they're just remains.'

'No; I mean it in a deeper sense. When Clive guided me through the temple in Luxor he didn't just say it represented a body. He said it was like a body when the soul had fled. He said that studying it was just – '

'Pathology,' I said. 'He's used the word often,' I lied.

She looked at me with suspicion and then, as if she had decided against query, moved on.

'As children we played games with objects that he said would mediate between us and the spirit world. He said mirrors were like windows into another dimension. And he made a planchette; do you know what that is?'

'I'm sorry, no.'

'It's a board with writing-paper and a loosely held pencil. Messages come through from the spirits and are written on the paper. Most children have a fascination with sinister games. For me the board did not work at all; for Clive, the pencil wrote name after name.'

'He was guiding it.'

'He swore he was not, and I believed him. Then he asked me to blindfold him and place his fingers on an upturned glass, and the glass moved of its own accord to letters arranged in a circle round it.'

'A ouija board. Lucinda, I know of two men who escaped from a Turkish prisoner-of-war camp by using a method like that. They pretended to be mad, but of course they were sane. It's easily faked.'

'This was not.'

'How do you know?'

'I *know*.' She waited a while before she went on. 'At first the glass became possessed by evil, and threw itself across the room. I was terrified, but after a while kindly spirits began to come through. One of them said it could speak through one of us if we held a seance, so we arranged it, just the two of us. We sat in a darkened room, out of the

100

way of everyone else, with the blinds closed. Clive had got hold of some incense from somewhere, so we burned that until the room was thick with a sickly heavy smoke. After a while his head tilted as if he were looking at the ceiling, but his eyes were rolled back so that the whites were glistening. And the spirit spoke through him.'

'Which spirit?'

'One from a long time ago.'

'Who?'

'He was an Egyptian.'

I could not believe that this intelligent, articulate woman would still believe in a ridiculous game played twenty years ago. To me it was obvious that Clive must have faked everything. He had always had streaks of devilishness and perversity within him; it distressed me that his sister was so trusting.

'I know you're a sceptic, Raymond. You'll not shock me if you say you don't believe me.'

But I did not know quite what to say.

'Maybe I shouldn't comment,' I said after a pause. 'You were there; I wasn't.'

'Why did you come to Egypt, Raymond? Interest? Chance? Opportunity?'

'A little of them all, I suppose.'

'Clive was destined for this place. His direction was pointed out to us a long time ago, in a series of childhood games.'

'And Rex? How did he fit into this pattern?'

'He didn't. He was a chance acquaintance that came along. By marrying Rex I was trying to escape from Clive.'

It was as if she had been shocked by her own confession. She was silent for a few seconds.

'I'm as weak-willed as the next person,' she went on; 'Clive is the one who is strong, the one with vision. While he was with the Bureau I lost my faith in him. Those were strange days, frightening and exhilarating at the same time. He sent me letters, and while I read them I was aware, all the time, that he might be already dead.'

'And you met Rex.'

'Met him and fell in love with him. Everything went so quickly, and there seemed no reason to wait. We were married only a few months after we first met, and already I was deceiving him. On my wedding night I pretended I had never seen a naked man before, because I could tell that the woman he wanted was different from the person that I am. A few weeks after that I was widowed. He was a good, kind man who did not deserve to die. Clive said he knew it would happen.'

'Lucinda, he can have had no idea that it would happen.'

'No? He told me that it was *bound* to happen. Fate swept Rex aside. I don't want the same thing to happen to you, Raymond.'

'But I'm not – '

She interrupted me. 'What if I'm not meant to have another man in my life? What if Rex had to die because, somehow or other, he was in the way?'

'I can't accept that,' I said; and then, more firmly, 'it's ridiculous.'

She stood up and dusted the last imaginary speck of sand from her palm.

'I didn't want you to be deceived as well,' she said.

But I thought it was Lucinda who was being deceived, and I did not have the courage to tell her.

Sayeed lived at the far side of a straggling village where men sat hammering at pieces of metal and the air smelled of burning cow-dung. Somewhere a press was being turned, and a woman squatting beside an open-air oven gathered up the hem of her veil to whisk flies away from her bread. A white dome stood on the village outskirts; a holy man had chosen that spot to sit in his rags and chant appeals to God, and after his death he had been buried on the very ground he had hallowed.

Sayeed's house was built into the side of a rocky mound; it had two storeys, whitewashed walls, and an external staircase leading to a flat roof with a dovecot. Brightly painted pictures of a railway-line, a steamship and the Ka'aba were painted on the walls. Sayeed wanted everyone to know that he had made the *hajj*, and proudly wore a green turban as additional proof. He sat waiting for us on a mud-brick bench outside his house while around his feet a few ragged-wattled turkeys strutted wearily.

He was a man in his late fifties, with a thin grey moustache and a pair of half-moon glasses hanging on a cord round his neck. Some of his teeth were broken or missing; the result, Oxtaby had advised me, of a stick fight in his youth. He welcomed us profusely and invited us inside. We removed our shoes before we entered, but Oxtaby would not leave his staff outside and instead brought it with him and stood it in a corner.

The room had benches covered with threadbare rugs, and on one of the walls was painted an imaginary Alpine scene, with impossibly sharp white mountains and vivid green fields. We were served with tea made from hibiscus leaves that was the colour of red wine. Sayeed placed a hookah in the middle of the floor, began to smoke, and then passed the pipe around. Only after this did we begin to talk business.

'My friend says you are a man of trust,' Sayeed said; 'a man, too, of discernment.'

'I'm proud to be his friend. I know that you also are a man of honour and fine judgement.'

He nodded ruminatively.

'A man with a collection of antika that even Carter might envy,' I added.

'It is Carter who is the envy of us all,' he replied. 'My collection is tiny; a man might even say petty. And I am forced to sell my valuable pieces because life is hard. But if you wish to see what I have gathered together, I will be honoured to show it to you.'

First of all he showed us a jar, a drinking bowl and several pieces of ornamented tile. We examined them and admired them for several seconds.

'These are fine pieces, Sayeed,' Oxtaby told him, 'but

often Europeans and Americans place greater value on things which are not so beautiful.'

'This is true; God has not given them true insight.' He shook his head with sadness at such blindness, and turned to Oxtaby. 'But you, effendi, you know true worth. When we have dealt in the past you have always bought well; never foolishly.'

'It is kind of you to tell me this,' Oxtaby replied straight-faced. 'Of course, we are like you. We cannot afford to keep the best pieces.'

Sayeed began to adopt a tone that varied between hurt pride and sly wheedling. 'But often you have turned away goods that I offered to you because you were my friend. I have thought to myself – Mr Clive is my friend, a good man, almost an Egyptian. I will offer him this, I will offer him that. And you have turned me down, even though my prices are the lowest on the entire Nile.'

'I cannot afford to buy what I like, Sayeed. There must always be someone else with a fatter wallet than I have.'

'And always, when you have turned me down, there are others who say to me – "Sayeed, we know you sell to the English magician. Do not deal with him; deal instead with us. We will give you *more* than he will offer you." That is what they say to me.'

'I see. And who are these people, Sayeed? Give me their names.'

Sayeed grinned widely. His teeth jutted from his gums at a series of extraordinary angles. 'That would be breaking trust.'

'Surely one of them cannot be Nasir,' Clive said.

'Effendi, Nasir is a famous man, much respected, a man who settles his accounts straightaway and in gold coin. I have known him since he was a small child. But he would have no interest in buying from me; he has grown rich on his own finds.'

'You worked with Mohammed Mohassib, didn't you? His uncle?'

'True.'

'Nasir would have been so small then that you could

have lowered him on a rope into caverns in the rock, into dark clefts, into places in the western hills that are still secret. No doubt he will never forget the friends who taught him everything he knows.'

Sayeed remained impassive.

Oxtaby drew on the pipe, passed it back to Sayeed, waited a few seconds, and then went on.

'Perhaps these other people you speak of have more money than true judgement. Perhaps they would not be honest with you. If a thing is valuable to the Europeans or the Americans, I tell you it is valuable. And what I have bought from you is always for others – great museums in New York and Chicago, collectors and scholars in Paris and London who want to have a piece of an ancient civilisation near to them so that they can reach out and touch it. But sometimes I *have* bought them because the things were beautiful, and I did not care what price you asked for them. Sometimes I *have* bought from you just because we are friends. And you have often told me you can obtain anything. *Anything.*'

Sayeed nodded.

'My friend speaks the truth,' I said.

Sayeed watched me carefully, the stem of the pipe close to his lips. 'You are both with the Antiquities Service. You will know much about truth and lies.'

'So I ask myself a question,' Oxtaby went on. 'If Sayeed can obtain whatever we want, where do his goods come from? Does he have a tomb which is known only to him?'

Sayeed inhaled the smoke. The cool water bubbled in the quiet room. 'Sayeed would be a fortunate man if this was so,' he replied. 'And if it was so, then I would have an official visit from the Antiquities Service, and your friends would tell me I was breaking their law.'

'We do not wish to pay you an official visit,' Oxtaby said; 'we respect confidences and secrets.'

'And they would tell me my valuables were not mine, but theirs. They would tell me they spoke for the country of Egypt, as if Egypt needs such men to speak for it.

105

And they would look through what I had, take what they wanted, and give back to me what they did not want and sneer as they did so. Why should Sayeed wish himself such fortune?'

'No one will know of the tomb you pillage,' Oxtaby said. 'Not me, not Murchison, not the Service.'

'Not Carter?'

'Especially not Carter.'

Sayeed nodded.

'We think,' Oxtaby continued, 'that you have collected together a large number of things, or have been given them by the nephew of an old friend. Some are of great value, some of little worth, and you have them hidden – perhaps in a great chest; perhaps in a room behind this house.'

Sayeed looked at us and laughed, half in protestation. 'The English have their heads full of dreams.'

I leaned forward slightly. 'No,' I said, 'our heads are full of truth.'

I was rather pleased with my simple response, but Oxtaby shot me a swift, despairing glance as if to warn me not to patronise Sayeed. Sayeed merely tugged on the pipe again as he waited for Oxtaby to continue.

'Only a few miles from here,' Oxtaby said, 'men are taking out of the ground richer treasures than you have ever seen; men whose names have travelled down the Nile and flowed back to Europe, to America, to every continent – Carter, Carnarvon – '

'Carnarvon is dead. He was cursed to death.'

I expected Oxtaby to answer, but instead he looked to me to respond.

'Carnarvon was a dying man finished off by an insect bite,' I said. 'And did his death make Carter stop excavating the tomb? Did he desert the riches because he feared an ancient curse?'

'If he did or if he did not, this has nothing to do with me.'

'Sayeed,' I told him, 'it has everything to do with you. It will alter the way you do your business. Already things are changing. After the excavation is finished, everything will be different.'

'If God wills it,' he said uneasily.

'You know I do not lie. When the shrines were opened, fake antika flooded into Luxor from Aswan, Cairo, even Alexandria.'

Oxtaby spoke again. 'You said to me yourself that these were inferior, and that they brought your trade into disrepute. Even forgers were embarrassed at how bad they were.'

'True.'

'In a market such as this,' I said, 'with an increasing demand for good work, and an increasing supply of bad, it is a wise man who knows what is valuable in his own home. Wiser still is the man who knows what is valuable in Cairo. Wisest of all is the man who knows what is valuable in New York. The Americans are not such fools as many think; they are learning. Day by day, they learn more.'

Sayeed did not respond, and we sat quietly for a few seconds.

'Murchison has seen every object taken from that tomb,' Oxtaby said. 'We will watch as the mummy is unwrapped, and I will count the amulets and the charms as they are taken from the layers of bandages. No one else who comes here will do that. No one else will have the knowledge that we have. You are a wise man, and yet you will not know what prices your goods would bring in New York.'

'I know what they bring in Cairo.'

'No. You know only what Nasir tells you is a fair price.'

He was still cautious. 'Perhaps.'

'You have your collection of good-quality antika,' Oxtaby went on. 'They are in a chest with bolts and locks, or perhaps they are kept within thick walls in a room behind this house.'

Sayeed shrugged as if it would be foolish to draw such a conclusion.

'The goods that have been found in the tomb of Tutankhamun will never leave Egypt,' Oxtaby said. 'They

107

will not go to London or New York, no matter how many English or Americans work at the excavation. They are all packed into large crates and sent to Cairo under armed guard. I have helped load such crates myself; Murchison took some down the river only a few weeks ago. The Cairo museum will keep every one of those treasures, from the coffins to the smallest clasp, from chariot to needle, from pectorals of beaten gold to dead flowers. Everything.'

'And still your people search for burial chambers in the West. Why should they do this if there is no profit in it?'

'A good question.'

'And its answer?'

'Esteem,' Oxtaby said; 'renown among scholars. Academic glory.'

'And you think this is why I should show you all I have to sell? I do not understand.'

'Everything must have been very easy until the steps were uncovered,' Oxtaby said. 'You had been good businessmen. You knew the value of your ornaments, your pieces of sculpture, your weapons and statuettes and portraits of the dead. All that has changed. A dust-storm is blowing from the Wadi Biban al-Maluk, and it is obscuring the roads in front of us. Many will misjudge the storm, and think they are running before it, but when it has passed over they will have lost their way, and have around them nothing but desert.'

'Now tell me,' Sayeed said drily, although I could sense the hesitation in his voice, 'what should I do to run before such a storm? Put my trust in the English?'

'We are the only people who know what is truly wanted,' Oxtaby said. 'In Europe and in America there will be buyers with pockets deep enough to hold thousands of dollars, thousands of pounds. And what will happen? They will want relics and they will not be able to get them. Why? Because the Antiquities Service will tighten like a noose on anyone who wishes to take anything out of the country. They will give licences to no one; they will stop trains and search them, and demand that all packing-cases are opened before they are loaded onto ships. Only experts can walk past barriers like that.'

'And you are such experts?'

I leaned forward. 'On your honour, Sayeed, tell no one else this; I have already helped Carter take away goods from the tomb of Tutankhamun. Goods that have never been catalogued, goods that have never even been photographed. They did not go to Cairo; they went straight into Carnarvon's private collection in England. I repeat, you must say nothing: no one else even suspects this.'

He stared at me for several seconds. I held his gaze until he turned to Oxtaby.

'You do not just want to cast your eyes across my poor collection. You want something very special.'

'True.'

'Tell me what it is.'

'Show us your collection, and I shall tell you if it is in there.'

'Why not ask Nasir? I am an old man; I do not care if he becomes the richest trader on the river. Ask him.'

'But we have always been friends,' Oxtaby said; 'that is why I am asking you. Out of friendship.'

Sayeed nodded.

His hoard lay in a room at the back of his house behind a door with a large Turkish-looking bolt and lock. Saws, awls, knives, brushes, and engraving tools lay just within the door along with two statuettes in different stages of completion. Roughly cut limestone tablets lay next to two lengths of planed and painted wood, and nearby was a heap of recently incised scarabs; they had been stacked carefully, as if by a child playing with pebbles on a beach. Before he sold them, Sayeed would make sure they had a patina of age, and to do this he would either leave them in the layer of droppings at the bottom of his dovecot or pass them through the digestive systems of the turkeys he kept outside.

Oxtaby shook his head sadly. 'Sayeed, a man should not mix trades.'

'How else am I to live?' he asked.

109

'By relics which are real,' Oxtaby answered. For here, also jumbled together on the floor, was a ransack of the past.

A painted mummy-case stood in one corner. Its lid was missing, and the trunk and head of a bandaged body lay within it like a macabre joke. The legs and one arm had vanished, and fragments of ripped bandage trailed across the emptied sockets. The wrappings were glued together by unguents, so a knife had been used to cut them apart in a search for hidden amulets and charms. The torso looked as if it had been bayoneted, and the cartonnage across the head had been torn to expose a dark area of fibrous skin and a yellow patch of bone.

'You're selling this for medicine,' Oxtaby said, pointing to the wreckage.

'Mummy flesh is very good. Very powerful. Even doctors say this.'

Oxtaby shook his head again as if loss had overcome him. 'Perhaps a hundred years ago they did. And you could have sold the case without breaking it apart.' He indicated the planks on the ground. 'What will you do? Saw them up, paint charms on the pieces, and sell them to ignorant tourists who come up the river?'

'They like them. My work has travelled to all of the world. Especially America.'

And Sayeed began to list a number of United States cities and states, accenting them in the American way, as if he was faithfully mimicking his customers.

Along with Oxtaby I knelt down among the items littered around the foot of the coffin. Among them were two cream-coloured stone jars.

'Canopic,' Sayeed said, and indicated his stomach with an open hand. 'For the insides. Genuine.'

'Only two?' Oxtaby asked. 'The four sons of Horus guard the internal organs of the dead.' He looked at the lids; they were Eighteenth Dynasty. 'These we can sell, Sayeed; for good money.'

'I paid much money for them.'

'But we can sell them for even more money if we have all the jars.'

'My supplier,' he said, and shrugged as if to indicate terrible unreliability.

Oxtaby put them back on the ground. We exchanged a quick glance. I was sure we were each thinking of the two canopic jars reportedly bought by van Diemen.

'And the wax figures of the four gods? You must have found those in the bandages.'

'The mummy was as barren as the desert. He was not an important man; merely someone like me.'

I sighed. What was on Sayeed's floor was a jumble from more than one tomb; perhaps it came from several, and had passed from hand to hand through the labyrinths of the antiquities market before it had reached him.

'The men with most money are those who know what they want,' Oxtaby said. 'They can tell by looking at an object which dynasty it was made in, and even which king was on the throne. But they ask questions which it is difficult to answer. They want to know where an object was found, and what was found with it.'

'You would have to say that you do not know.'

Oxtaby laughed and shook his head. 'That is no longer an answer which would be believed. Everything is catalogued now. To buy antika, a prudent man must know everything before he hands across his money.'

Now I picked up a spindle from a loom, which could have been thousands of years old or only ten; a terracotta waterbottle; and some fragments of tile which I tried to piece together.

'It is a pig,' Sayeed said, as I peered at the relief; 'very rare, yes?'

'Quite rare,' I said. 'I'm not even sure that it is a pig.'

He looked hurt. 'Certainly it is pig. Eighteenth Dynasty.'

I grinned. 'Pigs were never depicted before the Eighteenth. Probably this is later.'

Near to the coffin, partly hidden by a hessian bag, was a

111

roll of papyrus. I felt myself tense. Then, as nonchalantly as I could, I bent and lifted the bag.

The papyrus was fragile, and small grains showered from it as soon as it was touched. A section as large as my palm broke away as I lifted it.

'A good tradesman would not deny a sample,' I said as calmly as I could, and passed the fragment to Oxtaby.

'If you wish,' Sayeed answered. 'But I want fifty pounds for the complete papyrus.'

'Fifty?' Oxtaby asked, peering at the fragment. 'Never, Sayeed. Ten if it was good. Two because it is falling to pieces.'

'Forty,' he said. 'And that is cheap price because you are my friend. I can make much more than your offer by cutting it into pieces and saying it is cartonnage.'

Oxtaby threw the fragment back onto the roll. I dared not speak.

'Do that with it, then. This is beyond any salvation that a damp cloth and a sheet of glass could give it. Besides, it is only Ptolemaic; thousands of these have been dug up in the Fayoum. But if it was a good papyrus, if it was a *special* papyrus, then you would be paid more than fifty.'

'A thousand?'

'Five hundred, maybe. At the most.'

'And what kind of papyrus would be worth even more than five hundred?'

'You are a true believer, Sayeed; you know what happens when a man dies. The ancients had different beliefs. A papyrus about a man passing through the field of reeds and entering the Other World might be sold for five hundred.'

Sayeed shook his head. 'No. Carter bought a papyrus from Maurice Nahman for one thousand pounds. An Amduat papyrus would be worth much more than this.'

Oxtaby nodded grudgingly. 'Perhaps.'

'Not perhaps. Certainly. Much, much more.'

'And is there such a papyrus, Sayeed?'

'If a man searches hard enough, he often finds what he is looking for.'

Oxtaby turned to me as if our meeting had suddenly but irrevocably ended.

'My friend Sayeed is right. We must search harder for what we want. We'll take our leave and find someone else who could help us.'

Sayeed held up a hand to stop us.

'Perhaps,' he said, 'I could search for you.'

Oxtaby was lost in thought when we rode away together. He placed his staff crosswise on the donkey's back, resting one hand on it as if he drew consolation from its texture and shape.

The rubble and sand ended suddenly, and we entered the fertile land. To one side of us there was another small village resting on its tel, bund tracks snaking out from it. White ibis picked among the vegetation, and the waterwheels were gradually falling silent as buffalo were unfastened from their yokes.

'That man could be nothing but a dead end,' I said at last. 'He can't distinguish between the real and the fake. If a buyer wanted something in particular he would simply have it manufactured.'

'You think so?'

'It's obvious. He'll take a knife to cartonnage and a saw to coffin-wood. How long do you think that mummy has been in that corner? Ten years? Twenty?'

'He cannot forge what we want.'

'Perhaps not. But you must have known that forgery was his main source of income.'

'Sayeed is a forger *and* a dealer. Neither of us knows the network that links the genuine and the false. Those jars were real enough. A match for van Diemen's pair, do you think?'

'When I think of the jungle of material in that room, I doubt it. The coincidence would be too great.'

'Raymond, you are disappointed. Did you really think we would get an answer so soon? Isn't that too much to hope for? And if you had an answer, you would have begun talking money with Carter. There is little difference between you and the people you condemn.'

I bristled at his jibe. 'I'm not a mercenary,' I answered. 'If I have to serve anything, then knowledge is the best god I can think of.'

'This papyrus would go via Carter to the Metropolitan because they would pay over the odds. At least I deal only in order to live; you deal out of avarice.'

His offhand condemnation infuriated me. 'I should hit you for that,' I said bitterly.

'By your standards you should. There's still something of the schoolboy in you.'

I wanted to drag him from his donkey and pummel him about the head, but the thought of Lucinda's anger stopped me. That, and the possibility that he might split open my skull with his staff.

'Sayeed may be a crook,' Oxtaby said after a while, 'and in the eyes of the Service he may even be a thief, but he knows how to get hold of interesting items. I have never asked him about his suppliers. If those jars were matches for van Diemen's, then Nasir is definitely allowing him to trade some pieces.'

'*If*. And why would he not sell all four together?'

'So they are in a kind of partnership,' he went on, ignoring my objection. 'And if they are, then Sayeed could be our route to the papyrus.'

'Clive,' I said wearily, 'he's a liar and a forger. If he swore that something were genuine, would you believe him?'

'I would.'

'We have been following a whisper, nothing more. Our papyrus was probably that worthless roll rotting in the corner. Rumour has done the rest.'

'I will make you a promise,' he said. 'I will find out the truth about this rumour, and I will tell you what it is. And if the papyrus exists, I will make sure that you see it.'

'How?'

'I must start resuming my life among the villagers of the West Bank. I am more comfortable among them than I am among my own kind. Given time, I will find out.'

A man with an overloaded donkey passed by and greeted us. I waited until he was out of earshot until I spoke again.

'And Lucinda?'

'She has money to stay at the hotel for a short while longer. After I move to the West, I will continue to see her. Later she must decide what she has to do.'

'This is a bad move, Oxtaby. No one will like it.'

'The villagers will.'

'How long do you expect me to be your champion? Carter and Lacau don't trust you, and the rest of the team don't either. Even Carnarvon didn't trust you, and Carnarvon wasn't the best judge of character.'

'Carnarvon was an amateur and a fool.'

'And where would we be without Carnarvon?'

'Happier men, perhaps. I am not proud of what I do for the Service. Carter has done me no favours. And Lacau tried to do me harm.'

'Because he dismissed you? What choice did he have? Your behaviour had become intolerable.'

'I was a giant among pygmies. Half the team has no real sympathy with present-day Egyptians, let alone the ancients. They may as well have taken up big-game hunting instead of archaeology. I was bound to create resentment among them. They are people who have taken their childhood dreams of buried treasure and turned them into an academic sniping war.'

'And your childhood dreams? What did you do with them? Aren't you here for the same reasons?'

'I am here because I read history at Jesus College, which my parents wanted me to do; joined the University Officers' Training Corps, which Lord Haldane had said we should all do; spent two seasons digging with Petrie, which I wanted to do; and a few years fighting the Turks, which the army told me it was necessary to do. It's a life that's not too different from yours. And like you, like thousands of our kind across the world, when the war was over I found that England was a foreign country to me. Dirty, cold, with skies full of drizzle. A little nation, contemptuous of others, inhabited by squalid people foolish enough to think themselves free.'

I said nothing.

'You want to go back,' he said.

'No,' I lied.

'You want to go back because you have been too long on the Nile. Commission on a wealthy find would help you a lot, wouldn't it?'

'I've told you, I had my hopes; not any more.'

'You have no sense of fate. Everyone has a destiny; I'm sure of that.'

'Lucinda has told me about the games you played. She believes it was some kind of destiny that brought you here.'

'Games?' he asked, and for a moment it seemed as if I had caught him off guard, and that he believed I had been told a terrible secret.

'Automatic writing,' I reminded him. 'Messages from the beyond. Pretending that mirrors were mystical objects. Calling up the spirits of the dead.' With each sentence I was more scathing. 'There was even an Egyptian spirit. Supposedly.'

He gave a relieved smile, as if a crisis had been avoided. 'That's right. An architect; a builder of tombs. He was quite a character.'

I looked at him. For a moment he appeared modest and yet proud. We neared the two colossi with their shadows stretched out in front of them, lost in a field of clover. A flock of pigeons passed over us, their wings beating the air as they followed a long curve back to their tower in the nearest village.

'When the guide spoke,' Oxtaby said, 'it was a mixture of archaisms and Rider Haggard. I'd just read *She*, you understand. And our father's library was a trove for the raw material.'

'You invented this man?'

'Scarcely. You know he existed as well as I do.'

'I mean that you didn't really summon him from the dead?'

He laughed scornfully. 'Murchison, I know that you are smitten with Lucinda. That much is apparent to everyone who sees you in her company. Surely you didn't believe her tale of two lonely children playing secret games in darkened rooms, and somehow dredging from a hidden dimension the spirit of a man who died thousands of years ago, a long, long way from the dank fields and dirty factories of England?'

'She believes you did that. And you invented it, just as I thought you must have done.'

'Believes it? She never believed it. She's toying with you. Playing the cat to your mouse.'

We rode on in silence. I did not know what to think or say. At last he stopped his donkey and got down from it. On our left the broken towers of the two colossi were like abandoned messages from a sunken world.

'Raymond,' he said, 'let me speak to you as a friend.'

I dismounted and watched him warily. The declining sun stretched our shadows along the road, and white moths began to flutter above the crops. The last waterwheel suddenly ceased to creak, and in the silence I could hear the animal being unyoked and then led across the fields.

'Carter and you are both solitary men,' Oxtaby said. 'You have many acquaintances but few friends. I, too, used to be like this; perhaps in many ways I still am. But I know my sister better than any other person on this earth, better than the well-meaning dullard that she married, and certainly better than you. Men find her attractive, although some find her character to be like oil and water – a commingling of opposites, of shy femininity and confident abrasiveness. You will have seen those qualities within her, and perhaps even tried to judge them.'

I said nothing. The donkeys swivelled their ears as insects began to settle on them.

'Well?'

'What if you are right?' I asked.

'Confess it,' he said, with the fervour of an interrogator; 'you're like a lovesick schoolboy, wistfully lusting for the unattainable object of his fantasies and dreams.'

117

'You're being offensive. Not only to me, but to your sister as well.'

'If you call honesty an offence, then I plead guilty. Don't strike Edwardian attitudes, Raymond; they're out of date in England and completely out of place on this river.'

I could not look him in the eyes, and stared instead at a strip of land beside an irrigation ditch. A scarab beetle was rolling its ball of dung up a tiny slope. Filled with shapeless rage, I kicked out and booted them both into the field of clover.

'Lucinda is a most unusual woman,' Oxtaby said, 'but there is a certain devilishness about her. She goads those she has charmed, but they still cannot break the spell she has placed them under.'

'Metaphors of witchcraft and wizardry come easily to you,' I said.

He went on. 'In many ways what she does is no more than what many Englishwomen do – she flirts, teases, contradicts. But the difference lies in the intensity of those actions, and in her capacity to extend them for days, months, even years. And it does no good to confront her, for she will staunchly deny any evidence you may present. She's stubborn, too; she will only accept what she wishes to accept.'

'You're being both scathing and dismissive.'

'I'm being honest. And dismissive? Good lord, no. I would never wish to dismiss Lucinda. She and I can still talk a private language which admits no one else. But I sometimes think that she sees the world outside as a plaything. For her, only her own feelings, and perhaps mine, are real. The seances were a jest, a jape, nothing more. We both knew our Egyptian spirit came from one of the books on the shelves and was given a certain extra zest by my imagination. But it's a good story, good enough for repetition to anyone with an ear to listen. Rex Plummer was fascinated by it. I still do not know if he suspected the truth; perhaps he went to his death still believing that I had already developed psychic powers as a child.'

'So she's fooling me.'

He put on a wry expression as if he found the word distasteful. 'She's teasing you. I believe it's a form of flattery. She must be intrigued by your attentions.'

'You're still *close* to your sister,' I said, accenting the word like an accusation. I did not dare mention her nakedness on that night I had spied from the balcony.

'In the way that only a single man can be,' he answered.

'And do you still entertain her with music-hall tricks, still call up voices from nowhere?'

He smiled and looked back towards the escarpment. 'If people need entertaining and are willing to pay me for it, then I shall entertain them. For Lucinda I would give a free performance.'

'So there's nothing mysterious about your powers at all. You're an accomplished magician, practised in sleight-of-hand, voice projection, manifestations, suggestion.'

'Partly.'

'What do you mean – *partly*?' I asked. His portrayal of me as dupe to Lucinda's hurtful schemes had angered and embarrassed me more than I could ever have admitted.

'You know what the word means.'

'That some of those tricks are real? You're not always in command, and sometimes you're not the perpetrator but the medium? A puppet for something else?'

'Exactly.'

'If that were true, Oxtaby, then you would be no different from Sayeed. You would traffic in the real and the fake, and make no distinction between them.'

'Your prejudices are showing through. Does it never occur to you that you may be taking a very simple view of what goes on here?'

'I know what is genuine and what only pretends to be. That's part of my job. Yours as well.'

One of the donkeys suddenly brayed and then fell silent.

'Sayeed needs his goods to be of value,' Oxtaby said patiently; 'otherwise there is little point in having them. If he can gain by leaving the piece as it is, he will leave it; if he thinks it has to be transformed, he will do that. He has an economic relationship with the world, just as most people have. Ideas about authenticity and falseness are useful to him only if they serve that purpose.'

'And you pretend to be different from him?'

'No, *you* pretend to be different, because you work for the Service and say you believe in its principles, which I have ceased to do. Value is what matters in Egyptology, too. At first it was monetary value, a value given shape by strange Western ideas about cruelty and beauty and power. Lucinda has to paint works which sell; she understands that, even if you do not – but Lucinda has a more mercenary soul than you could imagine. Why, even the man in the street is fascinated by visions of such a past; why else are so many reporters in the valley? And Carter's vision? Carter will die a bitter man, believing he has been cheated out of his rightful share of plunder by a gang of French bureaucrats and self-important Egyptian officials. But Carter is the last of his line, and also the first of a new breed. From now on, the worth of a find will be measured in terms of its rarity. Appeals will be made to a kind of higher knowledge, as if amassing every piece of tile, every shattered votive jar, will somehow lead us deeper into an understanding. This is the argument that you put forward.'

He walked nearer to the colossi and gazed up at them. Their smashed faces were in shadow now, giving them the air of masked priests at a secret ceremony.

'I have a wider vision,' he said. 'What will happen when Tutankhamun is lifted from his coffin and put under the knife? Lacau will count the amulets like a greedy pawnbroker. Douglas Derry and Saleh Bey Hamdi will dismember the body as efficiently as eighteenth-century surgeons who have bought a corpse from bodysnatchers. And Harry Burton will photograph each stage of the examination, like the clerk of an inquisition.'

'If you find it so distasteful, Oxtaby – '

'It is still necessary that I attend.'

'Because of curiosity as well as duty?'

'Yes, if you wish to think no more highly of me than that.'

'You really do believe that you see more clearly and more deeply than the rest of us, don't you? Perhaps you think that you are somehow honouring the king by your presence; that in the arrangement of mummy ornamentation you will see significant correspondences that the rest of us will be blind to?'

'I need to be there, Murchison, even if I am the only honest man in a band of thieves. A man who has been dead for one hundred and fifty generations still deserves some dignity. If we do survive our bodies after death, then I like to think that my presence would make some difference to his lost soul.'

His self-esteem was breathtaking.

'I've seldom heard anything so self-righteous,' I accused him. 'We approach the problems in the only logical way. The days of archaeologist tomb-robbers have gone; Carter's professionalism has made others look like men from a past age. Intuition and guesswork no longer have a place.'

'Look, I have said before that Carter's dig will catch only a shadow of this civilisation. Its force turned on ritual, mystery, and symbolism. Think of what happens when a Christian priest puts bread and wine on an altar. A scientific man like you sees only bread, only wine; you would probably even wish to have them analysed. But you would be missing the reason for the ritual; you would overlook a great truth while searching for a small one.'

'You're confusing symbols with reality. It's a hopelessly romantic view.'

'Am I?'

'Of course.'

He walked up towards me and gazed into my eyes from a distance of only a few inches. His stare was so intense that I stepped backwards.

He lifted his staff in one hand and ran the other hand along it. I took another step away, fearful that he might strike at me.

121

'Watch,' he said.

He let the staff fall to the ground. I licked my lips nervously, and felt that time was coalescing around us.

Nothing happened for several seconds, and then I saw the texture of the wood shimmer as if a flame had passed along it, and the staff moved a little. At first I reasoned that there must be a slight incline which I could not see because of the low sun, and that the staff had merely slipped down it. But the motion was not an involuntary slippage; it was a willed, flexing motion.

I peered more closely, believing I must be witnessing some trick of the light. Oxtaby stood with one hand spread in the air.

The staff shivered, writhed, and then a hooded cobra lay in the sand. It was green and yellowish-grey, the length of the staff, with eyes that were as cold and motionless as jewels. It remained still for only a moment, and then it began to slither away.

Oxtaby reached forward casually, took it by the head to lift it, and the cobra was a staff again. He held it out to me for inspection.

'Illusion or reality?' he asked.

I felt weak and feverish, and would not touch the wood.

Oxtaby burst into laughter and smacked the staff against his leg. It hit the cloth with the flat, slapping sound of a length of wood, nothing more.

'I've impressed you at last. You look so foolish, Raymond; have all the muscles of your face loosened? It's the trick I promised you, a new one but an ancient one, and I have spent years perfecting it.'

'How did you do it?'

'You don't expect me to reveal my secrets, do you?' he asked, remounting his donkey.

'I'd like some kind of explanation, yes,' I said stiffly.

'Forget explanations,' he said gleefully; 'just observe. In a few weeks' time I shall be even better. I can feel power concentrate within me as if it has been loosed into the air

122

and I am drawing it back in. Often I feel that I could do anything. *Anything*.'

And he struck the donkey a sharp blow, so that it began to carry him rapidly through the evening fields towards the Nile.

Thuillier's surgery was on the lower floor of the small house he had bought on the far side of the souk. This was a quarter of Luxor that few Westerners entered; if he was needed, we usually sent for him. He had once told me that it was these visits, and his services to local headmen and officials, that provided his only substantial income. The rest of his time he devoted to people whose earnings could hardly even be measured in our terms.

Thuillier's house still had an intricately worked wooden screen masking the first storey; its neighbours had been stripped for sale to rich Westerners. The factory which had made the screens was only a few yards away, but its workers now spent their days carving smaller, more easily transported objects – chairs, fold-up tables, stools. If I visited Thuillier during the daytime I had to step around them, for the carvers always moved into the sunlight to work.

Thuillier had long, hound-like features accentuated by a grey goatee. I guessed that he was about sixty; he had practised in Egypt for as long as anyone could remember, and for the last twenty years he had been in Luxor. There were rumours that there had once been a Madame Thuillier, but he never spoke of her. Whenever we shared a cognac I usually told him things I would have told no one else, knowing that these confidences would be fully respected. And yet I always left without knowing much more about his own life.

We sat next to the screen; it trapped the brilliance of sunlight within the repeated complexities of its patterns, and it was easy to feel admiration for those who had carved it. Even the hot, stifling air from outside seemed cooler once it had passed through the fretwork.

I talked about the clearance, for Carter had always

humoured Thuillier's deep interest in the finds. Thuillier had often made a journey to the valley, ostensibly to treat a minor ailment, but really to be able to talk to us, or even to be allowed within the tomb itself.

I sipped the cognac with care; it was the first alcoholic drink I had had in weeks. Thuillier puffed rhythmically at a pipe, and its scent coiled about the dim room. He kept his tobacco in an alabaster jar on a shelf fixed to his wall. Although shaped like a canopic jar, it was evidently fake, for it showed a copy of the necropolis seal of Anubis and the nine bound enemies of Egypt.

'I am pleased that you are working again in the tomb,' Thuillier said. 'I spent more than a year worrying that the whole project would be destroyed merely because both Carter and Lacau are such stubborn men.'

'True,' I said. 'But it was Lacau who was in the wrong. Carter wanted to have the families of his team be first into the tomb, and Lacau refused. Why? There was no reason.'

But Thuillier had a reason.

'Because we are strangers here,' he answered. 'We may pride ourselves on being more civilised than many who have occupied this country, but we have all ransacked the Egyptian past. Sometimes we have even given it away, like children who give away their most precious toys merely to gain the approval of fickle friends. Take Mohammed Ali; I know you always speak of him as an Egyptian, but he was an Albanian. He squandered the past to maintain his control over the present. These people have had centuries of such policies; they deserve the support of the organisation you work for. They also deserved a nationalist government, but the British destroyed that as well.'

I laughed at him. 'You're being partisan. It's not like you to take Lacau's side. Although I suppose if the choice is between a Frenchman and an Englishman, then I would expect you to be on the side of your mother country.'

He pointed the stem of his pipe at me in a good-humoured way. 'You are better than many, Raymond, but you are still afflicted by colonialism. The choice is not between your country and mine, but between Egypt and its occupiers. In my own small way, I have sided with the Egyptians.'

Unlike most expatriates, Thuillier had not surrounded himself with nostalgic reminders of his country's past. 'You'll be content to die here, won't you?' I asked.

He nodded. 'I have my own place in the Christian cemetery; there are Catholic and Protestant spaces among all the rich Copts. Of course, I no longer believe in my childhood religion, but nevertheless I would like a ceremony to be performed. It gives one's death a certain dignity, even a kind of continuity. And I am sufficiently romantic to wish to be buried inside a protective wall. I would not wish my body dug up by jackals, as the poor sometimes are on the West Bank.'

I could hear an argument in the street; something about who should give way to whom. As usual it was noisy and dramatic, but would soon be over with. I peered out and saw two overloaded donkey-carts facing each other, their owners gesticulating wildly. Nearby a man chewing a stick of sugar-cane leaned idly against the wall. I thought of myself waiting in a dark street while Oxtaby coupled with the black girl behind a screen such as this.

'You have already buried less fortunate visitors,' I said.

'There are always those who die unexpectedly and quickly. Some I have buried here; others have been embalmed and their corpses sent back. It is no easy task evading a law that says the dead must be buried within twenty-four hours. And I sometimes wonder if their grieving relatives realise how little of their loved one is actually in those coffins, and how much I have had to destroy.'

'Like Carnarvon being shipped back to England, you mean.'

'Carnarvon was lucky to get as far as Cairo before he died. I saw him early that month; I have seldom seen a man so exhausted.'

'You told me that Mace was exhausted, too.'

'I warned Mace he must recuperate or he would follow in Carnarvon's footsteps. He did right to return home before he had to be shipped there in a palm-wood coffin.'

'He wouldn't have wanted to be buried here?'

Thuillier shook his head. 'He would have been returned like Carnarvon. Lady Evelyn and Carnarvon's wife wished to have his body back at their home. That is a constant through the ages, my friend; only the poor are left to be buried among strangers. The rich, the important are always taken home. Well, this is my home now, and my space is here.'

'If I'm still here I shall come to your funeral, doctor,' I said jokingly. 'I shall even pretend to be a Catholic, just for the sake of your memory. I'm afraid neither Carter, nor I, and not even Lacau could arrange for the kind of ceremony the ancients had.'

'A simple one in the French language will be sufficient. And I happily accept the fact of decay, thank you.'

He blew out some smoke, and seemed lost in memory for a few seconds.

'I once had a patient who was some kind of official from Lyon,' he said. 'There was an accident; a ridiculous one, for he had sunstroke and fell under a horse and carriage on the corniche. Every bone in his wrist was snapped, every piece of tendon and soft tissue was crushed. I fought to save the hand, but could not, and eventually I had to amputate. But the man could not bear to leave a part of him in a foreign country, so I had the dead hand pickled for him.' He pointed to the canopic jar on the shelf. 'I sent it back to Lyon with him in one of those. I understand he thought the event quite exotic. No doubt when he dies it will be buried with him, so that on the day of judgement he will rise as a whole man.'

He chuckled to himself.

'And such people say the ancient Egyptians were backward,' he added, 'but we have the same mad superstitions.'

'For them,' I said, 'spirituality was also bound up with the body. The place of burial was also a place where a complicated set of other selves was rooted. It was said that if you desecrated a tomb you freed the magical forces held captive within it. I know of people who still believe that.'

'Fortunately,' Thuillier said, 'you and I are men of science. Rationalism is all to us.'

'Yes. Although I have seen something happen which the evidence of my eyes tells me is impossible.'

'I did not think this was a professional visit,' he said.

I shook my head. 'Don't worry; I know there is a rational explanation. It's just that I cannot think what it could be.'

'And what was the evidence of your eyes, Raymond?'

I took a deep breath. 'I saw a wooden staff turn into a cobra, and then turn back into a staff again.'

He said nothing.

'It happened just a few feet away from me. The light was good but at an angle. There can have been no sleight-of-hand. And I was sober and calm when I saw it happen.'

He drew on his pipe and exhaled before he spoke, as if he had weighed what I had told him.

'But someone did this,' he said; 'as a trick.'

'Clive Oxtaby.'

'Ah, our amateur magician. I would not concern yourself. Magicians are expert colonisers of that no-man's-land between observation and intellect. If he had been on a stage, and pulled a rabbit out of a hat or made a dove appear in an empty cage, would you have been perplexed? Of course not. You may not have known the mechanics of the illusion, but you would have accepted it as no more than a piece of stage wizardry.'

'You're probably right,' I agreed. 'But it was the most eerie thing I've ever seen. Apart from something else I saw a long time ago.'

'Go on.'

'I've never told anyone this.'

'You should feel no compunction to tell me.'

'My sister died when she was only young; she had a short

illness, and died. She was placed in a coffin with an open lid. I couldn't sleep for thinking about her, so I went into the room where her body was. She was standing beside the coffin.'

'Be more explicit,' he said calmly.

'Her body was in the coffin, but she was also standing beside it. She was exactly the same – the same clothes, even the same expression except her eyes were open. I don't know how long I stared at her, but all of a sudden she was gone. I didn't even see her vanish; she was just there one minute, gone the next. There was just the dead body. It was as if I had imagined the live one.'

'Which you probably had.'

I turned from him and looked out onto the street. Three black-clad women were walking down it, steadying baskets on their heads.

'I knew you would say that,' I said.

'Most of my patients would say there was nothing exceptional with such a vision. Every person, they say, has a spirit double, a *karim*, which accompanies each of us through life. Sometimes it is the human self's friend, and sometimes it is a trickster and deceives its partner. But to you I must give a rational explanation. You were young and had been bereaved. It is probable that you had a sense of guilt, possibly for no cause; we know that bereavement can generate many contradictory emotions. It may be that, like many young people, you had wished your sister dead, and that you were overwhelmed with remorse when a disease killed her. Under certain conditions the mind can mislead us. It can see what we dearly want it to see.'

'You think that's true?' I asked, suddenly thinking also of Lucinda's reflection in the mirror.

'I know it to be true.'

'How?'

'A number of my patients have seen their karim. You and I know that such things do not objectively exist; but I would be a foolish man to deny that my patients see them. Perhaps they see what they most fear; perhaps, also, they see what they secretly desire. Girls who fall in love have

128

told me that their karim is pleased by the choice of husband. Would you expect me to say that there was no such thing as a karim? Of course you would not.'

'No,' I said, 'of course.'

'That is one of the many reasons I live here,' Thuillier said. 'Among people such as this, it is not always either their fault or mine if a man comes to harm.'

The funeral libations had flowed across the intricate golden surfaces of the inner coffins, filling the narrow gap between the sides of the third and the lower shell of the second. Dried to the colour and viscosity of dried tar, these oils and unguents were hard enough to prevent the removal of the third coffin from its enclosing cradle, but still sufficiently active as to fill the antechamber with a cloying, resinous smell.

For some days nothing was done to separate the two coffins, but eventually Carter decided he could no longer delay opening the third. The retaining tenons, each one of pure gold, were prised free, and the lid removed by lifting it by its handles.

Fitting neatly inside was the mummy of the dead king, dark with solidified oils. A scarab had been placed on the upper chest, a pair of golden hands with crook and flail had been fastened into the wrappings, and below them was the bird of the soul with opened wings. The wrappings were crossed by a framework of golden mummy-bands with small plaques and cartouches strung together by beads.

At the head, untouched by the oils, was a portrait mask of burnished gold inlaid with precious stones. Here again was the dead king as Osiris, with his *nemes* headcloth and the vulture and the cobra at his forehead. The eyes were made of obsidian and quartz, the pierced ears were covered with gold foil, and the beard was of gold and faience. On the golden face was a calm, resigned expression; Carter was later to say that it reminded him irresistibly of portraits of Akhenaten. The workmanship of the mask was so splendid that it silenced a team that had grown used to awe.

Through the sombre coating of the dried libations

the messages on the mummy-bands could still be read. They were the words of gods, and spoke of beauty and eternity, of divine love, of the heart living within the body for ever.

But our hopes were not high that the mummy would be complete and unharmed. Parts of the wrappings were already as perished and as dusty as the wreaths that had been strewn across them; the crook and the flail had already decomposed, and sections of bandage several inches square could be simply lifted away.

The mummy was still fastened within the double cradle of coffin shells, glued there by the tarry mass of consecration oils. Lucas reported that this could only be softened by heat, so the coffins and their contents were taken to the laboratory tomb. It took ten men to carry the load; as they did, armed guards ringed them, facing outwards with their guns at the ready as if they feared some kind of bizarre kidnap.

The coffins were placed on a trestle and left outside during the day as the valley temperature climbed higher and the golden metal became too hot to touch. We sat round, watching the shadows track across the dusty ground and noting the mercury levels in the thermometer columns. That day the temperature rose to almost 150 degrees F, but still the coffin shells could not be parted. The examination would have to be carried out with the mummy still fixed within its resting-place.

While we waited for the doctors to assemble, I took Oxtaby and Lucinda into the tomb.

The wooden scaffold with its pulleys and ropes was poised above the sarcophagus, which still contained the lower part of the outer coffin and a long bier with a lion's head on which the vast weight of the coffins had rested. Arc-lights cast a harsh glare into its depths and across the images on the walls, but the undecorated ceiling was a nest of shadows.

The paintings showed the king on his journey to the land of the dead, to divinity, to resurrection. The background was golden, the flesh tones reddish brown, the clothes white, and there were bright touches of green, red, and yellow. Everything was spotted with brown fungus which had been growing in the dark humidity for centuries.

As Lucinda began to draw copies of the images Oxtaby prowled the walls as if studying a testimony which only he could understand. In the empty antechamber behind us two guards squatted on the floor, their rifles leaning against the bare walls as they smoked the English cigarettes I had given them. Soon Adamson, the English guard, would arrive at his tent by the top of the steps with his wind-up gramophone and his records of Puccini, Offenbach and *Chu Chin Chow*.

'Look, Lucinda,' Oxtaby said, pointing to the north wall, 'this is the king's specially prepared body entering the Other World. This is his successor, Ay. He's tapping the lips on the coffin image; the ceremony is called the Opening of the Mouth.'

To me the paintings were less than perfect. Haste had marred them, and they did not have the detail and calm of others I knew. I saw Lucinda register my expression and then look down at her sketch-pad. Her fingers moved lightly across its surface. I could hear the faint rasp of the pencil, and thought of her as a child, watching as Oxtaby guided the automatic writing.

'They must have been done quickly,' I said; 'the king wasn't expected to die so young.'

Oxtaby continued his explanation as if my opinion were worthless.

'And here is something which looks like a man, but is not quite a man. This is following the dead king as he enters the realm of the gods. It's called the *ka*. The ka was a kind of spirit double, one of the constituents of the self along with the actual body, its shadow, and a soul represented by a bird. The idea of the double has survived down to the present day, although now it is called the karim. Like the ka, the karim is created at the same time as the child is born.'

I looked hard at the ka. For me it was as devoid of emotion as the rest of the paintings.

'And here,' Oxtaby continued, 'well, you'll recognise Anubis, with the jackal head. Priests used to wear Anubis masks when preparing the body.'

He stopped and turned to me as if he had just remembered something.

'Raymond,' he said, 'when I was crossing the escarpment on a donkey last week I witnessed something rather unusual.'

I looked at him. For a few moments he seemed to hang in a balance; he was wondering if it was wise to continue, but eventually he did.

'The sun was going down and glades of shadow were forming in the east-facing slopes. I wanted to reach the valley floor quickly, but sensed I was being followed. I turned and there was nothing there, but I kept checking. For minutes on end I saw nothing, but then, when I had turned especially quickly, I saw two jackals slink into the shadows. One was extraordinarily large.' He pointed to the figure of Anubis. 'I was reminded of the embalmer god.'

'Sunset distorts perspective,' I said; 'they must have been much nearer to you than you thought. You always have had an active imagination.'

'You think it was just a coincidence?' Lucinda asked.

'Of course.'

'At university,' Oxtaby said drily, 'Raymond studied William of Ockham. He has a logical explanation for everything.'

'I'm proud of that,' I replied.

Oxtaby turned back to the paintings and continued with his description. Here was Nut, the sky-goddess; Hathor, goddess of the west; Osiris, lord of the underworld. The section showing Isis greeting the king had been removed by Carter, he explained; it was the only way they could empty the tomb.

'You even had a rational explanation for the cobra,' he unexpectedly said.

I stared at him.

He moved so that he stood next to one of the lights.

132

It turned his face as white as burning phosphorus, and I could see no expression on it.

'What cobra?' Lucinda asked.

'I don't know,' I said, and felt sweat trickle down my forehead.

'Carter's pet bird and the cobra,' Oxtaby said. He had not meant his trick at all.

'I'd forgotten that,' I confessed.

'Yes. Rationalists always forget the important events.'

'Carter is a clever man, but difficult,' I told Lucinda. 'Like other solitaries, he likes pets. When this dig started, but before the tomb steps were uncovered, he brought a canary to his house. It was kept in a cage, and the local people said it would bring good luck.'

'In his terms, they were right,' Oxtaby said.

'But shortly after the discovery a cobra entered the house and killed the bird. I'm sure you can imagine what was said – the pharaohs were taking revenge, the excavation was cursed, and so on. So a chance event helped the spread of superstition. Clive would like to think this accident was part of a greater pattern.'

Oxtaby gave a predatory smirk, as if I had just condemned myself out of my own mouth. He turned back to the west wall.

I continued before he could speak. 'There were other rumours, of course. One was that the burial chamber would be empty but for thousands of cobras. Everyone forgets that story now.'

Oxtaby indicated the entire wall. 'This is the last wall of all. It's part of the Amduat. As you see, there are four lines, or registers. The top one shows the solar barque, the boat of the sun; underneath it are twelve squatting baboons, four for each register. They represent the twelve night hours, each of them occupying a different stage in the journey to rebirth, each leading to the triumphant appearance of the reborn sun in the eastern sky each morning. It's a process of magical transformation. Even the lowliest creature, the scarab beetle, is part of that process. The beetle rolls its ball of dung uphill in the sand, and larvae hatch from it. Life

133

arises from death. That's why the scarab is such a potent symbol, and that's why we find its image everywhere – and here, on this wall.'

He stood quietly for a while, one hand spread beneath his chin. All was silent but for the scratch of the pencil-point. I felt more sweat trickle down me, and could see Lucinda's skin shine with it.

When Oxtaby next spoke there was sadness in his voice. 'We're no better than tomb-robbers,' he said.

Lucinda glanced at me but continued to sketch. I rubbed my fingers along the base of my neck; my skin was covered in droplets.

'We're professionals,' I said; 'we do it for knowledge.'

'We do it for gain,' he responded. 'What knowledge do we take from this? Mere crumbs. This is no assembly of ignorance, no dark age of the mind. This is a journey of the soul as powerful as anything in Western tradition. It is allegorical, mystical, organised. It's not a dream, not an absurd private fantasy like Bosch; it's a manual showing how the flesh becomes spirit, and it lays responsibilities on the living so that the dead can make their journey.'

'The ceremony of the Opening of the Mouth?' Lucinda asked.

'That's one duty; yes. It was part of a cocoon of magic that was woven around the dead man, the burial ritual, the place of rest. Magic was the force that governed the processes of change; it started, steered, and completed transformations. It was in the rise and fall of the Nile, the dawning and setting of the sun and stars, the death and birth of men and women. It was bound up with the growth of food, its digestion and evacuation, the use of faeces and mud as fertilisers to aid new growth. Magic happened when something was burned, a meal was eaten, the moon rose, a beetle hatched from its larva, someone died. Look at these walls – serpents, hawks, scarabs, and gods beyond our understandings are accompanying the soul on the journey all of us must take.'

'He reads too much into it,' I said to Lucinda; 'these are

like misericords, like carvings under choir seats in medieval cathedrals. There are dozens, hundreds of received images; tomb painters copy them or work out elaborations from them.'

'I *do* believe it's a pattern,' he said, 'a pattern repeated in tomb after tomb and passed down among the peoples who succeeded the Egyptians. The ark of the covenant was the same shape as the shrines in this tomb. The blue we find on some images of Isis has been passed down in the blue dress of the Virgin Mary. Magical power can be found in shape and colour and function as well as rituals and individuals.'

'A pattern,' I responded, 'that begins in the pyramid texts, and becomes elaborated as dynasty succeeds dynasty and drought follows flood.'

'A part-truth, Raymond. These rituals must have had their roots long before they were written down.'

He turned to Lucinda and put out his hand to touch her on the arm; I saw her flinch.

'I've told Lucinda about the papyrus,' he said.

I was infuriated by this but dared not show it. Lucinda had already said I was secretive.

'I used to dream that one day we would find a complete codex,' he went on; 'a sacred hoard that gathered together all the funerary and magical texts of the entire civilisation. Then I thought that such a find was impossible, because there would always be part of the ritual that would not be written down but passed on, generation after generation, in a series of acts and pronouncements.'

I disliked the way he was speaking so freely; it made me uncomfortable. I thought of the guards who could be listening in the antechamber.

'The religion changed and was dispersed,' I told Lucinda. 'The Romans took it up in a simplified form. The true religion shrank, but lingered on at Philae until Justinian had it destroyed.'

'So your ambition can never be realised,' Lucinda said to her brother. 'This tomb is likely to be the last piece of evidence. There is no ancient Egyptian bible.'

'I spent years trying to accept that. Now I think that perhaps I was right to begin with. One should never dismiss dreams.'

'I think you can dismiss that one,' I said.

'We need more complete versions of the Other World and what happens in it,' he went on. 'We need clearer, more specific keys to the wall paintings. We don't even know the true functions of the gods, we half-guess at them. Until then, everything will be like Lucinda's work.'

'What do you mean?' she asked.

He turned on her like a master on a servant. 'I mean that you are no better than a writer of romances, and that you have forgotten what real truth is. Why, you produce nothing but pale impersonations of this art, and your thin copies are spiced with fictions of sacrifice and slavery so that they appeal to Europeans with a taste for the savage and exotic.'

'You're a cruel man, Clive.'

'Perhaps. But unlike you, sister, at least I am not a fraud.'

'I think you should take that back,' I said.

He wheeled round, and for a second I thought he would spring at me. Lucinda's pencil was poised above the paper, as if she had been magically charmed. Oxtaby's skin shone, and a bead of sweat formed on his chin, grew, and fell as I watched.

'I take it back,' he said, suddenly calm again.

I wanted Lucinda to reject his apology, but she did not. 'It's all right,' she said in a small voice, and lowered the pencil onto the sketch-pad once again.

The rest of our time was spent in awkward conversation, as if Oxtaby's casual insult had disrupted the relations between us. He rode down the valley with us but refused to return to the East Bank, and we left him near Qurna. After we had gone a hundred yards, Lucinda turned to wave, but he had already vanished. We rode back through the evening fields, with swifts and martins cutting through the air around our heads.

When we reached the river we hired a felucca making its

last crossing of the day. The sun was setting and a desert wind scoured the darkening water as if the air was being driven by immense wings. We sat on opposite sides to balance the boat, and found that we were staring into each other's eyes. The escarpment had become as black as pitch, and along its crest the last light of day flared with a dying brilliance. Above us the sky deepened through countless shades of blue, and the stars began to appear, first singly, and then in hundreds.

'I'll never forgive Clive for saying that,' she said. 'I'm not a fraud, and I never shall be.'

'You should have insisted on a keener apology.'

After a few seconds, she defended him.

'When he sees things like the tomb paintings, he becomes thoughtless with excitement. I'm in the wrong; I should just have ignored him.'

Water lapped on the side of the boat. I trailed my hand in it to cool my fingers.

'We had some trouble with him last year, in the Service. He talked out of turn and said stupid, regrettable things. Just as he said in the tomb.'

'I'm sure he didn't mean it,' she said.

'Probably not,' I said.

But I was sure he had done. I often wondered if I was right to defend Oxtaby, but by now it had become a force of habit. Our meetings had become unpleasant and characterised by argument and ill-feeling. But I could never forget how he had saved me; if he had not arrived when he did, I would have been put to death on a lonely dune beside the slaughtered bodies of a Bedouin family.

In the middle of the river the wind died, and everything fell silent. I could barely hear the creak of the mast under its heavy sail and the slight rasp of the rope around the tiller. The darkening waters parted before us with the faintest of liquid whispers, and I could hear the chatter of birds as they began to roost for the night in the trees on the far bank.

The felucca set us down at a ramp of stone beneath the corniche. I held Lucinda's hand as she walked down the gangplank. When she was safely on land I tried to pull away my fingers, but she gripped them more tightly and would not let go.

The hotel's upper corridors were busy with people. It was still early, but she bade me good night at her door. I went into my own room, wondering if there had been a farewell in her eyes.

I did not know what was expected of me. For a while I waited for a knock on my door, but when none came I turned on the shower and stood beneath it for some time. Afterwards I dressed in clean clothes, and only then did I go out onto the balcony.

Lucinda was standing beside her balustrade. Her arms were crossed as if she had been waiting for me, and her hair was damp. Her eyes had widened, as they had in Cairo when the lights dipped, and as they did in tombs.

'You were right,' she said.

My heart was in my throat.

'About what?'

'About the balconies. A man could easily step from one to the other.'

'Yes,' I said, 'I know.'

In the dim light I could not tell if the slight movement on her lips was a smile or a scowl, but when she turned and went back into her room she left the french windows open. Somewhere in the streets below a dog howled.

I stepped too quickly onto the balustrade and teetered for a moment; I did not know if I should go back or forward, and imagined myself falling to the garden and breaking my back because of my indecision. It must have taken less than a second for me to make the next step, but time began to thicken, and it felt like minutes.

I stood at her window and looked into her room. I was breathing heavily and a strange drifting sensation was in my head, as if my mind had been cut loose from moorings. The room was gloomy; Lucinda stood at its centre, her arms still folded. There was a darker shape in the chair beside the bed, and for a dizzying moment I thought that there was someone sitting there, but the shape had only been made by two rearranged cushions.

138

I wanted to enter the room but could not. A sudden fear overwhelmed me; what if I had misunderstood her completely? What if she screamed at my approach, or began to hit me with her fists, or wept like the victim of a rape? I waited for her to do something but she only stood motionless.

And now I had the sensation of time flowing away from me, as if the neck of an hour-glass had unaccountably widened and all of its sand was pouring into the lower chamber. I knew I must act before the sand emptied, but was too uncertain and too numbed to do anything.

She looked at me, bemused by my paralysis. Her eyes caught faint glimmers of reflected light and magnified them so that they shone.

And I could think of nothing but the shadow of Clive Oxtaby falling across us, of his extraordinary intimacy with Lucinda, of her confession that she would tell him everything if he asked. I even wondered if the argument in the tomb had been an act staged for my benefit.

At that moment I knew I should retreat. I tried to say something but could think of nothing, and I moved slightly away from her.

She crossed the space between us in four strides. Her feet were bare, and her thin clothes rustled as if they were being shed. When she had reached me she put up a hand and cupped it across my mouth so that I could not speak. As soon as she did the upper part of my body twitched as if a shock had passed through it. I could smell closeness, warmth, English perfume. I felt I was being drawn into imprisonment and knew I would do everything that was asked of me.

But I was amateurish and clumsy. No woman had ever loved me in such a way, and I felt unmanned. Everything about her was strange and new; the touch of her skin, the texture of her hair; even the articulation and musculature of her body was challenging and oddly foreign. I fumbled and hesitated before a multiplicity of uncertainties until she grew weary of my lack of initiative.

She whispered so close to my ear that the words melted

into the rhythm of her breathing. 'Don't move,' she said. Then she stripped me of my clothes as if it was a ritual she had performed every night. I expected to be senseless to everything but desire, but once I was naked I felt vulnerable, no better than a captive dragged before her in chains.

She lay me down on the bed so that I was looking at the darkened ceiling and then put her hand on my mouth again. This time she ran her fingers across my lips. 'This is too important to be anything else but right,' she said.

Lucinda took off her own clothes and knelt beside me on the bed. I thought I should embrace her, but when I tried she pushed me back onto the bed and ran her hands down my body. 'I can only just see you,' she said, 'your skin is darker than Clive's. He is so pale that at times he looks like a man who has died.'

Like a fool I wanted to answer, but she put her hand to my mouth for a third time.

'You can say nothing,' she said; 'your words cannot leave your throat.' And then she straddled my hips, pressing down on my ribcage with her hands. 'And I am the goddess of the sky,' she said, 'and my body is the vault of heaven.'

At some time during the night I dreamed of rain. The skies became bruised with cloud, and a vicious downpour began to fall across the land. I dreamed of flooded channels, of water spilling over rocks and cascading down gullies, of a rising slurry of mud that made clothing sodden and rose around the calves and thighs and up to the waist. There was no end to the rain, and I did not know if it was a benediction or a curse.

I awoke gasping for breath. There was no air in the room, and my imagination turned its bare walls into paintings, and my presence into entombment. In near-panic I made for the french windows, convinced that all air had been withdrawn from the chamber and that I needed to be outside to be able to breathe.

As I neared the window I saw, in the mirror, the reflection of a face watching me from my own balcony.

A fist of ice closed around my heart, but I walked out to face the man who spied on us.

There was no one there. Below me the town was quiet, sunk into the darkness of the witching hours. High above, a moon sharp as a blade hung in the sky.

I put my arms around my body to stop it from trembling. There had been no one watching us; of course there had not been. But for one dizzying moment I had not known if we were being observed by Clive Oxtaby or myself.

5

It took eight days to perform the autopsy. Each morning a team gathered at the entrance to the laboratory tomb; some of us were in shirtsleeves with the heat, others dressed in our uniform of Western suits with waistcoats, ties, and tarbooshes. Carter donned his glasses in readiness for several days of close, detailed examination. Each evening, after the day's work had ended, a statement was issued to waiting reporters and the steel gate of the tomb was locked, barred and guarded before we retired to our respective homes and hotels. Oxtaby went to one of his resting-places in Qurna; I returned to Luxor, where I joined Lucinda each night. She seldom spoke, as if the act of love was in itself too sacred for words. Afterwards she quizzed me about life along the river, but she never wanted to talk about her brother. I would rise before dawn each morning to take the ferry over to the West Bank.

Tutankhamun's body lay inside the lower halves of the inner coffins as if within a nest of cradles. These had been lowered into a simple palm-wood box, like a coffin for a giant, and draped with white cotton sheets. We bent over it, our heads dizzy with the smell of wood-resin, and peeled away leaf-shaped sections of bandage in a forlorn hope that the damage would be superficial. But with each removal it grew increasingly evident that a brittle decay had reached deep into the very fabric of the mummy.

Now a strange new libation was poured across the remains. Derry covered the entire body, apart from the golden mask, in a thin film of paraffin wax. When this had hardened he took a scalpel and sliced into the bandages. All was silent but for the harsh rasp of the fabric being cut apart by the blade. After the incision was completed the outer layers of linen peeled away like bark from a rotting tree.

Beneath these were further layers which had to be removed section by section from the feet upwards. Some of the inner cambric had become as black and powdery as volcanic dust. Lucas suggested that this was a consequence, not of the techniques of mummification, but of the liberal use of the consecration oils; over hundreds of years, a prolonged, scorching combustion had gradually incinerated the linen.

As the layers of bandage were lifted away they revealed amulets, charms, collars, rings, clasps and bracelets that had been secreted within the wrappings. Here was further gold, faience, lapis; here were yet more hawks, scarabs, vultures, falcons. The cocoon around the dead king had been packed with earthly riches that mirrored the divine heavens.

At each discovery Oxtaby bent forward, his eyes carefully noting the position of the find. Often Burton complained, and Oxtaby had to stand back so that the photographic record could be completed. And often it was Oxtaby who gently and precisely lowered his hand into the wreckage of cambric, dried oil, and paraffin wax so that he could lift a piece of polished gold from where it had lain for more than three thousand years.

Even Carter admitted that he had scant knowledge of the purpose of these charms. We all assumed they were to help the dead king in his journey through the Other World, but none of us really knew their precise function. Oxtaby shook his head when asked. He gave the impression of a man sinking into knowledge, as if the evidence was accumulating so fast that it would close over his head and he would eventually become dumb.

The oil in the coffin base had solidified into a mass so hard and intractable that it had to be chipped away; several times, for minutes on end, the tomb echoed with the sound of mallets striking the handles of chisels. Within this matrix, in a tangle of carbonised wrappings, lay the mortal remains of Tutankhamun.

And so the thin, sad body was slowly exposed to view – first the legs, and then, over a period of several days, the arms and torso. The flesh was dry as valley sand and had shrunk, and the joints of the bones had loosened. The stick-thin arms were folded across the chest. There was a closed wound running from the navel to the left hip where the embalmers had entered the body to empty it of its contents. The fingers and toes were capped with golden stalls, as was the penis, which was bound in an upright position in readiness for mating with the sky.

'He's no more than a boy,' Carter said with unaccustomed emotion; 'seventeen, eighteen at the most.'

Derry bent across the left leg and gently dislodged the kneecap. It came away in his hand, and he lifted it free of the leg-bones with a section of parchment-dry skin still attached to it. 'You are correct, sir,' he said, looking down at the femur and epiphysis; 'the cartilaginous bridge has not yet ossified; that happens at about the eighteenth year.'

Now that the wrappings had been stripped away, Derry and Saleh Bey Hamdi were able to have the body lifted piece by piece from its coffin. Each part of it was weighed and measured, and each piece of bone and dry tissue was examined intensively.

'Do you see what I mean?' Oxtaby murmured into my ear; 'it's as if everything can be reduced to statistics in an anatomist's report.'

The head of the king was apparently fixed fast within its golden mask. We considered several ways in which it could be loosened, but none of the more delicate methods would work. Eventually long knives were heated and inserted between the mask and the wrappings around the head, and in this way the head was partly cut and partly levered away from its housing.

The head was swathed in cloth, and around it was a diadem of gold and carnelian; beneath was a further band of polished gold which fastened a decayed head-dress; a further band held a cap in place on the shaved skull. The face itself was covered in fragments of decayed cambric and powdery scabs of natron. These were delicately brushed away until, at last, the entire features came into view.

The face was dark, with brittle skin. Its flesh had shrunk across the skull, making the cheekbones seem raised; on the left cheek was what could have been a bruise. The eyelids were partly open, exposing desiccated eyes that had sunk within the dry sockets. The nose had flattened under the tension of the bandages, and its nostrils had been sealed with resin. The mouth had also been coated with resin, and was opened in a mirthless smile to show the upper teeth.

We stood there for a while, each of us somehow humbled, silent before the ancient features. I noticed Carter suddenly turn white, and for a brief moment I thought he would fall, but Thuillier and Lacau steadied him. Someone made a weak joke about the heat and we all smiled.

I wondered what had passed through Carter's mind, for his expression was that of a man who had witnessed something profound and disturbing. It took him several minutes to recover, and all the time Thuillier watched him as if he feared he could collapse completely. Afterwards he cleared his throat as if nothing had happened.

The doctors transferred the head to a tray and continued their examination while Burton arranged to photograph it. Derry gave his commentary as the findings were made – the skull was empty apart from some embalmers' resin, hardened to the consistency of bone; the wisdom teeth had broken through the gum; the head itself was wide and flattened across the crown, a similar shape to the head of the Akhenaten mummy; the height of the body, calculated from the limbs, would have been five feet and six inches.

After a while Carter spoke. 'Dr Derry,' he asked, almost apologetically, 'could you hazard a guess at the cause of death?'

Derry pursed his lips; he had been waiting for the question. 'Impossible to say,' he replied; 'there's simply not enough evidence.'

'Tuberculosis,' Lacau said. It was less of a suggestion than a statement.

'You may be right,' Derry said. 'I cannot prevent you from speculating. All I can say is that the final mystery is, I'm afraid, beyond solution.'

Lacau looked at him disapprovingly and then turned to Saleh Bey Hamdi, who merely agreed with what Derry had just said.

'Why is the embalming wound where it is?' Thuillier asked. 'This is an Eighteenth Dynasty king; the angle should be from the hip to the groin, not upward to the navel.'

'Dr Thuillier makes an interesting observation,' Carter conceded.

'I can't answer that,' Derry replied. 'There seems to be no specific medical reason why the incision should be as it is.'

Lacau shook his head. 'There is no mystery,' he said. 'One must expect variations such as this.'

I saw Oxtaby smile. He wanted me to know that Lacau was dismissing important evidence.

For once I agreed with Oxtaby. But, although the angle of the cut must have been important, I did not really believe we would ever know the answer to Thuillier's question; the past would never reveal itself fully to us.

Oxtaby pointed to the lesion across the left cheek. 'Is this significant? Could it be a bite? Or a sting?'

Derry glanced across at Hamdi. 'Possibly,' Hamdi said, 'and possibly not. It may be something to do with the way the body was preserved.'

'An apprentice mortician, a botched mummification,' Lacau suggested. 'That seems an entirely reasonable conclusion.'

'An apprentice would not work on a god,' Oxtaby said scathingly, and Lacau cast him a quick, angry glance.

'A broken cheekbone?' Carter suggested.

'No,' Derry said; 'the skull is as it should be. Perhaps the mark is significant, more probably it is not.'

'Everything here has significance,' Oxtaby retorted.

Derry spoke again. 'Let me say again that I cannot prevent speculation. No doubt the gentlemen of the press are already eager to do that. But there is no pathological evidence to support any of the more, shall we say, unusual hypotheses.'

We all nodded. Witnessing the autopsy had forged a brotherhood between us; no one would question what Derry's report would say. But I wondered how many of us thought it possible that the king had been murdered.

'Please,' Oxtaby asked, 'let me hold the head.'

Derry looked questioningly at him, and then looked at Carter, who nodded.

Oxtaby stepped forward and lifted the head with all the strange, reverential gentleness he had shown towards the treasures within the wrappings. He gazed at the dead face for what seemed like a minute, holding it like a father gazing at a new-born child in a mixture of adoration and shock. No one spoke, but I felt that the air within the tomb was thinning.

Then Oxtaby returned the head to the examination tray as tenderly as he had lifted it.

'Thank you,' he said. I had never heard him speak so simply before.

'There is little more we can do here,' Derry said quietly. 'There remains only our official report.'

Near to the mouth of the tomb I asked Carter if he was feeling unwell. He shook his head. 'You'll think me out of my mind, Murchison, but quite unaccountably I felt I knew what it was like to be him.'

'Him? The king?'

He nodded but did not turn to me. I guessed that he wished to avoid looking into my eyes. 'It was the damnedest experience I've ever had,' he went on; 'just for a moment I wasn't here. I wasn't even *me*. I was back then, and I was . . .' His voice trailed away. 'Someone else,' he finished lamely.

'Howard, you're under tremendous strain. The years of working on this tomb, the trouble you've had with the Service and the press, the heat and the lack of air – it's not surprising you've had a slight feeling of unreality. It was an odd sensation to watch the autopsy, and you must have felt it more keenly than anyone else.'

'No; Oxtaby felt it more than me.'

I laughed uneasily.

'It's true. Couldn't you see it in his face? I had to give him permission to hold the head; it would have been vicious and cruel to refuse.'

'You never trusted him,' I said warily.

'I still don't,' he replied.

Oxtaby came towards us carrying his staff, but did not stop. He did not even look at us. Instead he walked straight out of the tomb and through the reporters who had grouped as close as possible to its entrance. He ignored them all, even the ones who had paid him in the past.

'Do you see what I mean?' Carter asked.

'I should follow him,' I said.

He nodded. 'Yes. He possibly needs his protector. It appears that soon he could be beyond anyone's help, even yours.'

I followed Oxtaby through the reporters, refusing all their questions. They all knew that Derry would issue a press bulletin later in the day.

I did not call to Oxtaby, but followed him along the dusty tracks towards the base of one of the fissures that scored the rock face. Soon he entered the area of shadow held within a ragged arc of cliffs. The shadow line was inhabited by swarms of tiny insects, and pairs of swifts swept back and forth to catch them on the wing.

When he was near the foot of the cliffs Oxtaby stopped. I paused where I was, watching him look up at the cleft.

He turned and sat on a broad, flat rock so that he was looking back down the valley. He gave no indication that he could see me, even though I was standing directly in front of him, fifty feet away. After a few seconds he put the staff on the ground beside him, picked up a stone, and gripped it in his fist. That was the last move he made for some time.

I moved to one side before I, too, sat down. Even though they were in shade the rocks were still hot.

We sat there as the shadow gradually slid further across the valley. I did not dare interrupt him.

After about twenty minutes he looked at me as if I had just arrived.

'Murchison,' he said, 'didn't you feel it as well?'

It was so quiet in this part of the valley that I could hear him clearly even though his voice was low.

I shook my head. 'I felt nothing.'

He threw the stone away in disgust. 'Even Carter felt something. At first I thought it was the position of the lesion, and then I saw his face change. Something even more important had happened to him.'

'The lesion? What about it?'

He laughed as if he could not believe I could be so obtuse. 'It was in the same position as Carnarvon's mosquito bite. Surely you realised!'

I licked my lips. They felt dry and cracked. 'A coincidence, that's all. The press will make the most of it but I'm sure Carter won't be worried. Like me, he probably didn't even notice.'

'He saw something.' He tapped the side of his head. 'Something in here.'

'The closeness of the tomb; the concentration; and who knows what could have infected us from those wrappings, that corpse.'

'It is not our bodies which have been infected; it is our imaginations.'

I moved closer to him and sat down again about ten feet away. He stared down the valley. Perhaps in his mind it echoed with the harsh blare of silver trumpets and was peopled with vivid processions.

'When we were in the war,' he said. 'That time we captured the soldiers who had murdered the family.'

'We agreed never to speak about that. I don't want to remember it.'

'You were sick – '

'Oxtaby,' I said warningly, but he did not stop and I still did not move.

'You froze so that you couldn't even get your own pistol. You waited to be killed, as if you wanted death, and afterwards you vomited until there was nothing left in your stomach.'

'I was stunned after pitching forward from the camel. And I was almost killed by those soldiers. One of them was only a few feet away when you fired. He could have murdered me like he murdered that family.'

'I should have felt close to those deaths, but I still didn't have the sensation that I had in the laboratory tomb. Even though the torture and the killing had just happened, I had no imaginative link with the fate of those people. Not at the time.'

'You still took the action that you did,' I said.

'I was cold about that, and very clear. Those soldiers were guilty; the blood was still on their hands. They had abused their power and broken the conventions of war. They had to die by the standards they themselves had set.'

But they had surrendered within a few seconds. Oxtaby had fired his revolver three times but not hit anyone, and the Arabs had still been taking aim when the Turks fell on their knees with their hands raised. We tied them up before deciding what to do with them.

It was after this that we examined the parents, butchered on the side of the dune. In the ransacked tent we found the raped daughter. She was little more than a child, and was naked from the belly down. Beside her was a younger brother with a single bayonet wound in his tiny throat. Blood was clotting on the rug we threw across them, and one bare foot stuck out from beneath it.

The five captured soldiers, each one with his wrists bound in the small of his back, pleaded their innocence and begged for their lives. They said they had been on patrol, bringing up the rear of a retreating column, and come across this atrocity; they would never have done such things. It was some other soldiers' fault. When I had come into view they had panicked and shot at me; if they had thought sensibly, they would have surrendered straightaway.

Our Arab companions pleaded for revenge while I trembled with shock and disgust.

Oxtaby unholstered his revolver. I had never seen him so possessed or so frightening.

He walked behind the captured men, paused behind each of them, and one by one he shot them in the back of the head while the Arabs cheered with approval. After the third soldier he stopped to re-load, and then he shot the remaining two. I was astonished and terrified, and yet I had wanted him to do it.

We had not mentioned anything in our report. Officially, we had merely completed our mission to spy on a retreating column. But Oxtaby had talked about it incessantly when we were alone together, and it had taken me days to persuade him that we should be silent about the incident, for ever.

'What I did was not revenge,' he said, looking down the valley. 'They deserved to die. I did it as efficiently and humanely as I could.'

'It was still unforgivable.'

'That was the day we came across the geode,' he went on. 'I didn't realise it at the time, but it was a sign to us. And afterwards I thought that, if the world ever found out what I had done, it would condemn my act as barbaric and unclean. But it was honest and just to execute those men. It even had a kind of purity.'

'Like your precious geode, you mean.'

'Yes.'

'You told me that at the time. You were always full of justifications. But I wanted to expunge the whole thing from my mind.'

'I'm reminded of it whenever I see necropolis seals.'

'There are always nine bound captives on those, never five.'

'True; but there were nine people killed that day – four

151

Bedouin and five Turks. Perhaps that was why you were allowed to survive, Murchison. So that, in the future, I would be able to see a pattern emerge.'

'Yes,' I said with as much sarcasm as I could muster, 'ten would not have been a magical number, would it?'

Oxtaby smiled. For him, my comment was so ridiculous that it did not require an answer. But I wanted to goad him a little more. He was my rival for Lucinda's love, and in that sudden, dislocating moment, I wanted to destroy him.

'I was the one who took your geode,' I told him. 'I took it down to the river and tossed it in. Its two halves are deep in Nile mud now.'

'I always suspected you had done that.'

'Your suspicions were correct. I thought that you would forget that piece of crystal, but you didn't. You still use it as an image, as a metaphor. I hate your doing it because it reminds me of those soldiers.'

'I could use it again now. About the king.'

'You would argue that his carcass somehow held the spirit of a marvellous past? That that poor emaciated body in there, drained of its lights and its brain, opened a kind of doorway to the world of the imagination?'

'The door opened for at least two of us. We sensed the power that had been released in that tomb; part of it soaked into our imagination. I don't know about the others. Perhaps even Lacau felt it.'

'Oxtaby, even if he did, even if *everyone* did, it would prove nothing. That kind of mass hallucination is a useless event, a frippery. Neurologists or psychologists might learn something; not Egyptologists. Whatever you saw, whatever you felt, had no basis in reality. It was nothing but a compound of the atmosphere in the passageway, the extreme concentration, your expectations, and perhaps what you read as a child.'

He picked up another stone, threw it a short way in the air, and caught it again.

'If it weren't for me you would have been buried in a sand dune in the middle of nowhere,' he said. 'You would be just like the nameless dead buried in unmarked graves along the desert edges of the Nile. There would have been no preparation and no ritual; you would have vanished just as Rex Plummer vanished.'

'Don't you realise that I cannot help but think about that?'

'The ancients knew that their treatment of the dead must reflect the hierarchy of power. The separation of the body from its internal organs was not just an efficient means of embalming; it echoed a principle we don't yet understand. As well as the identity of the dead man, the gods recognised the potency of the ritual. To bury an unembalmed man would be to condemn him. All nine of those people were condemned; you might have been, as well.'

'Whatever happened in this country's distant past has nothing to do with our work for the Arab Bureau.'

'The war changed everything,' he said. 'After what we saw, what we did, it's no longer possible to believe in the world you and Carter and Lacau were brought up in. Those ideas of objectivity and progress are finished, and yet none of you recognise it. Well, perhaps even Carter's complacency was shaken today.'

'Like rafts in a storm, those are the only ideas worth clinging to. Otherwise we're lost in black waters – magic, superstition, lies. We have to remain logical and objective.'

'You're like the rest of them, Murchison. You believe that somehow or other we are struggling on a path which rises towards a plateau of abstract, ultimate truth. You're deluded, and so are the whole gang of people who work on that tomb.'

'There is only one option for the man who thinks,' I said; 'you know which one it is.'

He looked at me with eyes that suddenly glittered like quartz. 'I turned my staff into a snake for you. You could do no such thing: you could not even begin to explain it. And yet your objectivity would tell you that I was merely performing a trick. Because once you have decided that, you need not worry that your belief in a rational, scientific world has been contradicted by real evidence.'

'It *was* a trick. You're an amateur conjuror who takes delight in confusing people. Your snake was as fraudulent as Sayeed's scarabs.'

'Was the mummy in his corner a fake? Or the decayed papyrus, or his canopic jars? Which was my snake – one of his scarabs, or one of his jars?'

'It was a trick. One out of antiquity, as you yourself said. Of course I can't explain it, because I don't have all the facts. But there is a rational explanation; there must be. If I saw the trick again, perhaps I would begin to understand exactly how you do it.'

'You would ask for a repeat of a miracle?'

'No, of an illusion.'

Oxtaby stood up and gazed at the red cliff that towered above us.

'Sense the world, Raymond; don't analyse it. Perhaps you'll find that your own intuition, your own emotions are more reliable guides than a fractured set of rules of analysis.'

He dashed grit from his hands, picked up the staff, and suddenly gave a charmingly disconcerting smile.

'I have to visit Sayeed,' he said. 'He may be a rogue, but at least he will not lecture me on virtue.'

'What do you mean?'

'His interests are purely monetary. After conversations such as ours, I find that rather refreshing.'

'You are involved in the market, too. It's a fact of life out here. You have no cause to feel superior.'

'I have every cause. The Other World papyrus – '

'It can't exist,' I insisted. 'If it did exist, we would have heard more by now.'

'I want to get to it before Nasir tears it into three or four parts.'

'He would not be foolish enough to do that.'

'No? He has been foolish enough to divide the four jars into two pairs, hasn't he?'

'Oxtaby, I should be meeting Nasir in two or three days; Ibrahim has arranged it. Give me a little time; if there is a papyrus, I'll find out very soon. Sayeed is just a liar.'

154

He spoke as if he had not listened to me.

'The amulets and implements that we found on Tutankhamun's body were part of an elaborate design; they must have been. Each one, and its exact position, had a precise magical function. Perhaps a papyrus exists that would tell us exactly what these functions were. That would be something for your museums, wouldn't it?'

'You know it would.'

'If I find it, I will not let it go to them. I have thought hard about this, and there is only one fair and just solution. I have decided to hand it over to the museum in Cairo. It belongs to this country's past; like Tutankhamun's treasure, it should stay here. If necessary, I'll even hand it to Lacau.'

'You can't do that. Carter has told me that in Cairo they cannot even assemble a chariot properly. A delicate papyrus could be ruined by them.'

'It belongs here. All the finds do.'

He began to walk down the bank of shale. The rocks clattered beneath his feet.

'You hate Lacau,' I said to him.

'Yes,' he said, 'but he is more honest than any of the rest of you.'

Nasir was a young man, perhaps no more than twenty-five, but he had already become portly. He smiled often and without warmth, and when he pretended to laugh he showed fillings in his teeth. He wore four silver rings, two on each hand; one of them was a seal-ring engraved both with his own name and an expression of trust in God. His two lieutenants, Akhmet and Deesa, made no pretence of friendship: they stood apart with expressions of sullen wariness as if even here, in the house of a cousin, their master could be in danger. Akhmet was big, muscular, strong enough to lift the heaviest of weights; Deesa was more wiry, with a thin moustache that emphasised the narrowness of his face.

Ibrahim showed us into a room and proudly indicated

155

six high-backed chairs. Before he sat down Nasir placed his hand on Ibrahim's shoulder, then flexed his fingers as they rested there. He seated himself carefully, almost demurely, and then told Akhmet and Deesa they could wait outside. They left in silence. We exchanged pleasantries while Ibrahim's wife served us with tea, sugarloaf and honey-cakes before she left us alone. I thought of the two lieutenants sitting on the bench outside, drinking tea and gazing impassively down the street. Perhaps they would forbid anyone else to enter.

'My cousin has told me how important you are, Mr Murchison,' Nasir said. 'For a long time I have known you to be a man of high principles and good taste. I am honoured to meet you.'

He must have thought that profuse civility was a guarantee of charm. I thought only of how sunlight can disguise dark water, but I thanked him and he went on.

'A man who stands at the side of others as they take old gods out of the ground. A man who knows the histories of the ancients and is an expert in the goods that they made. A man who knows *value*.'

'I like to think so.'

He waved his hand in a slight, feminine motion to indicate there could be no doubt about my virtues. 'Some of my customers do not know the difference between a genuine piece of work and a poor fake, let alone the difference between dynastic styles. For the last three years the antika market has been invaded by inferior copies, because now there are fools who visit this valley who will buy anything and everything. It is very frustrating for honest dealers; I have high standards and will not lower them. Why should I pander to those without true judgement? Surely it must also be frustrating for gentlemen such as yourself.'

'True.'

He shook his head as if the world were an infinitely gullible place. 'We are men of culture, and we are surrounded by vandals.'

I thought that he was the vandal, not those who bought from him, but I did not disagree.

'So I know,' he went on, 'that we understand each other. Yes?'

'I hope so.'

Nasir clicked his tongue and shook his head in faint disapproval. 'Not *hope*, surely. Ibrahim – do you say that we understand each other?'

'It seems to me that you do,' Ibrahim said.

'Good. So,' he went on, 'you have particular interests.'

'As you said,' I replied, 'I am interested in an entire civilisation.'

'Quite so. But one cannot collect the remains of an entire civilisation. Even the museum in Cairo could not do that. I have found that particular people want particular things. If a client wants, shall we say, statuettes, then I will do my best to obtain statuettes. If he needs faience, or tile, or fans, or boxes for kohl, then I will try to help him. With the fans, sadly, the feathers are always gone. And papyrus is always popular because Westerners feel that knowledge must always be folded up and hidden, as in a book.'

'There are those among us who would recognise at a glance which papyrus was important, and which not.'

He held the tiny cup of tea with a delicacy I had not expected from him.

'All these pieces from an ancient world,' he said, 'resting now in great houses in the West! I understand why scientists and lords and high officials want to do this. I understand it when they say, "our collection needs canopic jars, to make it more complete".'

'You have obtained canopic jars?'

'Of course.'

'But do you divide them between buyers, Nasir? If I was interested in such items, I would need all four. Two would not be enough for me.'

'Who would wish to buy only two canopic jars? Only the uninformed. But, if only two were available, then perhaps a little is better than nothing.'

'*Do* you have two available? Or three? Or four?'

He pursed his lips in an exaggerated parody of thought. 'I shall be honest with you,' he said.

157

'Good.'

'I did have two, very recently, but they have been sold. I do not know where their companions were; I never saw them. Sometimes, you see, I must buy from men who have no respect. They do not know what to search for, and do not recognise what they have found. To them, perhaps, one canopic jar looks very much like another. Perhaps they forgot the others, or broke them, or divided them between themselves – who is to know? It makes me sad to deal with such barbarians, but what am I to do? Let objects of such beauty be sold to tourists who would not appreciate them? I believe I should rescue them, no matter how incomplete, and offer them to the right people.'

'And at the right prices.'

'Men of knowledge can always agree on a fair price.'

'And you would not wish to tell me who bought these two jars.'

'I must respect confidences. So must you.'

'Agreed. So I could not tell you where I recently saw two others.'

'For sale?'

'Yes.'

'Eighteenth Dynasty?'

'Yes.'

'Ah, the ones I sold had animal heads and were Nineteenth. They were not the partners of your pair. Is this important to you?'

I shook my head. 'Not now.'

'The trouble with Sayeed,' he said, 'is that he does not know what he is doing.'

'Who?' I asked, innocently.

Again he made a gesture of the hand as if to dispel any kind of suspicion. 'A man called Sayeed. You may not know him. When my uncle was trading in the goods found in the Gabbanet al-Kurud, Sayeed had a sharp eye, a steady hand, a keen mind. Ten years have made a sorry difference. I try to help him because one must respect one's elders, but it is difficult with Sayeed.'

He glanced at Ibrahim, and then back at me, as he

decided whether or not he should speak the next sentence.

'I understand he has started to lie,' he said confidentially. 'No; that is the wrong thing to say. I understand he has started to believe things which are not true. He has heard of the riches that Carter and his team have taken from the Wadi Biban al-Maluk, and he thinks that he, too, can bring riches to light, simply by asking his friends to find and dig up whatever they can.'

'This is sad,' I said, 'but nothing to do with me.'

'But you would see that his illusion is as vast and as hopeless as the desert. You know what Carter has found. You have helped transport it down to Cairo. And Carter speaks to you on many matters.'

'True.'

Nasir tapped his head. 'Poor Sayeed. He is not correct. In here. It is as if robbers have entered the house of his soul, have turned order into confusion, have perhaps taken precious things away with them.'

I nodded, trying to appear polite but indifferent.

'But of *course* you know him,' he said suddenly; 'I remember now that you have been seen visiting his house. You and the Englishman who lives among the villagers of the west – what *is* his name?'

He continued pretending not to know Oxtaby's name until I told him.

'Of course,' he said, 'I remember it now. So it was Sayeed who was selling the jars? To you and Mr Oxtaby?'

I said nothing.

'Oxtaby,' he said again, testing the quality of the man by the sound of his name. 'I have heard as much about him as I have about you, Mr Murchison.'

'Have you not met him?'

'I am sure I would remember if I had.'

'He says he met you crossing a remote part of the escarpment. You, he says, and two others. Perhaps it was the men waiting outside this house who were with you.'

'When I was a youth I would perhaps cross those far mountains, but I have lost my foolhardiness. Mr Oxtaby

159

may not be scared of bandits, but I am. It was not me that he saw, but someone else.' He paused, then smiled confidentially. 'Unless perhaps it was my karim.' This amused him, and he chuckled to himself like a man laughing at a private joke.

'Oxtaby would not think he was mistaken. He remembers you very well. Do you know why? Because he suspects you have entered an unknown tomb.'

For a moment I thought I saw alarm within his eyes, but the emotion vanished as soon as it had appeared. Nasir shook his head. The motion was so slow it was almost languorous, and its deliberation was faintly unsettling. 'No, no, no,' he said, his voice like a weary chime. 'He is mistaken.'

'I am sure Mr Oxtaby is wrong,' Ibrahim said quickly.

I looked across at Ibrahim; there was concern on his face.

'You see?' Nasir asked, as if his case had been proven.

'Mr Murchison will tell him he is wrong,' Ibrahim said quickly, 'won't you, Mr Murchison?'

'If you wish it,' I said cautiously. I did not know why Ibrahim was taking Nasir's side.

'Sometimes Europeans think they are natives,' Nasir said ruminatively. 'This never happens with Americans. I do not know why. The English in particular are prone to this delusion. Perhaps it is something in their childhood. They make a romance out of what is, to us, mere necessity.'

'You think Clive Oxtaby is such an Englishman?'

'Surely you think so, too. A wiser man would have decided to leave this country by now. Only those possessed by some kind of demon would wish to stay.'

'Like Carter?'

'Carter is a great success; the greatest that the English have ever had. His demon is weakening as more and more gold is brought up from that tomb. But when his work is finished, he will leave. He will not be like Carnarvon, who let his obsession kill him. Unless he changes his ways, I am afraid your friend Mr Oxtaby could be like Carnarvon.'

'Clive Oxtaby is much tougher than Carnarvon.'

160

'But he is still a man who desperately wants to see a meaning, when there are merely facts.' Nasir smiled. 'You see, I have taken care to find out about him.'

I glanced at Ibrahim, who shook his head in denial.

'The Nile floods, the Nile sinks,' Nasir went on. 'Today we know it is because of rainstorms far, far away, beyond even the Sudan. And today we have the English dam at Aswan to release the water in the pattern of the old inundation. But that is not enough for your Mr Oxtaby. He wants to see such rhythms repeated in the beating of the heart. Just as he wants to see Osiris in the new growth of vegetation, Anubis in the jackals running in the wadis. He is in love with Egypt, and lovers are dangerous.'

'He threatens no one.'

'A man threatens himself if he thinks that the West Bank is a place of mystery. It is simply a place where people live and die. My people forgot the old religion two thousand years ago; today we follow the true way. For our villagers your friend's obsessions are tiresome, and his magic tricks a worthless diversion. To them the past is not a magical place or time, it is a livelihood. They see no romance in a newly discovered tomb, they see money. For them there is nothing symbolic about the path of the sun, it is just something that happens. There is no charm in poverty, only fate. And there is no poetry in violence; it is merely an act which often has to be carried out.'

I did not know what to say, because I did not know if I was listening to a threat.

Nasir yawned slightly and put up his hand, palm outwards, to cover his mouth.

'I apologise,' he said; 'I have had a long day. You are the second gentleman I have talked to today, Mr Murchison. The other was an American, here to view the body of the dead king.'

I nodded. 'There are always many Americans in Luxor.'

'Indeed. This one travelled from Amarna. I understand he knows you. I cannot quite recall his name.'

'Van Diemen?'

Nasir repeated his pretence of recognition. '*That* is

the gentleman's name. A charming man, but a little naïve.'

My mouth had gone dry. 'Nasir, I know that you trade with van Diemen.'

He opened his eyes wider, in mock astonishment. 'Mr van Diemen has not told you that.'

'Do not ask me how I know; I just do.'

Nasir's face darkened, but within a few seconds became bland again.

'Listen to me,' I said. 'There is talk along the Nile of a very valuable papyrus. One that concerns itself with the Other World. Van Diemen wants it; I know that he does.'

'Truly?' he asked, as if his interest was feigned. 'Is this what you really wanted to see me about?'

'It is. If that papyrus exists, then you should know several things about it. Firstly, it should not be split up or divided in any way. Secondly – '

'Mr Murchison, I know how to handle papyrus. Please do not lecture me; I understand that lectures are characteristic of your personality.'

'Then you have this papyrus,' I said, suddenly and illogically confident.

'Have I?'

'Yes.' I laughed with a sudden, heady belief that I was right, and that the papyrus was almost within my grasp.

'Raymond,' Ibrahim said warningly, but I took no notice of him.

'You have been offering it to people like van Diemen,' I said, 'and trying to establish a price. A very high price. Van Diemen is so desperate to buy that he has travelled here hoping to find you, hoping to stop you from offering it to others.'

'He *said* he was here only to view the king,' Nasir said urbanely, but I did not listen to his words.

'But you *will* offer it to others,' I said triumphantly. 'You are going to offer it to me now, because you know that Carter and I are a team. And that the home of this papyrus must be the Metropolitan in New York.'

162

'I think that would be a good home, yes.'

'I have to see it, Nasir. Before Carter will buy, the papyrus must be seen, examined, judged. You can forget about Clive Oxtaby's part in this; he will have none.'

'Truly?'

'Truly. So let us talk about the Other World papyrus.'

'Ah,' he said quietly, 'if only there was such a papyrus.'

He eyed me coolly. He was bluffing; I was certain that he was.

'I have been in this valley for many years,' I said. 'I am not like Oxtaby; I grow weary of it. Your advice is sound. I want to return to England before I forget what my home is like.'

He nodded approvingly.

'So I have little patience for delays, for feints, for all the devices of a trader's art. If you and I understand each other so well, then let us be honest. I will tell you the figure that you quoted to van Diemen.'

'I will be fascinated to learn it, since I quoted nothing. Not for a papyrus.'

I hesitated for a second, and then plunged ahead.

'You asked him for a hundred thousand American dollars.'

'Did I?'

'Yes.'

He looked at Ibrahim. 'This man Oxtaby; he must infect others with his madness.'

Ibrahim smiled thinly but said nothing.

'I must tell you,' I said, 'that the Metropolitan would not pay such a price, but that van Diemen would pay even less.'

'Mr Murchison, all this is very intriguing. And figures such as that are too great for my poor mind to grasp fully. But I do not have a papyrus of the Other World. I never have had. If I do find one, I shall come running to you and to Carter, because you will make me very, very rich.'

All my certainties began to fall away, and I felt for a moment that the ground beneath my feet was turning to water.

163

'No papyrus,' I said flatly.

'Oh, I have *heard* about such a thing; of course I have. But to me it was nothing more than a tale spun by others, a dream that would never become real. You have a saying about a rainbow's end, do you not? The new Amduat lay buried at the end of such a rainbow. At most it was a story to give encouragement, example, or amusement.'

'Like a tale of Goha,' I said, and could not prevent myself from nervously licking my lips.

'Exactly. Which is why I was astonished when Sayeed told me that you were searching for it. And I could not imagine why you should be on such a quest, because you must know that such a document does not exist. Why did you think it did?'

'I had heard about it,' I said weakly.

'Ah, you too had *heard* about it. The last papyrus I had I gave to Sayeed some weeks ago, and that was in Greek. You see, Sayeed is an old man and I feel sorry for him, especially now that his mind is becoming strange. Why, he even thinks that goods were stolen from Tutankhamun's tomb before it was officially opened. He goes so far as to tell me that you were involved – you, Mr Murchison, a man of incorruptible honour. Of course, I told him he must be wrong, and forbade him ever to speak such lies to me again.'

I said nothing.

'The papyrus was unreadable,' he went on, 'and falling to pieces. I imagine that Sayeed merely threw it into a corner. Possibly one day he will transform it into souvenirs for tourists; they like such small mementoes.'

'It was from the Fayoum?' I asked.

He shrugged. 'Perhaps. I find it difficult to remember.'

'Where did you get it?'

'It was not important and it does not matter. Besides, I could not tell you. My dealings are confidential, just as this conversation has been.'

He stood up and began to bid us elaborate goodbyes.

'I am pleased to have met you, Mr Murchison,' he said; 'now that we understand each other, we can perhaps do some business in the future. Unfortunately, I shall never be able to offer you a version of the Amduat. Of course I could have one forged for you, as Sayeed would have tried to do – but I am not a forger, and a man like you would spot fakery in an instant.'

'Yes,' I said, 'I would.'

'I have heard of very interesting finds being made in the mountains,' he said, dropping his voice to a conspirator's murmur. 'I do not know exactly what is there, but perhaps when we meet again I will be able to arrange that you see some examples.'

'If God wills it,' I said.

I was in a turmoil of uncertainty as I crossed the Nile by ferry. A black, battered Ford, one of the few cars to reach this far south, stood near to the landing-stage; the driver leaned knowingly against its dusty bonnet. Next to him black-clad women ignored him and chattered among themselves beside heaps of limes, melons, and guavas. Several tourists wished to hire the Ford, and at first the driver wanted to crowd us all together. I reminded him that I was with the Service, and he reluctantly left his other custom to haggle with donkey-cart owners and drove me to Carter's house. He was not there, so we drove up the road to the mouth of the Valley of the Kings. A cloud of choking dust rose in the air behind us.

Tutankhamun's body still lay near the entrance of the laboratory tomb. It was covered by a thin sheet, as if he had only recently died. Carter was further down the passage, standing beneath electric lights slung from the ceiling. Lucas and van Diemen were with him. On either side of them were trestle tables covered with glass bottles, wadding, and metal trays. On the floor were wooden boxes, carboys and large unopened rolls of material, like wrapped carpets. The narrow confines of the passage reeked with the smells of disinfectant, methanol, acetone, collodion, paraffin.

'Van,' I said with forced jollity as I walked to meet them.

They were surprised at my appearance. Lucas was noticeably put out; he was talking fluently about techniques of preservation, and found my unexpected presence an annoyance.

'Ray,' van Diemen said, 'it's great to see you again. How are you? And how is Mrs Plummer?'

I told him we were both well. He began to tell Lucas about our visit to Amarna. Lucas set his face into an expression of genteel boredom.

Carter looked enquiringly at me while van Diemen talked, but I could not respond to his unexpressed question. He had realised that I must have good reason for my uninvited arrival.

'I'm sure you agree this is fascinating, Van,' I said with forced comradeship; 'Alfred's skills of chemical analysis and preservation are incomparable. The expedition has lost far less of the recovered goods than anyone expected. Below one per cent, is it?'

'Far less,' Lucas said moodily. 'The funeral pall was a disaster, but we bear no responsibility for its condition. Professor Newberry and his wife salvaged what they could from that.'

Then, as if he was now resigned to having another observer on his tour, he carried on talking about how he and his team had gone about his tasks.

For the next ten minutes I tried to behave as casually as I could, but all the time I was wondering what I would say to van Diemen.

'It's really fortunate that you have the support of the Metropolitan on this,' van Diemen said as the tour reached its end. 'I wouldn't like to cost out this operation.'

'If we had a civilised arrangement with the Service,' Carter said drily, 'some of those costs would be offset by the value of the finds. As it is, we contribute money and time for no financial benefit whatsoever.'

Van Diemen nodded sympathetically. 'Well, maybe things will turn out better than you think. Maybe the government will reimburse you. I wouldn't be crass enough to ask what your costs were, Mr Carter, but I guess that in sterling terms they must be climbing well over, say, fifty thousand by now.'

Carter set his face firmly. He wanted no part of a discussion such as this. As if he had suddenly lost interest, Lucas wandered away to study some objects that lay in a treatment bath some distance along the passage.

Oblivious to the discomfort he was causing, van Diemen continued. 'At Amarna I used to sit at night and go over our estimates time and time again. Of course, the whole budget is written down officially, but the longer we dig the more variances I find.'

'Costings are not an exact science,' Carter said, with the gruffness he adopted when uncomfortable.

'You're so right, Mr Carter. Why, a few months ago I listed the new estimates for our two seasons. When I added them together, the total came to one hundred thousand dollars.'

I dared not look at Carter. 'Is that right?' I asked, hoping my voice did not tremble.

'Give or take a few dollars. But I'm sure I shouldn't say, so keep it under your hats.'

I cleared my throat. 'And did that figure include antika?'

He immediately became wary. 'Am I in a court here?' he asked, in the voice of a man suddenly and unjustly accused.

I shook my head. 'Of course you're not. Carter and I both swear to keep your confidences. Don't we, Howard?'

Carter was put on the spot by this unexpected turn in the conversation. He agreed, but I could sense his anger rise at my impetuousness.

'This has nothing to do with either of you,' van Diemen whispered. He looked down the passage towards Lucas, who was now several yards away. 'Him neither,' he added.

'You're right, it doesn't. But I have someone's sanity to think of.'

He looked at me hard for a few seconds and then began to grin widely. 'This is some kind of English joke.'

'I'm afraid it's serious. I'm talking about Lucinda Plummer's brother.'

'Oxtaby? He always was a little, well, strange. Are you being honest with me, Ray? Really?'

'Really. Van, you don't have to tell me anything you don't want to. But I know you liked Mrs Plummer and wouldn't want her to be unhappy.'

I had no scruples, I thought to myself; I was using Lucinda to find out the truth about my own fantasy.

'Go on,' he said. Beside him, Carter had squared his body and was leaning on his cane like an aggrieved country squire.

I breathed deeply to steady myself. 'Before we visited you in Amarna, a man called Nasir had come to see you. I met him today; he told me you had arrived in Luxor.'

Van Diemen was deeply suspicious, and merely stared at me.

'Did you buy from him – '

'Hold on now, Murchison. Has your little spy Laurent been telling tales? I thought as much. He's so bored up there that he sees things that don't happen and hears words that are never spoken. I'm going to complain to Lacau about this; see if I don't.'

'Please don't do that. Lacau knows nothing, and will be told nothing. Van, I don't need to find out much, but I do need to know if Nasir's canopic jars were Eighteenth or Nineteenth.'

He stared at me and said nothing.

'Please. It really matters.'

'You swear?'

'I swear.'

'All right then, Nineteenth. You'd better not be setting me up, Ray.' And he looked in appeal at Carter, who shook his head in mute, angry disapproval.

My heart felt as if it was held in a ribcage as fragile as a bird's. 'And was there a papyrus? A papyrus about What Is In the Other World?'

He seemed genuinely puzzled. 'Amduat? Is there such a thing?'

'You tell me, Van.'

'The only papyrus that was mentioned was the one I traded in as part of the deal. I don't think our friend was all that bothered about taking it, but he told me he would give it to an old relative who would use it. I don't know what for – fuel for the cold nights, for all I know.'

'What was it, Van?'

'Nothing. It was nothing.'

'What kind of nothing?'

'Look, I'd bought it for thirty dollars when we were passing through Cairo, and I thought maybe we could preserve it. But by the time we got to Amarna it was too far gone. In fact it was in one hell of a state – fragile, in pieces, unsalvageable.'

'Greek?'

'From the Fayoum, I would guess. And about a thousand years younger than anything we would like to see.'

I leaned against the nearest laboratory table. Sensing that there was nothing left to say between us, Lucas came ambling back along his lines of equipment.

'You're satisfied now?' van Diemen asked. I could sense an edge of bitterness in his voice, as if he had been betrayed into breaking a trust.

'Van, I appreciate what you've told me,' I said.

Angry at me for having questioned him, and annoyed at himself for having answered, van Diemen's temper broke. 'You English think you own the whole damn world, don't you? You want to run the whole show. Well, things aren't like you want them to be. The war has finished Britain; we have taken the lead now.'

We stood watching each other. Lucas picked up one of his own glass jars and began to examine it intently, demonstrating that he had no part in this disagreement.

'Mr van Diemen,' Carter said, 'I'm afraid I do not know why Mr Murchison has asked you such questions. I'm sorry that you have been subjected to what I can only call churlish behaviour.'

Van Diemen shook his head. 'I lost my temper,' he said; 'I shouldn't have done that.'

There followed several minutes of apologies and acceptance, during which I said all the right things but was unable to mean them. Eventually van Diemen shook hands with us all and said he had no hard feelings, but his face was still flushed with anger.

We said goodbye to him at the entrance to the tomb. Carter gave me a blunt, wrathful stare. He was gripping the handle of his cane so tightly that I thought he was about to brandish it like a weapon of punishment.

'That was not the action of an Englishman,' he said.

'It was necessary, Howard. I'm sorry.'

'Murchison, I no longer care for your friendship. Please do not be so familiar with me. If you do not act like a citizen of our country, have the grace to abide by its etiquette. I am *Mr* Carter to you.'

'Look – '

'Please say nothing more. It is disgraceful to pry into another man's business affairs, and to use an innocent lady as your excuse. Van Diemen should have refused to tell you anything. I don't quite know what you were trying to discover, but it appears that you have been wasting time pursuing – what? A chimera? A will-o'-the-wisp? And that somehow you wished me to become involved in this farrago. Am I correct?'

'It was worth trying. If that papyrus really had existed – '

'*If?*'

'When you calm down you'll see things differently.'

It was the wrong thing to say. He seemed to bristle visibly, and then his face set even harder.

'When I calm down, as you put it, I shall be pleased not to see you standing in front of me. What were you going to do, Murchison? Involve me in some absurd trap, the kind you and Oxtaby used to hatch in the Arab Bureau? Did you perhaps wish to ingratiate yourself still further with Lacau by seeking to show me as a man with a greed for illegally acquired grave goods?'

'Howard,' I said, deliberately stressing his first name, 'this is not the first time you've let anger take you over. There was trouble enough before; don't let it happen again.

Think of all the favours I have done you; you know that what you say now is not true.'

He snorted like a newly penned animal recognising that it cannot escape. Then he made several long lines in the grit with the tip of his cane, and scored across them to erase them.

'I do not like this constant rumour-mongering,' he said. 'It seems as if everyone now is talking about the Other World papyrus, and it is no comfort to realise that it is nothing more than the figment of a French imagination. I do not wish to be involved in this in any way whatsoever.'

'At least the rumours will die now,' I said.

'I think not. It will become a true story, as the curse of the pharaohs has become a true story. Evidence will not matter any more.'

He took a sudden, vicious swipe at a stone with his cane. There was a sharp click, and the stone hurtled through the air for several yards.

'You raised my hopes, Murchison,' he said, and there was bitterness in his voice. 'Your friends in the Ministry, and their stooge Lacau, have pinned me down with their contracts and their new laws and their maddening passion for bureaucracy. I am better and more important than any of them, and yet I am a Gulliver roped down by midgets. I allowed myself to think that quietly, unofficially, I would take out of this country something that would change the way we see the Egyptian past. Not gold, not jewels, but hard, indisputable *information*. And all you have been able to produce is rumour – a baseless, wanton rumour, but one that still divides as fiercely as a sword.'

I stood beside him. I had helped Carter in the past and wanted to help him now, but I could not. At that moment it seemed that his own summation was right. He was a sad, lonely giant, for ever condemned by his own stature. I thought of the colossus, fractured and made dumb, still gazing out towards the sunrise.

My mind went over and over the whole pitiful, stupid series of events as I crossed again to Luxor. Ahead of us

171

the columns of the temple glowed reddish-brown in the evening light, and a wisp of pink cloud floated high above them, but I was too preoccupied to notice. I thought all the time of my conversation on the bank at Amarna.

Laurent was young, inexperienced and imaginative, and Lacau had posted him to a bleak and windswept site where the only finds were patterned bricks, shattered tiles and unidentifiable rubble from broken statues. His colleagues had been withdrawn to supervise easier and more exciting digs, and he had been left on his own. The Americans were polite but clannish, the villagers unfriendly, van Diemen naïve but ambitious. It was little wonder that Laurent had begun to see intrigue, wealth and danger behind the simplest of confidential transactions. Made rich by isolation, his imagination had flourished unchecked; a jotted set of figures had been transformed into the arithmetic of trade, and an unimportant, unwanted papyrus had become the most valuable document ever found in the history of archaeology. And Nasir, who was nothing but an overweight dealer and village tyrant, had undergone a metamorphosis into an entrepreneurial robber with a secret hoard of priceless objects.

I tried to blame myself for not rejecting the story when I had first heard it, but I could not. It was Laurent's fault; he should have shown more care and less licence. I was so angry and frustrated that I daydreamed of being magically returned to Amarna, where I could accuse, judge, and systematically punish him.

I tried Lucinda's door before I knocked, but it was bolted. When there was no answer I listened carefully and could hear a faint, unidentifiable sound coming from inside. I knocked again, this time rapping on the wood like a policeman demanding entrance.

I was half-deciding to go into my own room and cross the balconies again, and then the door opened.

Clive Oxtaby stood in front of me, clean-shaven and smelling of English soap, naked to the waist and with his hair damp.

'Raymond,' he said. His voice had a curious, drugged quality, and his eyes glittered.

I was shocked by his presence, and gave a small laugh of embarrassment and uncertainty. I could hear a rustling from within the room but could see nothing because he was blocking the doorway.

'You did not think I would be here?'

I shook my head, still looking behind him but seeing nothing.

He glanced back into the room as if to satisfy himself that everything was all right, and then he stepped back so that I could enter.

Lucinda sat on a chair by the window. She was fully dressed, but she was sitting with her legs slightly apart and there was a bloom of sweat on her skin. A straw hat was in one hand, and she listlessly wafted it in front of her face. The mirror was missing, but its brass hook was still fixed into the plaster. Months of afternoon sun had bleached the paintwork so that there was an oval shadow where the mirror had hung.

'What's going on?' Oxtaby asked me.

I looked blankly at him. It seemed that I should be the one to ask such a question.

Oxtaby cleared his throat, and when he spoke again the laziness had disappeared from his voice. 'There's something happening that you haven't told me about,' he said.

I walked across to Lucinda. 'Are you all right?' I asked.

She looked up at me. Her face was strained and tired. 'Of course I am,' she answered, 'why shouldn't I be?' Her voice was like a veil drawn across the truth.

Oxtaby ran his fingers through his hair, and then lifted his shirt from the back of a chair and began to put it on. I watched with a kind of horrified fascination, imagining the process in reverse, seeing it taking place, here, only a few minutes ago.

'You should be frank with me,' he said.

I licked my lips nervously.

He walked across the room and stood in front of

173

Lucinda. 'Am I presentable, do you think? Would I pass for a gentleman again?'

'Your hair has grown too long.'

He put his hand on the back of his neck and patted it. 'Do you think people back in England would think me a disreputable brigand?'

'They would see you for what you are.'

He laughed. 'Perhaps I could be a corsair in one of your more adventurous watercolours. And our friend Raymond could be a merchant, terrified that his gold will be taken from him and his wife ravished.'

'I didn't think I would find you here,' I said, rushing my words out like an accusation.

'Why ever not? Why shouldn't I call on my own sister?'

I stared mutely at him, waiting for his falsehood to crack, but it did not.

'For heaven's sake, Murchison,' he said, exasperated, 'I haven't grown completely used to bathing in the Nile. Not just yet. Hot water and English soap still hold an appeal.'

'You came here to use Lucinda's shower?'

He raised his hands and clapped them together with heavily ironic slowness. 'You *are* slow on the uptake. You even misunderstand evidence of everyday activities.'

I felt like an intruder, but was determined to stand my ground. 'How long have you been here?' I asked.

'As long as it takes to greet my sister, share a drink with her, have a shower. Is this anything at all to do with you? Why should you be so suspicious?'

I shook my head rapidly but refused to meet Lucinda's eyes. 'Of course not.'

'But I,' he said, and there was a tigerish pounce in his words, 'am suspicious of you.'

I could not count the number of thoughts that ran in my head at that moment, but they were all to do with Lucinda. Oxtaby suspected us, and I did not know if our affair had become evident to him, or if she had confessed, or if he was merely testing us out. I did not know the extent and nature of his love for her, and I thought that

174

he might tell me a truth I would be half-eager, half-scared to learn.

'You've been getting more deeply involved in certain things,' he said, 'things that you should have told me about.'

I looked quizzically at him, prepared to out-face a direct accusation. And then I remembered his sudden, merciless decision to kill the captured Turks, and I grew cold at the thought of the violence he might wreak.

He walked calmly across the room and stood in front of me. 'The papyrus,' he said.

I became weak with relief. 'The Other World papyrus?'

'There is no other.'

I laughed, but I must have sounded strained, perhaps even a little hysterical. 'Not only is there no other, there's no such thing.'

'You saw Nasir, Ibrahim, van Diemen *and* Carter today. What are the five of you arranging?'

'Nothing. And how do you know that?'

Oxtaby smiled. 'So it is true.'

'I have no need to keep such things secret. I suppose your men on the West Bank must have told you.' But I could not see how news could have reached him as quickly as this.

He walked into the bathroom and brought out the mirror, which he carefully hung back on its hook. The glass dripped with condensation, and he wiped it as reverentially as a priest cleaning a sacred image. Then he stepped back and looked at himself. His reflection was smeared and uncertain, like a watercolour abandoned in rain.

I looked at Lucinda. She was still wafting air with the hat, but as soon as I looked at her she pointedly turned away.

'Clive,' I said, 'the only papyrus is the Ptolemaic one in Sayeed's house; the one that's beyond recovery. The rest is all misunderstanding, exaggeration, wishful thinking. Van Diemen knows nothing about it, and neither does Nasir. Carter's right; this has been nothing but a wild-goose chase. The real treasures, the only ones, are those being brought up from the tomb under Service supervision.'

175

Oxtaby studied me. 'You know,' he said after a while, 'I don't think you're lying. You really do believe what Nasir has told you.'

'I do. On this occasion he has no reason to lie.'

'I know nothing of his reasons. But I know that he was furious with Sayeed for talking openly about secret things. So furious that he had his henchmen break two of Sayeed's fingers.'

I felt suddenly, icily cold.

'Does Sayeed say this?' I asked.

'He says he had an accident. A slip, an awkward landing on an outstretched hand.'

'Isn't that likely to be true, then?'

'No. Nasir helps him out of respect for the old, but Sayeed talked about the papyrus to us. The Other World papyrus, not the Ptolemaic wreckage on his floor. He thought he was doing Nasir a good turn, but Nasir must have some other purpose in mind. In talking to us, Sayeed must have compromised a secret deal. He has acted like a fool, and been punished for it.'

I turned to Lucinda, but she stood up and walked towards the balcony as if we were not even present.

Oxtaby leaned on the wall next to the mirror, raised one hand, and gently tapped the glass with his fingernail. Droplets of water trickled slowly down the surface.

'I saw it in here,' he said; 'the clouded mirror.'

I wanted to jeer at the absurdity of his claim, but could not. I remembered what I had seen in the mirror and thought was real.

'Mirrors tell you what is hidden,' he said; 'their surfaces give you spaces you cannot touch. Even the image of a face is reversed, strange, illuminating. You do not see yourself but someone else, someone who is not quite you.'

He nodded slowly as he considered his own words.

'If the glass is misted or dark, if the light falls on it indirectly, then it can draw images from beyond vision. Only a wise man knows if such images are fantasies or portents.'

I thought of Lucinda, naked within the oval frame, and

the watcher on the balcony who had not been there. I felt feverish and strange, and wondered if Oxtaby was infecting me with his madness.

'You didn't see me in that mirror,' I said. 'That's not how you knew I had met the others.'

'I guessed you had, because I saw the papyrus.'

'Oxtaby, you can't have seen it. Face up to facts; you're having hallucinations. What you see is as meaningless as a dream. This place, the tombs, the rumours — they've affected everyone, but you most of all.'

'Clive says he's not ill,' Lucinda said.

'And what do you think?' I asked her, but she shook her head and looked away again.

'It's in a box,' Oxtaby said; 'a box like a casket, in the same shape as the burial shrines, as the ark of the covenant.'

'Where?'

'In darkness.'

'The darkness of a tomb?'

'Yes.'

'If there is no light, then how can you see a reflection? And how can you see into a closed box?'

'In the same way that I knew there were crystals inside the geode, or that a human body contains a heart, lungs, stomach, brain. The external world is just a shroud, Raymond. It's a mask, a pall. You can do nothing but study how the corpse is wrapped, but I can see the world it lived in.'

'Lucinda,' I said, 'I've always tried to help your brother, but now he rejects me.'

'Rejection?' he asked, suddenly becoming agitated. 'You're the one who is rejecting me. To you my knowledge is tainted and my insights nothing but dangerous fabrication.'

He began to pace the room as if trapped within it.

'I am surrounded by the blind,' he said fiercely. 'The ancient world is not dead, and its history still courses through us today. All around us are rhythms, vibrations, patterns, events that repeat and echo, resonances that

177

carry across days, years, centuries. There are repetitions drumming like a pulse through the whole of existence – the dawning and setting of the sun, the rise and fall of the Nile, the birth, death and regeneration of beetles, hawks, men. The ancients understood. They understood enclosure and secrecy, and most of all they understood a world full of such endless variety that they had to populate it with a host of divinities. They would have seen our lives as mean, colourless and poor, because we have withdrawn from all that is true. We can no longer hear the drumming, no longer feel the pulse. We blind the darkness with electric light, build houses and machines to rob us of the seasons, invent a god whose omnipotence is too generalised and too impossible for anyone to believe in. We are like hermits in the cave of our own failings.'

As he continued, Oxtaby's pacing became more frenetic. Lucinda looked directly at me for the first time, but I could not read what was in her eyes.

'Clive,' I said.

'The ancients left evidence of their wisdom on temple walls, in the wrapping of the dead, on pieces of papyrus, in tales of sorcery. They filled tiers and registers with images of strange gods and complex ceremonies, they made testaments of allusion and subtlety and elaboration, and all we do is plunder them for our need to feel that we have advanced.'

He grabbed Lucinda's arm. The force in his grip showed in the very stance of her body, and I could see a sudden terror appear in her face.

'They're not like her paintings,' he said, 'they were honest. They were real.' Lucinda stood dumbly beside him like a manacled slave.

'Clive,' I said, 'let go of your sister. You're hurting her.'

He peered strangely at me.

'You're ill,' I said. 'You need to see a doctor. Let me take you to Thuillier; he'll help if he can.'

'You're a fool,' he said flatly.

'Maybe. But let go of Lucinda.'

178

He loosened his grip. Lucinda pulled her arm free and stepped back.

'The Other World papyrus,' he said carefully, 'is a list of rituals, symbols, and celebrations, some of which we have only been able to guess at. It is hidden in a tomb from the Eighteenth Dynasty. The tomb was dug in a valley where only the graves of monkeys and cats have been found. It is deep within a natural cleft, well out of reach of robbers, near where I saw Nasir and his men last season. They have begun to empty the tomb, and have already taken the canopic jars and a head of Osiris. The papyrus is still there. If it had not been there, I would not have been able to see it.'

'This is lunacy,' I protested.

'Lunacy?' he asked. 'And how is the moon, Raymond? Is it waxing or waning?'

'It doesn't matter one way or the other.'

'You see,' he said, congratulating himself like a pedant, 'I can tell you exactly what it looks like. I know its phase *precisely*.'

In the Arab Bureau there had been a man who had gone insane; he, too, had switched topics with an unnerving speed, and prided himself on arcane scraps of useless knowledge.

I turned to Lucinda. 'I'm sorry,' I said, 'but I am very concerned about your safety. I do not think it is wise for you to remain with your brother.'

'Your safety?' Oxtaby repeated, shifting the word into a parody of my pronunciation.

'There's a kind of mania in you, Clive,' I said, as firmly as I could. 'I've seen it before. It can be very frightening, because a man can feel justified in doing anything. *Anything*.'

He thought I was talking about the Turks.

'I was following a thread, a pattern, although I didn't know it then. Those nine dead bodies were part of a lattice that extends back in time for thousands of years. And tomorrow, and the day after, and next year, all of those times will see other repetitions. I'm certain of it.'

179

'Clive, the nine captives on the necropolis seals were not individuals; they were symbolic of the nine enemies of ancient Egypt. They don't fit your argument at all. You've become the kind of person who will say that everything that happens is somehow pre-ordained. You belong with those hopeless romantics who believe in a pharaoh's curse.'

He shook his head. 'Not pre-ordained, no. There are events which respond to the action of the will. The priests knew that, but they let their talents become corrupt. Moses proved the better sorcerer.'

'You prove it,' Lucinda said suddenly.

I looked at her in surprise. She walked across the room to Oxtaby and glared straight into his eyes.

'Make something happen,' she demanded, 'make something *change*.'

'He has a trick with his staff,' I began, and she turned on me.

'I don't want a trick,' she spat; 'Clive has surrounded me with tricks since I was a child. I want an end to uncertainty. One way or the other, I need a *proof*.'

Oxtaby seemed gripped by indecision, but then he turned to me. 'We must cross the Nile,' he said; 'I know what it is I have to do.'

'It's pitch-black. No one will take us.'

'Ibrahim will.' He turned back to Lucinda and put his hands on her shoulders. 'Trust me,' he said, 'I can do it. I can bring the Other World into the light of day.'

'Good,' she said. 'And then, perhaps, I can be free.'

I felt that we were present at the very creation of the world. The river ran dark and silver under a bare moon, and its waters flowed around us in a chill, electrifying silence. Ibrahim, still yawning as he had done when we had roused him from sleep, steered us past an island that rose from the surface like the body of a massive sea-creature. Its mud was already stippled with the marks of a hundred vanished birds.

Near the far bank we came to shallows, with black spears

of reeds protruding from a surface glittering like the scales of a fish. Beyond them was a motionless line of grasses with grey stems and marble-white heads. They rustled drily as the felucca parted them, and suddenly two ducks flew from under the bow and whirred panic-stricken into the night. As we disembarked onto the dried silt of the riverside, an animal or a man coughed twice within a grove of palms on our left.

Oxtaby woke a man sleeping beneath one of the palms, and hired three donkeys for our journey. The man asked no questions and was not surprised at our presence. In another few hours he would be fully awake, hiring out his animals for the ferryboats of tourists flocking to the Wadi Biban al-Maluk. As he settled back into his shelter, a rifle was fired a long way away. It was nothing to worry about, the donkeyman said with a sleepy grin; nightwatchmen always believed they had seen either a robber or an evil spirit, but when dawn came there was never anything to be found.

None of us spoke while we rode, for the night demanded silence. New crops were growing on either side of the road and the air was filled with the smell of vegetation and mud. When we rode past the colossi they were grey, the colour of ash, while ahead of us the limewashed houses of Qurna resembled pale apparitions ranged on the side of the dark escarpment. Above the ridge the stars shone with an icily vivid clarity, and as we rode further west I watched them fall out of view behind the black hills, as if the entire world was sliding into the unknown.

We were passing across rock, sand and grit when the first rays of sun touched the highest point of the western hills, turning them from slate-grey to pink, then rose, and then red. Life came back to the escarpment, and as the colours of day slipped down the limestone walls I heard a strange, resonant sound, as if someone within the village behind us had struck a copper gong with a hammer. The noise bounced from the hills, spread out across the plain, thinned, and vanished as if it had been imagined.

I did not look at Oxtaby. I knew that he would think

181

that the sound had been made by the colossus as the dawn touched it.

Soon we were well beyond all habitation, and moved through a desolate landscape vivid with the shades of rust, sand, and quartz. We ascended a faint path on the very edge of a wadi and emerged onto a high barren plateau where we covered our heads against the sun. Kites screamed above us as they swooped through the vivid air.

After half an hour, perhaps more, we descended again. Loose rock rolled away from our donkeys' hooves, and I found that I was sweating heavily.

We came to the mouth of an unfamiliar valley and turned into it. Perched on the summit of a rocky knoll at its far side were three sleek-winged vultures. As we looked up at them they shifted lazily in the mounting heat.

I unslung the water-bottle from my neck and passed it round. The contents had become tepid but they were still welcome. I wanted to turn back, but knew I dared not suggest it.

The valley was deserted, and echoed even the faint noises made by our donkeys as their hooves clicked against stones. The path was narrow and wound between tall banks of debris, but at one point it undercut the cliff itself. Most of the debris must have been carried down from the plateau over thousands of years, but some parts of the mounds seemed new. The banks led up to red walls that were pocked and scarred, with deep fierce gashes running down them. These fissures resembled fresh wounds, but I knew they had been made centuries before the time of the pharaohs. Each one was marked by the stains of bat droppings. As we rode, prisms and needles of light shimmered in the banking as tiny pieces of hewn limestone caught the sun.

After some time Lucinda complained of feeling faint, and we stopped beside a massive oblong boulder that lay beside the path as if it had just fallen from the walls. There was still an area of shadow on its western side, and we edged within it while the donkeys stood listlessly in the brilliant sunshine.

'You should never have come,' I told Lucinda.

'I had to,' she answered.

'There are tombs in these rocks,' Oxtaby said; 'tombs you do not even suspect.'

As I scanned the valley I licked my lips and tasted salt. The rocks seemed both as ancient as time and raw with newness. They were stripped of all life, and yet awaited life. The valley's high, jagged rim stood out sharply against a sky whose deep cobalt blue was so flawless and unbroken that it seemed both without depth and endless.

As I watched, something moved along the skyline.

Oxtaby walked out into the sunlight and, lost within his own imaginings, put the fingers of one hand to his temple. The other hand grasped his staff.

'Lucinda,' I said, and pointed at the cliff-top. As I did, I saw movement again; a speck of black moved lower down the layered rocks beneath the summit crags. 'Can you see it?' I asked.

'See what?'

'A man; perhaps two men. Just there – do you see? I don't know what he's doing up there.'

'A bandit?' she asked.

'Perhaps. If he follows the ridges he'll be able to drop down into any of the valleys,' I said.

As I spoke there was another movement, slower this time, and a black dot became smaller, as if it had been partly obscured.

'They're birds,' she said. 'Kites, or maybe vultures.'

'No,' I said, 'it's a man. Maybe more than one.'

'Perhaps they're tomb-robbers. Clive, can you see?'

He did not answer.

'Maybe,' I said, 'but there are only animal tombs in this valley. Family pets – cats, a few monkeys, that's all.'

Oxtaby turned suddenly to look down the path we had travelled. A dust-devil raced towards us, scattering grit and sand, and then moved towards the head of the wadi.

'It's starting,' Oxtaby said, and fell to the ground, knees first. He knelt weakly in the sand with his head bowed.

Lucinda bent and took his face between her hands.

183

'Clive,' she said urgently, as if he were slipping away from her.

I imagined that he had brought us here because his mind was so crowded with fantasies that he could no longer think straight. Perhaps in his delirium he believed that we were witnesses to some majestic discovery or event. 'Oxtaby,' I said, 'it's time to go back now.'

He swivelled his eyes towards me. I was shocked by his expression, for he looked like a man severely concussed. 'Go back?' he said vaguely, like a man repeating a fragment from a language he did not understand.

'Yes,' I said firmly, 'there's no point in staying here, and it would be dangerous to go further. You never know what those people up there might do.'

'It's over with, Clive,' Lucinda said gently, 'it's all over with.'

She spoke as if, at last, she and Oxtaby had reached the end of a road they had followed for years.

'No,' he said, 'it's just beginning.'

I knew we should never have come on this insane and hopeless mission, and was furious that we had humoured him, and that he had led us here, miles from anywhere, among desolation and animal graves.

'Lucinda,' I said, 'we have to get your brother back to Luxor. It's for his own good. Thuillier must see him.'

Oxtaby regained some of his self-control, but remained kneeling in the sand. Lucinda stood beside him, stroking his hair.

'I'm going up the wadi,' he said. 'All my life has led me here, to this moment at this place.'

'You'll not find any undiscovered tomb,' I answered. 'All you'll find are rocks and barren soil and perhaps the mummy of an animal. And there are people up there.'

He nodded.

'Don't pretend that you know who they are,' I said angrily. 'And don't tell me they are Nasir's men, either. It could be anyone. Whoever they are, they're not likely to be your friends.'

He got to his feet and swayed, overcome by dizziness.

Lucinda supported him, one arm clasped around his midriff. They looked like lovers. He dug the point of his staff into the ground and leaned on it.

'Where are these men?' he asked.

'I'm surprised you can't see them,' I answered scathingly.

'Perhaps I can. Where are they?'

I turned to point at the valley rim, but I could no longer see the black dots.

'I've lost them,' I said after a few seconds. 'I didn't invent them, Oxtaby. And I wasn't seeing things. Lucinda saw them too.'

'I thought they were birds,' she said. 'Vultures, maybe.'

'They are creatures who are not quite men,' he said, and eased himself from Lucinda's grasp.

I cast a despairing glance at her, but she was staring at Oxtaby. Sweat glistened on her skin like a film of oil.

He did not acknowledge her, but instead gazed obsessively at the high ridge. Suddenly I noticed that its outline had become less clear, as if the reds and blues of a watercolour had begun to bleed into each other. 'There,' he said, in a voice of cracked triumph. As soon as he had spoken a line of thin cloud began to spill across the ridge.

I grabbed hold of his elbow, but he swung at me with his staff. It struck me on the upper arm. I was only slightly hurt, but the shock of his attack made me clutch the injury and step back.

'You're insane,' I said.

'Tell that to the creatures we shall meet,' he answered.

'No one is going with you, Oxtaby. I know as well as you that a storm is going to break over this valley. The sooner we get out of it, the better. You would meet no one up there other than bandits sheltering from the deluge.'

'There are no bandits. What is up there belongs to me. One of them is closer to me than any friend, closer than a sister. I knew that some day he would come to meet me.'

By now the upper half of the far wall was completely obscured by a thickening cloud which flowed nearer to us along the high ridges. We stood within a pocket of intense sunshine, but it was narrowing around us and would soon disappear.

'Lucinda,' I said, 'we have to get out of here. This is dangerous. A wall of water could sweep along this track.'

Oxtaby took a dozen steps further up the valley and then stopped. Lucinda called his name sharply; I thought he might turn back, but he ignored her and began striding purposefully towards the approaching storm.

'I'm going with him,' she said.

'You can't,' I said.

'You can't stop me.'

'He's just your brother,' I said fiercely; 'I should mean more to you.'

The sun vanished quite suddenly, and the land around us began to darken. As Lucinda began to follow Oxtaby the cloud lowered itself into the valley and seemed to compress the air. Large drops of rain began to fall spasmodically onto the sand and glisten on its powdery surface.

I ran after Lucinda and caught her by the arm. She tried to wrench it free but I held on tightly and then grasped her other arm. Hatred and frustration were in her eyes as I pinioned her so that she could not move. For a moment I thought that she would spit in my face, but she only struggled to follow Oxtaby. When at last she gave up, he was disappearing into a thin, curdling mist that had begun to rise in the valley.

Everything around was softening, cooling, turning into the drab colours of silt and dung. A squall of rain passed across us, soaking us within the few seconds before it eased. The valley floor shone like tidal sand after a receding wave, but then more rain began to fall and it became as grey and streaked as battlefield mud. The mist rose around us, shrinking visibility to less than twenty yards.

'Lucinda,' I said, 'we have to leave. Clive has chosen to take his chances. We both did what we could to stop him.'

186

'You think he might die,' she said bitterly, 'but he made this happen. This is his proof to us.'

'If he did, then he has put you and me in danger as well as himself.'

I half-marched, half-dragged her to the donkeys. As soon as she was mounted I slapped the animal's flank, and then followed her on my own mount. Oxtaby's donkey cantered behind us with a weary patience.

Rain began to fall more steadily. Soon it became torrential, shrinking distance further and filling the air with a muffled liquid heaviness. The rocky banks shone with pale, steely light, like raw magnesium cut by a knife. Broad pools began to form in our path and I could hear rivulets falling onto the mounds from the high cliffs.

I urged the donkeys onward, lashing at them until they began to bleed. The rain was even heavier now, and fell so thickly that I was half-blinded. From behind us I could hear the noise of torrents pouring down the gullies as if released from a dam.

The way turned so that it passed directly beneath the cliff before veering away between the mounds again. The cliff was the colour of old brick, and water poured ceaselessly onto the path from a high lip of rock. A pool whose depth I could only guess had formed in front of us and was building up against the sides of the mounds.

The donkeys would go no further no matter how much I beat them, so I dismounted and led mine through the pool. The water came up to my waist and was as cold as death. Then I returned and led Lucinda's donkey across. She sat astride it, shivering with fear, hair streaked across her face, her drenched skirt clinging high on her white legs.

As we were about to remount there came from behind us a strange vibrating roar, both liquid and grating. I seized Lucinda's wrist and tugged her onto the highest bank of debris. She screamed and fought but I pulled her higher up the slope. The rocks clattered beneath us and we often slipped heavily, but at last we scrambled onto the summit. I felt sure there would be no hope for us on the track, but did not know if the bank would be a haven. Below us the donkeys stood unhappily; Oxtaby's was still at the far side of the pool, its hooves already submerged.

The noise grew louder until it was deafening, and then a mass of brown water came speeding round a bend between the mounds and coursed unstoppably down the track. Its front was a ragged, turbulent wall about four feet high which tore at the lower slopes of the banks, churning and rattling the stones. Two of the donkeys were bowled over and vanished immediately; the third made a desperate attempt to climb the nearest incline, but the force took its hindquarters and it, too, disappeared beneath the foam. Behind the wall came a wild, eddying swell as opaque as sand, and within a few seconds the entire visible length of the track was submerged beneath a headlong flood.

Lucinda began to shake like a malaria victim, and her eyes were dilated with fear. She grabbed hold of me as if I were her saviour. The rain hissed all around us, moulding our clothes to our bodies.

The river rose again; a bulge like the wake of a sea-serpent bore along it, scooping huge sections out of the banking and carrying them away. I watched as it approached us and the mounds cascaded into it, tensing myself for the shock when it struck the hillock on which we had taken refuge. When it did there was a roar like a landslide and a motion like the lift of a wave; I was certain that all the stones beneath us had suddenly become suspended in water. The grinding noise intensified as debris was hurled around. I waited helplessly for the entire surface to slide away and take us with it.

I do not know if the mound sank by a few inches or if we slipped downwards, but we began to slither away from the rock wall. I scrambled for it, hitting my knees and my elbows on stones, clawing at the rock with my fingers, breaking my nails as I searched for a hold. Lucinda had one arm fastened around my shoulders, but she lost her grip and slipped beneath me so that I was half-lying across her. I could feel the frantic beating of her heart, the feverish strength of her limbs, the sudden fragility of her body, and I thought helplessly of Virginia.

188

The limestone was friable and broke away like rotten wood when I gripped it. Panic-stricken, I reached and clutched again, this time finding in the rock a shallow recess with a firm ridge at its lip. I fastened one hand onto this and braced myself as best I could. I was ready to take both my own weight and Lucinda's if the mound shifted and fell, although I knew that such an act would be useless; if our shelter collapsed into the flood, we would go with it.

Water streamed down the cliff-face and hit my shoulders and neck with the force of a hose. I could not escape, and closed my eyes as it drummed and pummelled me. Shock and the expectation of death loosened my mind, and I drifted back to boyhood.

When I trapped Virginia in my bedroom she began to cry, so I cupped one hand across her tiny mouth to silence her as she struggled. A cold frenzy made me tug and yank at the unfamiliar clothes, not caring if they tore, until she was stripped from the waist down. Her nakedness both disappointed and disturbed me; I had never seen an unclothed girl before, and had not known quite what to expect. Instinct and hearsay led me to straddle her, my hand still across her mouth as she twisted and kicked underneath me. I must have reached a climax immediately but I hardly knew I had done so, and stared in a kind of dazed puzzlement at my own seed as it lay scattered across her belly. Only when I had threatened her again and again did I dare lift my hand from her mouth. I said to her that if she ever told anyone about this, or even if she thought bad things about me, she would be punished. God would be furious with her, she would catch a terrible disease, she would die.

The rain turned to squalls which played across us with changing intensities. My entire body ached. I felt that we were creatures from a mythology, trapped on the very edge of annihilation, doomed to live out eternity on a bank of wet, broken, hazardous rock. And then, with a hope that I knew was foolish and absurd, I imagined we were living at the start of the world, humans left on a bank of stone and mud after the great river of creation had begun to fall.

I was convinced that Clive Oxtably must have drowned by now. At first I was exultant that he was out of my way, but then I felt spiteful and petty. Another squall of rain drove across our refuge and struck the cliff wall. I had begun to lose sensation in my fingers.

Whatever Oxtaby's faults, and however selfish he had become, he was a man made unique by his very extremity. His actions and beliefs carried frightening risks, were often detestable, and belonged to no one but himself. I was scared of him and yet I admired him; he believed what no one else dared believe, and did what no one else had the selfishness or brutality to do.

It was some time before I realised that the rain had stopped.

I eased my body painfully from Lucinda's so that I could look around. As I did, the sun burned through a thinning patch of mist and the valley's drenched surfaces began to glow and shine. Even the water still falling from the high rims began to sparkle.

I looked down onto the new river. Its force had lessened and the level was already beginning to fall. I took my hand out of the fissure in the cliff. My arm felt useless, as if all the muscles had wasted.

'Lucinda,' I said.

She looked at me, startled and numb.

'We've come through,' I said.

We stared at each other in the tranced realisation of our own survival. The saturated grit had stained us a pale red from head to toe, and Lucinda's white, stunned face was smeared with pink, like a birthmark.

She tried to speak, but as soon as she did her teeth began to chatter uncontrollably. I put my hand to her mouth; her lips were cold. 'Clive,' she said, and began to shake again. I put my arms round her as she trembled. A last drizzle of rainwater spattered over us from the cliff-top.

We sat wordless for a long time as the river gradually fell. At one point a snake, belly-up, was swept past. The banks

190

began to steam in the heat so that the valley filled again with a white mist whose humidity caught the throat.

All the time I was thinking about Clive Oxtaby, who had always done what I had never dared.

After about an hour we descended the incline on our haunches. It slipped beneath us like unstable scree. The lower part of its slope had been cut away and we half-slid, half-fell onto a path submerged beneath six inches of sand-coloured water. Lucinda stumbled and pitched forward, and would have fallen if I had not caught her. Suddenly, crazily, I felt desire for her. The very fact that we had survived had keyed up all my senses.

'I don't think I can walk,' she said. Her lips had swollen and she part-mumbled her sentence like an injured child.

'Let me see,' I demanded.

She sat on a collapsed mound of stones and extended her foot. I did not take off the shoe, but could see plainly that the ankle had been damaged. She winced as I ran my fingers over the swelling, and I had to check my insane fantasy of making love to her among the mud and the water and the sharp, hostile rock.

The water-bottle was still on its sling round my chest. I gave her a little to drink and replaced the stopper.

'We have to get back,' I said.

She shook her head. 'We have to look for Clive.'

'You can hardly walk, and Clive could be anywhere.'

'Then you must look for him, and I'll wait here.'

'Lucinda, you're injured and in shock, and we're miles away from help.'

'I'll never forgive you if you desert him. Never.'

The impulse came over me again, but this time spiced with a desire for violence. I realised that I did not know what I felt about Lucinda; passion, certainly, but also anger. She had given me pleasures I had never experienced before; she had opened a future for me; but she could also have lied, and had probably betrayed me with her own brother.

Quite suddenly I saw a correspondence between her and Oxtaby; they had each been a kind of salvation, and I had felt responsible to them both, but they had each exploited me ruthlessly.

I stood up and felt the water flow around my ankles. Beneath the damp strands of her hair, the stain on Lucinda's face was like washed blood. I handed her the water-bottle.

'Wait here,' I said, 'I'll go.'

I waded and splashed through the dying stream, moving against its weakening suction and drag. The pool beneath the cliff was chest-high, and I felt my heart thump as I crossed it with my arms held clear of the turbid surface. I half-expected to tread on a body, but beneath my feet there was only an unstable layer of tumbled rock.

I followed the path further, and after a few yards stopped to shout Oxtaby's name. The mist swallowed my yell, and there was no response.

I moved into the shadow of the cliffs and the mist thickened. The path was strewn with rubble and I could scarcely find any secure footing. I stumbled several times and fell twice. All the time I was terrified that I too would be injured, possibly even break a leg, and that I would be dead by the time that anyone found me.

I was exhausted and weak, and it seemed suicidal that I should be struggling through this wrecked, barbarous landscape. I was convinced that Oxtaby was dead and that my search was pointless and absurd. I made up my mind to turn one last corner, take one last look up the misty valley, and then return.

Water had begun to drain from the path, leaving quiet pools and beds of soft gritty sand. I sank within the sand; it coated my legs like silt, and I felt it could draw my entire body within its glistening surfaces and cover me for ever.

I looked up and saw Clive Oxtaby standing on top of the nearest bank of rock.

He was motionless, apparently unharmed, and gazed down on me with a mute, quizzical expression. In his hand he still carried his staff.

'Oxtaby,' I said, astonished, but he did not respond.

I began to scramble up the bank towards him. The

surface was sodden and unstable, and I slipped and fell several times before I reached the place where he had been standing. He had already vanished.

I was gasping heavily and had to lean against a dripping wall of red limestone. I looked all round, but there was no sign of Oxtaby, and nothing to prove that he had ever been there.

I called his name several times, but knew it was hopeless. Afterwards I sat down and put my head in my hands. Around me the mist was dispersing, and as its strands dissolved the sharp cruel details of the valley were appearing.

I made my way back to where I had left Lucinda. She was still sitting on the eroded bank. As soon as she could see me I shook my head, and when I was nearer I shook it again.

'There was no sign,' I said.

She looked down to hide her face from me.

'We have to think of ourselves now,' I said.

I supported her as she got to her feet, and then she put her arm round me. Together we began to hobble down a ribbon of silt towards the mouth of the valley.

After some time she spoke.

'He's still alive,' she said.

'Maybe. But I doubt it.'

'Clive was an expert; he wouldn't be killed by something he himself started.'

'Don't talk,' I cautioned her; 'save your energy.'

'It's true, isn't it? Tell me you agree with me.'

'All right, I agree with you.'

The surfaces of drying sand were as contoured and smooth as mixed cement. We trampled and furrowed them as we made our way. At one point we came across a low dune with a tiny irregularity running across it like a fractured line. Suspecting what it could be, I kicked at it and brought a broken staff to the surface.

'It's his,' I said, and thought of the snake I had seen carried past us.

'Pick it up,' Lucinda ordered.

I was nervous, but the wood was nothing more than wood. Oxtaby's staff had been burst rather than snapped, and its middle section was splayed outwards as if massive pressure had been applied to each end. I could not imagine what had happened, and thought of a tree struck by lightning.

'It's useless now,' she admitted sadly, and I let the staff fall.

The corpse of one of the donkeys lay round the next bend. It was lost beneath vultures who flapped reluctantly into the air as we approached and then eyed us from rocks only a few feet away. They had already opened wounds in the thick fur, and the head was a mass of flesh and exposed bone. As soon as we had passed I could hear the ungainly half-beat of their wings as they settled back down onto the dead animal.

Further down the wadi we came across some villagers. They had seen the storm and were entering the valley to search for whatever had been brought to the surface. Already they were combing the drying flood channels, picking their way through the silt with legs and hands coated, like Victorian children scavenging the emptied basins of the Thames.

They were our rescuers. They ran towards us, shouting excitedly at each other, and stood around us as our strength drained away. By now Lucinda was dazed and scarcely conscious. There was a curious lightness within me, and I felt that my very bones had become more fragile and that air moved within my veins instead of blood.

Everyone was talking to us, asking us where we had been, how they could help us, what they should do. The sun shone with an intense, giddying brilliance, and I had the sensation of being watched by someone who stood outside the circle, mute and unrecognised, before the mud surface gave beneath my feet and I slipped helpless into a net of strong, trustworthy arms.

I was in a room, propped up on a cushion that felt like silk, stretched out on a divan covered with rugs. My clothes had the crumpled, uncomfortable feel of drenched cotton that has dried against the skin. From somewhere outside came the sound of water being drawn from a well. The divan ran round three of the four walls; Nasir sat opposite, looking at me with a concerned expression.

'You could have been killed,' he said, 'both of you.'

I tried to struggle to my feet, but he nodded to someone standing at my head. Akhmet put his fingers on my chest and gently pushed me back down. I noticed that there was sand under his fingernails; he had been digging with his hands.

'I think you should not trouble yourself until Dr Thuillier arrives,' Nasir continued smoothly. 'He will see to you both.'

Lucinda sat opposite me. A blue shawl had been wrapped around her; she had twined its tassels around her fingers to cocoon herself within it. It was the same blue that had been painted on the figure of Isis at Abydos.

A girl came into the room carrying a tray with glasses and tea. I guessed she was Nasir's sister, or possibly his wife, but she did not speak and backed out of the room as if she had been in the presence of lords. Nasir gave a tiny shrug to signal to me that he found it politic to accept such outmoded servility.

'Very few strangers have entered my house,' he said; 'you are privileged. But when I heard that you were exhausted and in distress, I wished to offer you my full hospitality.'

He indicated the tea to Akhmet, who poured it and handed the glasses to us, but did not drink himself. Lucinda sat with one hand around her glass as if it would be dangerous to let go.

'Tell me,' Nasir asked, 'why were you in that wadi? There is nothing there that would be of interest to you. Mummified pets from long ago cannot excite your curiosity, surely?'

'Clive Oxtaby asked us to go,' I answered.

He nodded slowly. 'I see, but I do not understand. The place is desolate, a haven for scorpions and jackals, nothing else. Even the graves are high up in the walls, and a long trip for no reward.'

I looked across at Lucinda. Her eyes were dull. She pulled the edge of the shawl up around the lower half of her face to hide her mouth.

'He's convinced there is a tomb up there,' I said. 'An Eighteenth Dynasty tomb. One that will only be found when rainwater washes down the rock face.'

'So he believed a storm would point to the entrance, as it did ten years ago in the Gabbanet al-Kurud?' Nasir paused to consider this point. 'He must be a man who can see such storms before they gather,' he said at last; 'this one broke only within that one wadi, nowhere else.'

I nodded.

'But he will have found nothing,' he added with a sweeping confidence; 'as a boy I scrambled up and down many of the hills within that valley. The most I ever found was a mummified cat that the moths had burrowed into.' He turned to Lucinda. 'I am sorry, Mrs Plummer. I know you have a great love for your brother. But he is mistaken.'

'I just want him to be still alive,' she whispered.

Nasir looked at me and raised his eyebrows slightly. It was a signal to me – we are men of the world, it said; we know how little chance Oxtaby must have had.

'It doesn't look good,' I said. 'We found his staff. It was split.'

'Really?' he said. I expected him to ask how it could have been broken, but he did not.

Lucinda shuffled into a corner of the room and drew up her knees, wrapping the shawl more tightly around herself. Her hand and the glass protruded from its fringe.

'Woven by my family,' Nasir said, indicating the cloth like a salesman. 'They are happy to give this to you, Mrs Plummer. As a gift.'

'Thank you,' she answered in a small, quiet voice.

'You are welcome. If there was something else I could give you to make you feel better, I would gladly do it. And you as well, Mr Murchison.'

196

'A papyrus,' Lucinda said; 'a papyrus about the Other World. If you had such a thing, then we would not be here now, and Clive would not be lost.'

He raised a finger as if in admonishment. I wondered if this was a signal, for at that moment Akhmet went to the door and opened it. Deesa sidled in without a word and leaned against the wall with his hands behind his back. His thin features were impassive.

Nasir ignored both men. 'I have already sworn that I have no such thing,' he said. 'Is this what you were seeking?'

'Yes,' I confessed. 'Oxtaby is convinced that it is hidden up there.'

'But why?'

I shook my head. 'I don't know. It's difficult to say.'

He leaned back expansively and laced his fingers across his chest. 'I have often found that Westerners are driven by a need to possess. Of course, that is how I make my living – but I could not do it if you had not already created such a demand. You need to have *things*. Experience and knowledge are never enough for you. Not even the certainty of God is enough.'

'Clive Oxtaby has the same kind of argument,' I said.

'Ah, but you say that he, too, wants something. He wants a papyrus so badly that he will endanger his own life and the lives of the people closest to him. Is this not true?'

Neither of us answered.

'Even the ancients knew that all truths could not be counted and numbered and chiselled on a wall or painted on a scroll. They knew that no man could ever know everything, not even the pharaoh, not even one of their gods. And yet you live here, in conditions that you find unpleasant, and you devote your lives to accumulating even more detail about our past. Why? Where does it lead? Does all your excavation make you happy? Do you understand more deeply how the world turns? I think not. I think you do it because you do not know your own souls.'

197

He placed his empty glass back on the tray. I heard a faint chink as it touched the metal.

'I, on the other hand, know exactly what I am.'

'Good,' I said neutrally.

'I understand what I have to do so that I might prosper. The grand schemes of life, theories of what it means, a passion to step outside what you already know to be true – none of these concern me. I live by simple rules. And I understand that, if I break these rules, someone will punish me. That is the way that life is.'

There was a sudden cloudiness in his eyes, and then he smiled again.

'Are you trying to say that Clive has been punished?' Lucinda asked.

Nasir waved his hands as if to dispel any such suspicion. 'Of course not, dear lady,' he said with the fussiness of a valet, 'of course not. Unless, in breaking rules he pretends not to understand, he punishes himself.'

Lucinda put her glass on the floor and then ran her hands through her hair, which had dried into lank swatches. 'He's very clever,' she said. 'He loves living here. And he understands life on the West Bank.'

He nodded. 'It is true that I have heard that Mr Oxtaby is a very clever man. He can make voices speak out of nothing and confuse his watchers so they no longer know what is happening. He worked with Sheik Moussa, ridding the tourist hotels of snakes before the new season; perhaps he learned from the Sheik how to turn snakes into rods, rods into snakes. But Mr Oxtaby is not content with such party tricks. I have heard that he believes he holds within his grasp all the powers that Moses learned from the ancient priests. But such days are history; there can be no plagues of Egypt now, no river of blood, no death of the firstborn. Men with such talents would destroy themselves. They would reach too far; perhaps they would conjure up something which they could not control.'

I searched his face but it was opaque.

He shrugged and held out his hands fatalistically; no one could ever understand the will of God.

'If you wish to live here,' he went on, 'you must be very careful not to betray a trust. And yet sometimes I think that my friends from Europe and the United States do that all the time; it is a part of life for them. They break trusts within their own families, with businesses such as mine, and even with governments. A man cannot lie and expect to live without retribution.'

He stared directly at me, and then smiled.

At that moment there was a shout from outside the room. Nasir motioned to Deesa, who opened the door.

Ibrahim stood there, dishevelled and breathing heavily. I thought he would look first at us, but instead he glanced at Akhmet and Deesa as if he dared not speak in front of them. They remained impassive, and I felt my whole body tense. Finally he looked at Nasir. There was both a plea and desperation in his gaze.

'Please,' Nasir said, indicating Lucinda with his opened hand.

'Mrs Plummer,' Ibrahim said quickly, 'Raymond – they have found him.'

The world stopped for an instant. We all stared at Ibrahim; he shook his head to show there was no hope; the world moved on.

'They are bringing him now,' he said.

Lucinda got to her feet mechanically, the shawl still wrapped around her. We went outside into the afternoon sunshine. The Nile was vivid and silvery in the distance, and the fertile strip a bright, drenched green. Men were walking up the road towards the house in a small group. Their djellabas were dusty and some of their turbans were awry, as if these had slipped and been hastily rewound. The men were all talking rapidly, and often shouted at each other. In their midst was an improvised stretcher made of lashed-together poles, and on it was a body covered by a square of dirty grey linen. The stretcher was too small for the body and the feet protruded over its edge. Although there was still a shoe on one foot, the other was bare. I felt ice melting within me.

Next to me Lucinda swayed as if overcome. I took hold

of her hand and elbow, ready to support her if she fainted. 'There is no need for you to see this,' I said.

'I have to,' she replied.

'They found him high in the wadi,' Ibrahim said as the men came closer. 'He was fastened between rocks and almost covered by sand and grit. I think one of the banks must have weakened and slipped onto him, perhaps after he drowned. It was as if he had been buried within a mound of mud.'

'Ibrahim,' she asked in a fragile voice, 'what does he look like?'

'Do not be afraid, Mrs Plummer; he has entered death easily. There are no marks upon him.' He hesitated, looked at me, then back at her. 'Apart from one,' he added.

Lucinda stiffened and I gripped her more tightly. The procession was nearing us; the closer it got, the quieter it became.

'The man who found Clive could only partly dig him out,' Ibrahim went on. 'He ran back down the wadi for help. Everyone came as quickly as they could. But in that time a vulture had found him. One man tried to shoot the bird, but he missed. Others said that it could not be hit because it was a magic bird.'

The men stood a few feet away from us. Now that they had arrived at their destination not one of them spoke, and they looked at us with their round brown eyes, suddenly unsure how to behave.

Nasir told them to put down the stretcher and they lowered it too quickly onto the ground. The impact made the body rock slightly.

'Are you sure you want to see him?' I asked Lucinda. 'No one will think any less of you if you don't.'

'I came this far with Clive; I must see it through to the end.'

Nasir gestured to Deesa, who stepped forward and lifted the cloth without hesitation, like a man innocent of any involvement with Oxtaby's death. His expression did not change, but I noticed that there were bruises on his fingers and skin missing from his knuckles.

Clive's dead face looked up as if he was staring at the high arch of sky. His skin was as pale as ash. Gritty sand had partly filled his eyes, caked across his teeth and stopped his nostrils. Across the left side of his head, close to his ear, there was a gash where the vulture had begun to tear at him with its beak.

'Cover him,' I said quickly. Deesa put the cloth back over the face. I was scared that, if I looked on him any longer, I would still see Clive Oxtaby's face before me when it was my turn to die.

Nasir walked forward with an expression of neighbourly concern. He held out his hands towards Lucinda but avoided touching her, as if painfully aware that he was not her equal.

'Dear lady,' he said, 'this is the most terrible of shocks for you – and for Mr Murchison also. Please, come back into my poor home until Dr Thuillier arrives; he will do what he can for you. And he will also – ' He broke off, suddenly unwilling to use Oxtaby's name, and gestured to the body lying beneath the makeshift pall.

'Wait,' Lucinda said.

No one moved.

'He belongs here,' she said; 'on the West Bank. He should be buried here.'

'I am sorry, Mrs Plummer,' Nasir said, 'you are right, but it cannot be allowed.'

'There is no place for strangers here,' Deesa said. They were the only words I ever heard him speak.

'There is a Christian cemetery in Luxor,' I told her; 'we can arrange that Clive is buried there.'

She shook her head with a sudden fury. 'He doesn't belong with journalists and tourists,' she said.

'Perhaps this can be discussed with Dr Thuillier,' Ibrahim said tactfully.

I tried to lead Lucinda away, but she wrenched her arm from my grasp and dropped on her knees in the sand beside the stretcher.

'Lucinda,' I said, but she ignored me.

She held the cloth by its edges and then lifted it from

Oxtaby's face and folded it across his chest. As we watched she began to clean his face. The sand and grit had dried so that much of it could be dusted away from the skin, but the mouth and nostrils had to be cleared with her fingers. She did not know what to do with the eyes, and seemed scared to touch them. Unexpectedly, Deesa reached down and closed them with his thumbs. She glanced up at him, and for a moment I saw that she was grateful. He caught my stare and looked down. High overhead a red kite screamed.

Lucinda took hold of the cloth again, but before she covered Oxtaby she put her fingertips on his lower lip and then kissed him. It was not a short kiss of farewell, but a long, lingering one on lips that had been dead for hours. I was light-headed and nauseous, but I stood my ground.

When she was replacing the cloth her body suddenly convulsed as if a massive shock had passed through it, and she gave a high, wailing cry that made me shiver. Saliva dribbled from her mouth and dripped from her chin. The cry ended, she drew in air shudderingly, rackingly, and then she called again. Her grief spread out across the barren land, and I felt I could sense her anguish drift across the fertile plain like a thin cloud.

Ibrahim looked at me. I did not know what to do.

Lucinda spread her hands on the ground and clawed it, all the time giving her shrill, unearthly cry. She lifted handfuls of sand, poured them across her scalp, began to rub them into her hair. Grains cascaded down her face onto the blue shawl.

Nasir bent down and lightly placed his fingers on her shoulders. He had an expression of embarrassment, and I wondered vaguely if this was the most genuine emotion he had ever shown.

I reached forward and knocked his hands from her. He seemed relieved rather than angry.

'Lucinda,' I said roughly, 'get up.'

But she would not, and the men who had recovered Oxtaby began to edge away. I grabbed her wrist but she pulled it away from me in fury, and snatched another handful of sand.

'Let her do it, Raymond,' Ibrahim said. 'She is like her brother, nearer to our people than to yours.'

The circle around Lucinda and Oxtaby moved further outwards and I walked with it. When, after a few yards, it seemed that we had reached the right distance we all stopped. Minutes passed as we watched. Lucinda raked the ground again and again, and her terrible broken cry went on and on as if it would have no end.

6

I lifted the mirror from the wall and held it with the reflective surface turned inwards.

'Clive's dead,' Lucinda said; 'it's just a piece of glass and wood now.'

'That's what it has always been,' I answered, but I still took it into my room and put it on the bed with the mirrored side facing down. I dared not leave it pointing up, because I was half-afraid I would see someone else standing behind me.

I went back into Lucinda's room. She was dressed as she had been when I first met her, months ago, but she was thinner now and there were dark patches under her eyes from lack of sleep. Her packed bags stood beside the door next to a travelling chest filled with her paintings.

'Should I call for the boys,' I asked, 'or do you want to be left alone for a few moments?'

'I already know every part of this room,' she said; 'I'll not forget any of it.'

I nodded and rang for Hamid's porters.

'I wish I could be here later today,' she said.

'Don't worry, it will be done. You have a train to catch; Ibrahim will come with me.'

'You've always been able to rely on Ibrahim, haven't you?'

It was true, but I had always thought of Ibrahim as dutiful rather than loyal. 'Yes,' I said, 'I suppose I have.'

'And you'll do it when the sun goes down? That *is* the right time.'

'I promise you we'll do it then.'

'And you'll thank Mr Carter and Monsieur Lacau again for me. And, of course, Dr Thuillier. All I had to do was sign the official forms; it was their influence that made things go so easily, and I'm grateful.'

'They have spent their lives dealing with bureaucracies; they've had to be experts.'

'I don't suppose I'll ever meet them again.'

'Carter will be lecturing in England soon. We can go to hear him.'

Carter had been of great assistance but had maintained his coolness towards me. And not only was he a man who held grudges for years, but he was being slowly destroyed by his life's work. I thought it unlikely that we would meet again after the end of this season.

'He and Lacau will be at the station,' I said. 'They need no further thanks. But, if you wish, after the train has left I'll make certain they're aware of your gratitude.'

I would have to tell Lacau today; tomorrow I was officially summoned to appear before him at the Winter Palace.

Two porters came to the door and stood with their heads bowed, looking uncertainly at us and hesitating to interrupt. I pointed at Lucinda's belongings; they picked them up and took them to the lift.

I looked at my watch. 'Almost time to go,' I said. 'I don't think the journalists know much yet; we'll keep them in ignorance for ever if we can. Ignore them if they ask anything. Do you want to take one last look at the horizon?'

We walked to the balcony and looked out across the river to where the hills disappeared in a bluish haze. Below us a carriage waited in front of the hotel. Beside its emaciated horse the driver was eating seeds and occasionally spitting onto the ground. The beggar woman sat on her own under the sycamore, one hand permanently outstretched.

'Look,' Lucinda said, 'on the tree. It's a chameleon. I didn't see it for a while.'

I nodded.

'Raymond,' she asked, 'are we doing right?'

I did not answer for several seconds.

'I don't know,' I said. 'I hope so, for both our sakes.'

'We're each other's last chance, aren't we?'

'We deserve to return home,' I said. 'Despite what has been said about the English who go native, most of us yearn for village squares, church bells, and railway stations with geraniums in window-boxes.'

'And brass bands in parks where people stroll on Sundays,' she said. 'But you don't really know if you could settle there, do you?'

I shrugged. 'Life is richer here,' I confessed.

There was a silence which stretched and tightened between us. On the road below the porters were carefully stacking Lucinda's luggage onto the carriage. Even from this distance, I could hear the springs creak beneath the weight.

'It's time to go,' I said; 'I'll come with you. Remember, if anyone asks you a question, say nothing.' I was surprised at how curt I sounded.

'You never really appreciated how close I was to Clive,' she said.

I was stung by her words. 'No,' I said, 'but I watched you carefully. I studied the evidence.'

Her face showed puzzlement for an instant before she composed herself, and then she spoke as carefully as a witness before a court.

'There has only been a small number of men in my life,' she said in measured tones, 'and to begin with, I did not want to love any of them. But I could not help what happened. The circumstances were always extraordinary.'

'You mean an extraordinary childhood? And after that the war to end all wars, during which you met a man who happened to look like Clive anyway?'

'And then a voyage up a river I had always dreamed of sailing. You are the only man I have not lost, Raymond; the others died alone in barren landscapes. Don't betray me now.'

'There are a lot of things still to do here. The lower

halves of the second and third coffins still have to be separated; after that they will have to be carefully treated. Carter wants to return the body to the sarcophagus within one of them. At the end of the season, I promise you I will be in England.'

But I could be back well before that, and Lucinda knew it. Lacau had already told me that the last thing the clearance had needed was another death. I did not know if he would post me to another site or simply dismiss me.

Lucinda put her hand on top of mine as it rested on the balustrade.

'I've been a fool for love,' she said.

The word *love* made me uncomfortable. For me it was an idealised absolute, unattainable by the very people who used the word so often.

She went on. 'Rex was kind but shallow; a man unable to understand the force a passion always has. When I met you, I worried that you might be the same – self-important and yet doubting, honourable but a little unwise. When I talked about love Rex thought I meant duty, or respect, or responsibility. He was unable to see it as the cause of everything. He had no idea what I would do for love, how I would be willing to jeopardise my life, how I needed it so much I would behave in ways that he would never understand.'

'You loved him – ' I said, and the fateful word hobbled my tongue so that I had to start again. 'You loved Rex so much that you pretended to be someone you were not.'

'I don't know what you mean,' she said.

I shifted uneasily, uncertain if I should continue. 'When you married him you pretended to know nothing about men; you pretended to be innocent.'

'Because it made him happy.'

'You faked your reactions, Lucinda. You hoodwinked him.'

'Of course I did,' she said, seeming to be amazed that I should make such an obvious point. 'Anyone with any sense would have done the same. A small moment of fraud, a white lie – they're nothing, not when compared with love. By veiling one small part of my life I helped Rex reach contentment. I like to think that for a few weeks he was truly happy. I'm proud of that.'

'But it was only a few weeks.'

'Because he was destroyed by events outside of us, and not started by either him or me. We didn't have a destructive love. It wasn't like my love for Clive.'

'You can't blame yourself for what happened in that wadi. Neither of us can.'

'Can't we? Didn't we both love Clive in our different ways? Didn't we humour him, indulge him, want him? For a time I believed that he carried us along with him. Now I think it may all have been our fault, yours and mine. We could have stopped him.'

'Clive could never have been stopped.'

'There must have been another way of ending all this. *Must* have been. In one way or another, we should have been able to call a halt at any time. But we didn't. We failed him, Raymond.'

'Clive was his own man.'

She shook her head. 'No. Clive was desperate to live a different life from the one he had. Surely that was obvious in everything he did.'

I took a deep breath. 'I don't know what kind of life he had,' I said.

'How can you say that? You were his oldest friend. You shared more than ten years with him.'

'I had a sister who died when I was very young,' I said suddenly.

She stared at the misty horizon. Feluccas and a steamer were crossing to the West Bank, a place she would never visit again.

'You never told me that,' she said.

There was a catch in my throat; I had to cough before I could speak again.

'I never told Clive; only Thuillier knows. But I have a reason for telling you; I want you to know that I realise what an intense brother-and-sister relationship can be like.

You were overcome with grief when Clive died, and he once told me you would do anything for him.'

'Clive had made his peace with our love. I don't think I ever did.'

'Are you trying to tell me that you were reluctant to let him share your bed?' I asked.

Her face was already pale; now all blood drained from it, and she was white as the finest alabaster.

Immediately I wished I had not spoken, and a part of me ached to have the last few seconds of our lives erased. But I had spoken the words, could not retract them, and knew that we had to pass beyond them.

'You did that for him as well,' I said, pursuing the truth relentlessly; 'you still did things you began to do as children. It was a game then; he probably told you a pack of lies just to get what he wanted. Maybe his fake spirit guide ordered you to pretend to be a pharaoh's sister-wife. But why did you humiliate and disgrace yourself by still doing it now?'

She hit me hard across the face with her right hand. I saw the blow coming, but did not avoid it. I had not realised she could be so strong, or that the ring on her finger would hit me so violently. The impact knocked my teeth together with a bony crack. I reeled to one side with my head spinning and had to lean on the balustrade to get some stability.

Immediately she was onto me, embracing me feverishly and begging me to forgive her. My head was still ringing from the blow; she took it between her hands and kissed my face, calling me her love, her darling, her only one.

I nodded vaguely, still not able to think straight.

'Raymond, how can you ever forgive me?' she asked. 'I should have learned from Rex that jealousy makes a man think mad thoughts. Those are wild, idiotic imaginings. Please don't ever mention them again, please don't even think about them. I hadn't realised you felt so left out; there's no need to torture yourself with sick fantasies.'

I wondered if it was saliva or blood that was filling my mouth.

'In England everything will be different,' she continued rapidly, still holding my face between her hands. 'Everything will become clear to both of us. We'll know what to do with the rest of our lives. Do you know what I think will happen? I think we'll get married, have children. A little girl. Wouldn't you like a little girl? We could give her a name. I've always liked Virginia; we could call her Virginia.'

I had the dizziness I had felt when I saw Lucinda's body reflected in the mirror. Suddenly I wondered if she was already pregnant.

'Yes,' I said, 'we could call her Virginia.'

She kissed me again, and this time I knew there was blood in my mouth. When she drew away I looked down. The carriage driver was looking up at us, and even the beggar woman had changed her position so that she could stare at our balcony. On the branch of the sycamore the chameleon had begun to move with a languid, cold deliberation.

By the time we pushed the felucca from the bank Lucinda was far away from us, settled in her carriage with tinted windows as the heavy train pulled north towards Cairo. She would be looking out across the fertile lands and into the west, waiting for the sun to touch the far horizon. At the rear of the train two men with rifles would be sitting on the floor of a bare compartment stacked with trunks, labelled boxes, and Clive Oxtaby's coffin. His eviscerated body had been filled with preservative, and the coffin had been tightly made and packed with linen, but a smell of formalin would still seep into the van.

'I think this is not allowed,' Ibrahim said. He let his cigarette fall into the water, and then braced his feet on the felucca's stern and tightly gripped the guide-rope.

'It's a small crime,' I said; 'no one need know.'

Ibrahim rested his forehead on the heel of his hand, but did not turn the craft away from its destination. 'At least

I have business to take my dahabeyah upriver tomorrow. Aswan and Abu Simbel will never have seemed more welcome.'

I smiled at him, and shifted my weight as the felucca tilted and its mizzen swung.

'What if we are seen?' he asked.

'Then we are seen,' I said. 'Everyone will understand, even Nasir. Only Lacau and Carter would not understand.'

'Thuillier must be as crazy as you,' he muttered; 'I have often suspected this.'

The boat tilted as Ibrahim tacked around the new island of mud, and our spades clicked together in the bottom of the boat. I watched the island slide past. Already fine green stems of vegetation had begun to sprout on it.

'There is blood on your face, Raymond,' Ibrahim said after a while.

I scooped a handful of water from the river and splashed it on my left cheek. When I rubbed the skin with my fingers a patch of dried blood came away.

'It looks better now,' he said. I was glad he did not ask me why I had been bleeding.

'Ibrahim,' I asked him, 'do you think Oxtaby was murdered?'

He hauled on the rope and looked ahead. We were almost in the middle of the river, and a long way away from the nearest sandbank.

'Clive drowned,' he said; 'you read Thuillier's report. His lungs were full of water. A man would have had to be a Noah to escape such a storm.'

'That isn't what I asked,' I said, 'and Lucinda and I weren't Noahs. We escaped.'

'True,' he said, and glanced at one of the bags at my feet. It was the one containing the alabaster jars.

'I'm sure Clive can't hear you,' I said.

'It is the only answer I can give, Raymond.'

I nodded. 'I understand,' I said, but I thought again of the sand under Akhmet's nails and Deesa's bruised fingers. 'I asked Thuillier if he had been murdered. He said there

211

was no evidence to support speculation. I think he must have picked up the phrase from Derry.'

'Maybe. But now it is useless to think of what might have been the cause; merely accept that everything happened as it did. The past cannot be altered.'

'I don't know if I believe that,' I said.

'Of course it cannot,' he said; 'Carter and his team are discovering a past that has not been altered for three thousand years.'

'That's just evidence, Ibrahim. We have evidence but no understanding.'

'Just as with Clive, you mean? I have told you before, Raymond, that men always want what they cannot get. Do not worry your head about what can never be known; just give thanks that you are what you are, and that you have done what you have done. What good does it do a man to ask nothing but questions? Better by far just to live, for the more questions he asks, the more answers he will not know.'

'Yes,' I said quietly.

'We will be at your chosen place before the sun goes down behind the ridge,' he said; 'you need not worry. Clive will sleep a long time before he is disturbed again.'

In the middle of the river, where Ibrahim thought it ran the deepest, I reached into the bottom of the felucca and picked up one of the canvas bags. As he watched I slid the mirror out of the bag, holding it by its sides with the glass facing downwards.

Ibrahim was silent, as if he was watching an impenetrably obscure act. He angled the boat so that, as I leaned over the side, the surface of the river rose to meet me.

I had not intended to reverse the mirror, but at the last moment I did. For a moment its bright surface seemed liquid. It flashed an incandescent sun and then a high, endless sky, with the tip of the felucca sail pointing like the image of a distant pyramid.

I slid the mirror into the water, releasing it as carefully as if it were alive. It slipped away from my hands, an oval patch of silver dimming as it fell. I watched it drift down, becoming smaller and increasingly obscure, until our course took us past its grave and its image was lost in a dazzle on the water.

The felucca sail caught the wind and we sped towards the western shore. I narrowed my eyes at the brilliance of the sun as it began to fall towards the western escarpment. Soon we would pass through a thicket of tall, waving reeds and land on the far bank. It would not take us long to reach the place where the colossi looked out across the flood plain towards each dawn.

CHRISTOPHER BURNS
THE CONDITION OF ICE

In 1936 Ernest Tinnion leaves England for Switzerland to climb, with his childhood friend Hansi Kirchner, the awesome north face of the Versücherin. As they prepare the ascent, unforeseen pressures mount: from Tinnion's lover, who has left her husband to join him; from a too curious, menacing German photographer; and from a rival Italian team. In a breathtaking climax, Tinnion is forced to weigh survival against loyalty, neutrality against love and friendship, and to recognise ominous parallels with the looming global conflict.

'Christopher Burns' harsh, beautiful novel employs a number of unforgettable mountaineering images to dig deep into the condition of the European soul on the eve of the war'
Kazuo Ishiguro in The Sunday Times 'Books of the Year'

'Put Burns' imagination on a perpendicular cliff of stratified black rock with the cracks filling with snow and he'll have you feeling for a toe-hold in the carpet'
Nicholas Shrimpton in the Independent on Sunday

'Burns writes with a marvellous lightness of touch . . . a novel whose living perfection is triumphantly removed from the icy rigidity that is its subject'
Savkar Altinel in the Times Literary Supplement

'Excellent, exquisitely crafted . . . One of Britain's finest writers has written a gripping, many-layered story'
Val Hennessy in the Daily Mail

'That rare thing: a novel of action and emotion which is also a novel about the way people think . . . it is a tremendous achievement'
D. J. Taylor in The Independent